AN UNCOMMON LOVE
By M.J. Schiller

CHAPTER ONE

Adriana lifted her head, straining to see past the thorny bramble of the bush she lay behind with Garin. Her father's Royal Commander plucked a leaf from her hair.

"What is it, love?" Garin asked, still wearing the silly grin she put on his face.

She could barely make out the sounds of jeers and cries coming from the outer courtyard of her father's palace, the Castle Ramport. "What is that? What is happening?"

"Oh. It must have something to do with the commoner who struck Derrick."

She gasped. "Somebody struck Derrick?" Even though he worked for her father, she was terrified of the hulking beast of a man.

"Aye," he answered with a chuckle. He looked over to where the crowd was entering the grounds, too. "But he is probably sorry for it now, the poor fool."

She frowned, noting there was little pity in his voice. In fact, his words sounded mocking. The princess tugged at the gold laces which held her bodice together, trying to thread them quickly through their looped cording. When she attempted to struggle to her feet, he sought to press her down.

"Adi, honey." He touched his lips to the skin still accessible above the low cut of her neckline, but she was no longer in the mood.

The noise of the crowd surged and she again tried to make out what was happening, but saw only snatches of color and movement between the branches surrounding her. Her heart was racing.

"What will they do to him?"

"Oh, I do not know," he said, shrugging. "Whip him or beat him or ..."

"What?" Incensed, she succeeded in scrambling to her feet.

Garin sighed, gazing at her with ill-hidden lust. He sat, bending one knee and languidly resting on one elbow, his shirt left half-opened.

"Adi, I do not know if I can make it to our wedding night. The very scent of your skin these days sends a fire burning in my groin." He rose hastily. Pushing aside her fingers, he helped to tie her bodice. She fumed at the delay, half-ready to fly, tied or not. He smiled at her. "It is so strange how these feelings have awoken in us. Forever you have been my best friend, the one who explored the creek with me, who fought with me, who fished with me, who got in trouble with me. Soon you will be my lover, and that thought consumes my mind throughout the day. And tortures my nights." He stilled and gazed into her eyes. Gesturing to the patch of earth they had just abandoned he begged, "Adi, darling, come back and lie with me." He seemed not to care about how unmanly the pleading made him.

"Garin," she scolded. "I cannot lie with you in the grass while some man is being tortured within my hearing."

He grabbed her even as she turned from him, and pulled her in roughly, his strong fingers claiming ownership of her hip bones. He pushed his groin against her and brought his mouth to the base of her ear. "You *will* give me some time later," he growled.

She twisted her head toward him, her arms crossed in front of her, hands covering his. She leaned against his lean body, her lips curving up in an effort to seduce. "Would you doubt that?" she asked, her voice stroking him needlessly.

He chuckled softly in her ear and changed his grip, sliding along her bodice in order to cup what she had hidden away from him. "You will be mine soon, Adriana, and then there will be no running away."

The sound of his voice thrilled her. The need she heard in it was intoxicating, his touch, masterful, even as he clutched at her desperately. She whirled in his embrace and urged his head into a position to press her warm, open lips to his. She parted from him and watched the haze of passion lift from his eyes. She ran a finger from his temple to his lips, her gaze traveling its course. He nipped at it playfully and she lifted her head to peer into his eyes. "It will be worth the wait," she promised.

"Had I any doubt, I would have taken you on the grass today despite your protests."

"Oh. You, wicked boy." She spun toward the sound of the crowd and fought free of his hold. "Come, now. Hurry, Garin. I must see what is happening."

With that, she broke from his grasp and lifted her skirts to free her feet. Running across the stone pathway that curved around the corner of the building, she followed the uproar. As she ran, parallel to the crowd on the road, she peered amid branches of the oak trees planted at regular intervals to edge the garden. She could see a man with his wrists tied in front of him, struggling against his captors as he was shoved and dragged forward. He wore a loose-fitting, beige-colored linen shirt. His blond hair was long on top, and flew in front of his face as he swung his head violently. He seemed to be trying, at the very least, to injure someone with his skull.

She hastened her steps, and was actually the first person to reach the courtyard, angled as it was in her direction. She broke from the tree-line and stood just beyond the edge of the wide, hexagonal, stone court. High above, a small balcony jutted out from what she knew to be her father's conference room.

She continued to hear the whistles and cheers of the crowd, though they were briefly out of sight up the roadway, and it filled her with apprehension. In the past, her father had never let her see the goings-on in cases such as this, and now she understood why. It frightened her. Her heart beat faster as a few guards poured into the courtyard, walking backward as they took in the actions of the mob that trailed. She could see Derrick, her father's Captain of the Guard. Even from this distance the purple bruising on his chin was obvious. He held the rope tied to the captive and jerked it, a cruel move that sent the man crashing to the stone pavers.

Adriana gasped, but then covered her mouth. She stood, barely visible, at the fringe of the trees. If her father or his men saw her, they would order her away, of that she was sure. The man struggled to his feet and defiantly shook the hair out of his face. His white teeth flashed as he bared them, glaring with disdain at Derrick. His heavy work pants were torn at the knees, whether from the fall she had just witnessed, or from some other fall, she could not tell.

The prisoner's gaze lifted and caught hers. For several seconds it was as if no one else was there besides Adriana and the stranger. The air seemed to shimmer between them with the intensity of their stare. The noise of the crowd thundered in her ears, but was now accompanied by the sound of her own blood pounding through her veins. His eyes were the most startling blue, reminding her of the flash of a blue jay she sometimes caught a glimpse of in Ramport's gardens.

Adriana's cheeks grew warm. She peered at the stranger, her mouth hanging open. He was easily the most gorgeous man she had ever laid eyes on. His shirt, which should have been tied at the neck, was torn and open, revealing his well-muscled chest, which glistened with sweat in the late afternoon sunlight. The veins on his powerful arms, captured on each side by a guard, bulged as he fought to free himself, despite being wildly out-numbered. Adriana felt an unfamiliar acceleration of her heart-beat when he, despite the flurry of activity surrounding him, did not take his eyes from hers. His face at first seemed open, thoughtful. But then, as his gaze trailed over her gown and the thin circle of gold and jewels laced in her hair, his jaw became set. His stare became cold, almost hostile. Adriana pursed her lips, uncomfortable with the change.

Her father stepped out on the balcony, and she at last tore her eyes from the prisoner's and focused above.

Garin appeared, grabbing her about the waist and trying to steer her away from the scene. "You should not be here."

Adriana slapped at him. "Leave me be, Garin," she whispered, her voice hoarse and tense. At her words, his eyes flashed, and he pulled his hands away, holding them aloft in a sign of surrender.

The crowd quieted as one, and all faces tilted upward as the king spoke. "Why is this man brought before me?"

Adriana stared at her father. She did not recognize his voice as it rumbled forth from on high, so uncaring, so...icy. As she spun her head to hear Derrick's response, she noticed another face in the crowd. A woman was observing intently, covering her mouth, her eyes filled with tears. She was beyond beautiful, with huge, meadow-green eyes and long, wavy hair the color of deep mahogany. She had high cheek bones and a delicate nose, and she was watching the prisoner with rapt attention. So, he had a girlfriend, or wife, she surmised, taken aback by the wave of disappointment that swamped her heart.

"Sire, this is the commoner who assaulted me earlier today."

"Has he not been scourged?"

The attractive brunette in the audience winced.

"Aye, Sire." Derrick answered with a wicked grin.

Adriana thought her father's lips curved up as well as he nodded. "And...?"

Here, Derrick's formerly cheerful countenance clouded. "The prisoner refuses to apologize."

The king's eyebrows rose in surprise. "Perhaps a trip to the river will change his mind." His tone was ominous. The brunette gasped and a woman nearby grabbed her arm to support her as she seemed to swoon.

Adriana twisted to question Garin. "What does he mean?"

"Adriana, you should not be here—"

"Garin," she hissed, desperate to understand what was going on, "*what are they talking about?*"

He shrugged. "They will take him down to the river and hold his head under water until he apologizes or until he drowns."

"What?" She stared at him in disbelief, her stomach dropping like a bucket in a well.

"You wanted to know," he responded blandly.

She rotated slowly to catch Derrick chuckling, and her father viewing the proceedings in—what appeared to be— amusement. Fear flitted over the prisoner's face briefly, but then it became like stone. He looked at the dark-haired woman apologetically, but seemed resolute. The group as a whole turned to leave.

"Wait!" Adriana shouted, her voice ringing out across the expanse. Without even realizing she was doing it, she had stepped out of the shade and into the open courtyard.

"Adriana?" The king gave Garin a hard stare. "What are you doing here?"

"Father." She caught her breath. "You asked me what I wanted this morning for my birthday—" She thought quickly, chancing a glance at the prisoner, who was peering at her now with wide eyes, his mouth hanging open a bit.

"Ana—" The king responded affectionately, and, while dismissive, his voice sounded more like what the princess was used to, "—we can discuss this at dinner." He pivoted to go inside.

Angered by his condescension, she struggled to contain her voice. "Nay, Father!"

He circled and stared at her, eyebrows lifted.

She stepped forward so as not to be heard by the crowd. "Papa," she cajoled, switching gears, "I want you to free this man, *please*."

"What?" He took another glimpse at the commoner bound before him. "What is this man to you, Ana?"

Her cheeks blazed as if she had been sitting by the fire for hours. She purposefully did not focus on the others, only gazing into her father's eyes. "Nothing, Father. Nothing. I just... I do not wish to see him hurt."

"Ana, this is none of your business—" he began.

"Father, this *is* my business," Adriana stated firmly, but softened her voice, noting the anger spark in her father's eyes. "This is your business, and so it is mine." She stepped closer, almost within the shadow of the balcony. "I do not wish to anger you." Now she chanced a glance backward and saw Derrick glaring at her with conspicuous irritation. "But, if I am to celebrate my birthday this evening, I cannot do it knowing this man is suffering."

"He will not be suffering long," she heard Derrick murmur under his breath.

"Are you sure this is what you want, my Ana? I had picked out something very special for you, a piece of jewelry from your mother's collection."

"I am grateful, Father, as always, for your generosity. But I know all the work you have put into making this evening special for me, and I only wish to enjoy it as you meant for me to. I cannot do that knowing this man is to be tortured." She gestured in his direction and then paused, holding her breath.

The king seemed to consider her argument a moment. He shrugged indifferently. "Well, if that is what you want." He smiled at her, waving above the gathering beneath him. "Release the prisoner."

There was a cheer from the small part of the crowd that had come in support of the accused commoner. The brunette rushed to the prisoner, jumping into his embrace.

Adriana was about to leave, when the prisoner raised his head from where he had laid it on the woman's shoulder and studied her. Her breath felt tight in her chest.

The man's arms, which a guard had been working to release with a small dagger, came free and he swooped the woman up, closing his eyes for a beat, and then saying something to her with a tender smile. He set the woman on her feet and hugged her to his side. He glanced in Adriana's direction one more time as he turned to go.

She dropped her eyes, filled with confusion. When she lifted her gaze again, all she could see was the man's back. His shirt was ripped to shreds and bloodied from the blows he had received, but he walked away with a happy ease she found enviable.

Garin clasped her shoulder. "Why did you do that?"

"I do not know," she answered honestly.

"It could not possibly be because the commoner was—" he quirked an eyebrow, "—somewhat handsome."

"Nay." Feeling her response was a bit too adamant, she hurried to add, "I just did not want to see anything happen—to anybody, boy, girl, good-looking, or not." *Besides he is not somewhat handsome, he is gorgeous.* She peered over her shoulder just as the object of her thoughts was passing under the stone gate of the castle's outer walls and sighed wistfully. Then she spun to Garin with a smile. "Let us go get ready for my ball."

He smiled in return and gave a little half-bow. "After you, m'lady."

CHAPTER TWO

Seth Hobbes sat on a bench at the kitchen table with his sister, Lea. She peeled the shirt from him with care, but it felt like she was ripping off a layer of skin.

"Ouch!"

"I am sorry. The blood has dried and the shirt is practically sealed to you in places." She worked for several seconds more in silence, but when he again sucked in his breath, she scolded, "If you were not out tangling with such dangerous men..."

He knew that her irritation only masked her concern, but pain spurred his own aggravation. "Are you going to lecture me, now, Lea?" His voice was almost a growl.

She sighed. "I was not going to lecture, little brother." Finally lifting the remains of the shirt from his back, she reached for the rag in the bowl of water by her side to clean the wounds. She dabbed gently at the abrasions and welts that had risen on his skin. He could not help but flinch and she withdrew momentarily so he could catch his breath. "I do not understand why you would want to strike—"

The water felt like fire. He jumped to his feet, almost upsetting the table the bowl was on. Wheeling about, he gripped his hips and glared. "I am not Tristan, you know. I can make my own decisions without having to come home and be schooled by you." Even as he barked at her, he felt bad for speaking unkindly, but his temper was amplified by his worry, and something else...something he could not quite get a handle on. "Where is Tristan, anyhow?"

"He is next door at Demetri Parish's. Why?"

Seth walked over to the wide fireplace and, resting one fist on the mantle, stared at the blazing logs. "Just wanted to know. Has he been home today?"

"Briefly. Why?" Lea's green eyes now held suspicion. "Why suddenly this concern over Tristan's whereabouts?"

"Just wondering. I am going to take a walk." He rushed to the door.

"What about this salve for your cuts?"

He heard her call after him and swung around. As she went to put the bowl away on one of the shelves, he stepped behind her and placed his hands on her shoulders.

"I am sorry I yelled at you. Bad day, and all." He shrugged, trying to humorously downplay the beating he had taken.

She smiled. "You are entitled, every now and then." She spun to regard him sternly, though a slight twitch of her lips betrayed her. "But you need to tell me exactly what happened today—" Seth moved away from her and she had to raise her voice so he would hear the rest of her sentence as he walked away "—to make Derrick want to turn ye into his new whipping boy."

Seth strode through the door. "Later," he called over his shoulder.

He marched along the dirt path past his blacksmith's shop to the pond, trying to come to grips with whatever it was that had gotten under his skin in the courtyard. He did his best thinking by the water. For some reason, it seemed to calm his nerves. The cooling evening air made his cuts sting and he shivered. His thoughts drifted to the princess who had undoubtedly saved his life, as he knew his stubborn pride would have cost him had he been taken to the river. When he arrived at the pond's edge, Seth crouched and skipped a rock across the water's surface, counting its hops idly. He rested his arms on his thighs, looking a little like a frog as he stared out over the water.

She was definitely pretty, that one. Fair-skinned, hair a rich chestnut, well-formed... He sighed. But, the king's daughter. How about that? He was sure what had seemed like compassion on her part was just...something else. Why would she have sympathy toward him, a mere commoner? He was certain in her eyes he was considered less worthy than the scrambling ants he now noticed at his feet. So why come to his aid? It was curious.

Though determined to get her out of his mind, he could not. The way the curling tendrils had framed her sweet face was quite fetching, and her eyes, striking in their blue-grey intensity. Yet, surely there was a haughtiness in her gaze, though he did not detect it, a coolness in her voice, although it had seemed both musical and sincere. And who was that nobleman who had touched her shoulder so familiarly and led her away? No doubt someone who was courting her, or perhaps they were already betrothed. Why did this thought make his stomach sour? A shout cut into his reverie.

"Uncle Seth!"

Seth pivoted to see a sandy-haired youth running among the tall, golden shafts of wheat in the field surrounding the pond. "Tristan," he called with relief.

The boy ran until he was a few yards from Seth, and stopped to bend over and catch his breath. He raised his gaze as he panted, squinting one eye because of the angle of the setting sun, and assessing his uncle.

"Are ye well?"

"Aye, Trist. Are you?" Seth was careful to keep his injuries hidden from the boy as he went over to put his arm over the lad's shoulder, rubbing the long hair Tristan wore in the same fashion as his own.

"Aye, sir. I was just scared. Are ye certain you are well? Why are you out here without a shirt?" Tristan leaned and peeked at his uncle's back. "Oh!" Tears sprang to his eyes and his face took on such a green tinge for a second Seth was afraid he was going to be sick. "That is my fault."

He moved in front of Tristan and, bending slightly to look him squarely in the eye, grasped his shoulders. "Nay, nay, Tristan. 'Tis my own temper that caused this. Nothing more, do you understand?"

Tristan nodded obediently, but seemed unconvinced as he hung his head. Seth rose and walked slowly toward the house with his hand on Tristan's shoulder. He glanced ahead. "Let us not speak any more of this. Your mother has been through much today." Tristan nodded silently beside him. "Trist," Seth added, trying to sound bright, "how about after we eat dinner, if there is still enough light, you and I try to catch a couple of fish?"

"Are you sure you are up to it, Uncle Seth?"

"Of course I am, son. Or are you afraid I will catch more than you?" He raised his eyebrows as he peered into Tristan s face.

He grinned. "I doubt that, Sir."

Seth rumpled his hair again. "We will see about that."

ADRIANA FELL INTO THE pillows, exhausted. She and Garin had danced every dance together and she could not remember a time when her feet hurt worse. But, although she was truly spent, sleep would not claim her. She tossed and turned on her bed, sometimes so violently she sent the sheer curtains that hung down all around her flying away as the covers fanned them outwards.

Garin was right. She had not belonged in the courtyard today. The alien sound of her father's harsh voice amazed and bothered her at the time and now echoed hellishly in her empty bed chamber. She had never known her father to be anything but kind. Since her mother had died when Adriana was ten, they had been very close. When he had remarried, their bond had remained unbroken, despite the efforts of her step-mother to drive a wedge into it. She loved her father, truly and deeply, and had tried to love her step-mother for her father's sake. He had been destroyed when he lost his most cherished wife to illness, and anything that gave him a small measure of happiness was prized by Adriana.

Her mind returned to the scene in the courtyard. What, then, had happened today? Had her father been ready to torture a man just for getting into a fight? The man had not appeared dangerous in any way, he had simply looked...

...incredible. She allowed her mind to stray to more pleasant thoughts of the man brought before her father. He was slightly taller than average, and exceedingly well-built. Virile...virile was the word that entered her mind when she thought about the stranger, and all the various connotations of the word had her quivering. She smiled at her own silliness and flipped to her other side.

Still...he had an intensity...like a rip tide. His eyes, she was sure, would have had any woman simpering after him like a fool...and the appealing way his sunny, blond hair fell into his eyes...ooooh, he was worth every minute she spent thinking of him.

Who cared when she kissed Garin good night she pictured the stranger's full lips commanding hers, rather than Garin's thin, more complacent ones? She had never really felt dissatisfied with Garin, or had any doubts about their relationship, but now something small nagged at her like a pebble in a shoe. Certainly, the match between Garin and her had been made before either of them had spoken their first word, but she had been able to transition from considering him as a brother to envisioning him as a lover easily. He was good at arousing her, in his way. His kisses were pleasing, his touch, soothing, they were compatible in that way. Perhaps her heart did not exactly skip a beat when they were together, but maybe that was because they had always been together...and would always be together...until the end...

Why did that thought seem suddenly terrifying? Adriana tossed again, huffing and throwing off the covers to get up and cross to the balcony. Perhaps it was just the stuffiness in the room making her feel smothered, she conjectured hopefully. She flung open the doors to her balcony and stepped out, leaning on the outer edge of the stone wall bordering the balcony and gulping in the deliciously cool air as the curtains flapped in the breeze. The wind also blew her lacy nightgown and licked at her thick, loosely-curling hair. She sat on the cold stone ledge that penetrated the thin fabric of her dressing gown, giving her goose-pimples, and stared at the full moon in rapture. She rubbed her arms, then closed her eyes and imagined another one touching her.

Her eyes opened after a bit, and she gazed longingly at the full moon. *Is there magic in you, fair Moon? Before many of your sisters have come and gone, I will be an old married woman, married to Garin. Is that what I want?* Though the moon bathed her in its pearly glow, it did not answer her, as she yearned for it to. What were these doubts of hers? Just this afternoon she had been so sure her happiness at Garin's side was secure. What changed that? Adriana's eyes scanned the grounds below, where the moonlight laced its way among the tree branches, casting mysterious shadows. Who was she searching for, in the depths of the night?

Her questions went out from her heart but returned, unanswered. She drew her feet in, balancing on the ledge and hugging her knees to her, suddenly morose. She had always been a good girl, doing just as her father told her, and her father had told her Garin was to be her husband. At twenty, she would be considered an old bride. Even her youngest sister, Kate, had already wed and left Ramport at sixteen. Adriana put off her marriage for one reason or another. When her father told her of the arrangement on her sixteenth birthday, she asked for more time to become accustomed to the idea of Garin as her husband. Later, she used Kate's wedding as an excuse, stating that she did not want to steal the light from her sister's glory. But for Adriana to continue on, unwed, would soon be deemed scandalous. Now as she peered out over the fields of wheat, the ponds, and thatched roof cottages of the village, she felt the castle walls confining. The fact she had rarely left them seemed all at once to be ridiculous. There was so much more of the world out there, so much more for her to learn, so much more for her to discover. Was she to waste her life within these frigid walls? She stood and turned from the view, strangely pained by it. She ran her hand along the chilly, hard walls of the castle, and began to feel like the proverbial princess, locked away in a high tower, waiting for her prince to come to her rescue.

Shaking her head, she reentered her room, closing the doors behind her. She ran to her bed, jumping in it with a bounce and pulling the covers to her chin.

She would think of it no longer.

And as the moonlight silently crept across her floor, drawing nearer and nearer to her bed, she fell asleep.

CHAPTER THREE

Adriana woke. Had she heard something in her chamber? Her heart beating wildly, she sat and searched the deep shadows of the room, but saw nothing. Her eyes were drawn to the motion of the curtains where her balcony doors stood wide open. Had she not closed them? No wonder. With a sigh, she swung her legs out of bed and crossed to the door.

"Princess…?"

Her scream pierced the air and then her mouth was covered as she was pushed back to the wall, her left arm clasped firmly by the intruder. Pressing against her, the man's gaze flashed to the door, his forehead creased. It was the man she had saved in the courtyard earlier.

"Why did you do that?" he asked.

Her reply was muffled by his hand. He removed it cautiously.

"I was not expecting visitors to my bed chamber this evening," she retorted sarcastically, breaking free from him and crossing the room to pull on a satin robe over her gown.

"Is that so?" he mumbled under his breath as if he doubted it.

She stiffened. "What?"

"Princess! Princess Adriana!" Fists hammered on the thick wooden door she had barred before retiring. Watching the door, she returned to his side.

"Who is that?"

"My guards," Adriana remarked matter-of-factly.

"Your <u>guards</u>? Are you such a heavy threat they have to keep you under guard to ensure you do not escape?"

"Me, under guard?" She stared at him, confused. "Nay. They are guarding *me* from intruders—" she punched his chest for emphasis, "—like you."

"Princess Adriana! Open the door this minute or we will break it down!"

Alarmed, she responded, "Nay, everything is fine. I...had a bad dream is all. Sorry to have bothered you." Seth and Adriana exchanged hopeful glances, praying her answer would satisfy them.

"I would like to see ye are well for myself," a deep voice insisted.

"Derrick," she whispered in a panic to Seth, grabbing his elbow.

Again, the deep voice rumbled through the door. "I thought I heard a man's voice."

Adriana studied Seth. "You have to get out of here. Quickly!" she hissed. She walked with him to the edge of the balcony, calling over her shoulder. "Derrick...you know I would have no man in my bedchamber...at this hour, or any other."

"Then you will have no reason not to open the door so I can see for my-self," came his answer, sounding as if he were smiling.

Adriana gaped at Seth again. The moon danced in his hair as he gazed in-to her eyes—his eyes the bluest blue of the evening sky—and his lips parted. For the briefest of seconds she imagined kissing those full lips goodbye, but as she did, he stepped on the wall and grabbed on to a length of rope he had looped around a section of the battlement to scale the walls. "You must flee as fast as you can. If they catch you—" Adriana squealed as the door rever-berated with a loud *crack*. Wood splintered as those outside rammed it with something large. "You must take me as a hostage."

"What?" Seth almost lost his grip on the rope just as he had begun to de-scend.

"If they catch you, you must be able to barter with me for your freedom." Adriana scrambled onto the parapet.

"What? Nay!" Seth stared up. The princess grappled with the rope above him. He tried to focus elsewhere when the wind blew her gown out, allowing him full view of her bare legs. He continued to shimmy lower as fast as pos-sible, afraid the rope would fail with the strain of the added weight. When his feet hit the bottom, he peered overhead and saw the princess awkwardly traversing the wall. With an abbreviated scream, her slide accelerated. Seth stepped forward to try to catch her, his heart thumping, but after several feet she managed to wrap her legs around the rope tighter and slow her descent. Seth said a silent prayer of thanksgiving he had not killed the princess; he de-cided that would undoubtedly be a bad thing for him. She descended the rest of the way more gracefully, and when she was close enough, he grabbed her hips and helped to swing her to the ground, trying to ignore how his hands glided over the satin covering her curvy figure. She turned, and held very still, considering him. The wind blew her hair gently and he didn't release her hips as they stood frozen. "Princess..." he began, his voice oddly hoarse.

She grabbed his arm and raced toward the castle's gate. "Hurry! We must flee before they discover I am gone." Having no other choice, he raced after her as he heard the sound of the door crashing and several shouts over finding the princess was missing.

They flew across Ramport's confines, jumping short fences and dodging statuary, listening for sounds that they were being chased. Once beyond the gate, Seth took the lead as they rushed through an orchard, just beyond the castle's walls, brushing against low-hanging branches, and finally, into the wheat field outside of his home. No one seemed to be following them, but they did not slacken their speed, their feet pounding across the landscape without ceasing. When he reached the house, Seth threw open the back door, and entered, dragging Adriana behind him. They stood, panting, unable to speak to each other, their eyes wide.

"Seth?" Lea called, approaching with a candle held aloft, worry straining her voice. When she caught sight of Adriana, she inhaled in sharply. "The Princess! Seth Hobbes, are you crazy?"

Adriana stepped in front of him, still gulping for air. "Nay...it...was...my idea."

"*Your* idea?" Lea glanced from her to Seth, incredulous. Seth shrugged, but seemed like the little boy who was discovered after breaking a family heirloom.

As she tried to catch her breath, Adriana looked from Seth's face, to the woman's, then stopped, enchanted by how the candle and the fire, which had burnt low in the hearth, made the mesmerizing green of the woman's eyes glow even more brightly. "You are so beautiful," she murmured.

Seth and Lea exchanged expressions of astonishment.

"Did she hit her head?" Lea asked tentatively.

Seth shook his. "Not that I know of."

Adriana flushed. "I am sorry. It is just...even all of the ladies of the court, with all their expensive artifices, cannot compare to you."

"Well...thank you," Lea replied slowly. She seemed uncomfortable with the compliment, and still unsure about Adriana's sanity.

Adriana shook her head to clear her thoughts. She studied Seth. "Can I ask you something?" He took a step in the opposite direction, but nodded. "Why did you strike Derrick?"

Lea moved to the princess' side. "Aye, I would like to hear the answer to that myself."

Seth peered from one to the other hesitantly, and finally let out an exasperated sigh. "I hit him because he was about to cuff Tristan."

"Tristan?" Lea clutched her stomach.

"He did not tell you?"

She shook her head, feeling her way as she sat on one of the benches at the kitchen table. She set the candle down. "I have not seen him all evening. He is spending the night next door, at the Parishes'." Seth took a seat across from her, gesturing to Adriana to sit beside him. As Adi joined him, she noted how carefully he watched the woman's face, obviously concerned for her.

"Who is Tristan?" she interrupted as the candle-light drew the three into a tight circle.

"My fourteen-year-old nephew."

"My son." Lea answered at the same time.

She tipped her head to one side. "You are not man and wife?"

"Nay!" they both answered vehemently, and then laughed at their duplicate reaction.

"This reprobate is my little brother." Lea grinned at Seth, reaching to squeeze his arm across the table. It was apparent the two cared deeply for one another. "Seth has lived here with me and Tristan since my husband passed two years ago."

"Oh, I am sorry for your loss." A wave of remorse hit Adriana for having accidentally breached such a sad topic.

Seth regarded her curiously but she ignored it.

"Thank you," Lea responded quietly.

"Why was Derrick—"Adi forced herself to swallow her anger, "—why was he going to hit Tristan?" The image of the burly figure towering over a cowering boy had her stomach churning.

Seth answered, but kept his gaze on his sister. "Because...he was mad about losing a bet." A quick fury ignited in Lea's eyes. He held up a hand to keep her from cutting in.

"He bet Simon, another one of your father's men—" he explained to Adriana, "—I could not lift this enormous log. And when I did," he added, seeming a little smug, "he was angry. Tristan had a hard time holding in his laughter and Derrick stepped forward, and I, well...swung the tree at him."

Lea's mouth fell open. "You struck him with a tree?"

"Aye, I suppose so." He grinned.

Adriana felt the blood drain from her face. "Derrick was going to hit a fourteen-year-old?"

They both stared at her. "Aye," Seth said, "but that is nothing new. That is how they always work." He studied her face. "I should see you home to the palace."

Adriana nodded dumbly, and Lea and Seth traded a look.

"It was nice meeting you, Your Highness," Lea said slowly.

"Oh, you as well. Please call me Adriana, or Adi." She rose from her seat, still feeling shaky, and allowed Seth to lead her to the front door. But when he opened it, they all heard the shouted order outside. "Search every house until the Princess is found."

Seth pushed Adriana away from the door, closing it to within a crack, and peering out. A dozen horsemen, some holding torches aloft to light the way for the ones on foot, roamed the dirt streets of the village. Doors were being banged on and sleepy villagers roused from their beds.

"What are we going to do?"

"We will go out the back." He grabbed Adriana's elbow and ushered her through the house. But when he opened that door, he had to shut it just as quickly. Horsemen patrolled the pond and wheat field, watching for anyone who tried to escape from the village.

"Now what?"

Seth sighed. "Now I turn myself in, before they harass any more people, and the princess goes home."

"Nay!" she and Lea cried at the same time.

The terror Lea felt was etched on her face. "There has to be another solution."

"This is my fault!" Adriana wailed. Seconds passed while they all tried to devise another plan. Adriana's face cleared. "You can hide me."

Lea and Seth shook their heads. "They will search the house. There is really no place to hide in here."

"Then I will wear a disguise."

Seth snorted, and Adriana shot him a dark glare. She took Lea's hands. "Do you have something I can change into?"

"Aye, but..."

"Princess, even dressed in a potato sack, these men would recognize you," Seth finished his sister's statement for her.

Adriana's gaze never left Lea's. "Not when you cut my hair."

"What? I could not." Lea shook her head, shocked.

"You must," she stated vehemently, dragging her into the room. "And you must do it quickly."

Seth appeared unconvinced.

"With that, a change of clothing and a little luck, it might be enough. The lighting is dim...I think it could work."

He continued to gape at her for a beat, peered again outside, and responded with an air of resignation, "I will watch the front door."

They rushed now, knowing it would be mere minutes before the king's men worked their way around to them. Lea scrambled up the ladder to the loft with Adriana hot on her heels. "I cannot believe I am doing this." She fished in a trunk at the foot of the beds Seth fashioned for her when Tristan was born, and brought out a plain, coarse, blue dress.

Adriana quickly disrobed and slipped the stiff dress on over her head. Without another word, she crossed to the ladder. As she twisted to head down she saw Lea shake her head, running her hand across the intricate beadwork on the beautiful nightgown and robe.

Lea stuffed the royal garments into the bottom of the trunk, covering them with quilts and pillows, then hurried to follow Adriana.

When Lea spun around, Adriana was sitting at the table. Seth was staring out the door. He turned now, his face tense. "They are next door."

Lea fumbled in a drawer and produced a sharp knife. Adriana went cold, but she bent her head and gathered her hair.

"Are ye sure, Princess?"

"It is Adriana," she replied tersely, "and ...aye."

"I cannot believe I am doing this," Lea said again, her voice high and desperate this time. She grabbed ahold of the mound of Adi's softly-curling, gleaming brown tresses, and began to hack away at it with her knife. Not a sound could be heard for several seconds except for the knife as it sawed through thick locks. Seth glanced over from his post at the door as Adriana fought back tears. Despite her best efforts, Lea was pulling some out by the roots. It hurt more than Adriana could have imagined, but she could not alert those outside by screaming. Instead she tried to release her pain by clenching and unclenching her fists.

"I am sorry. I am sorry," Lea mumbled over and over again as she struggled feverishly with the mass of curls.

Seth looked away.

He shut the door and sprang to the table. "They are coming!"

"Well, I am finished," Lea said mechanically. She held a length of the last strands as she gazed at the results forlornly. She rotated and threw the remaining hewn fibers on the hearth, hauling over a wooden crate that held logs to hide it. Seconds later, the door was thrown open without even a preliminary shout. Four armed men walked in, studying at the trio with suspicion.

The tallest of the group, who had entered last, eyed them suspiciously. "Why are you all awake at this hour of the night?"

"We heard your sweet voices in the common area, and thought we may as well rise and get dressed to greet you," Lea answered, with barely-concealed contempt.

"Is that so?" The man smiled smugly. He paced while his men tore about the room, searching. "You have two women? What is your trick?" he asked Seth suggestively.

"This is my sister," he spat, "and my cousin, here for a visit."

Adriana kept her head low, avoiding eye contact, but the man approached the table. He grabbed her chin and tipped her head up so he could get a better view of her in the firelight. He leered at her, offering a toothy grin. "Welcome, Cuz."

With terror seizing her heart, Adriana tensed and stared at the man's hard features. Seth and Lea simultaneously grabbed her hands under the table and squeezed them to comfort her, but then they all were distracted by the sound of dishes hitting the floor and breaking.

The destruction incensed Adriana. She lost all fear in an instant. "Stop that!" she burst out, her voice imperial in its fervor. She stood and raced toward the man who was throwing items out of Lea's cabinets. "What do you think you are doing?"

The man who had grabbed her, his jaw tight, now maneuvered so that he was between her and the other man.

"Please!" Lea called out frantically. "My cousin has been sick." She grabbed Adriana and tried to pull her back. "Poor dear does not even know what she is saying." Lea raised her brows and shook her head, letting go of Adriana for a second, to tap her temple with one finger, indicating her "cousin" was mentally diminished.

The man glared at Lea for a second, then returned his gaze to Adriana. In a flash, he slapped her across the face, sending both women stumbling into the mantle. "Ye need to teach her some manners, then."

Seth started forward, anger impugning his judgment. But Lea swung an arm out to detain him, and it was enough of a delay as the next instant all of their attention was drawn to the soldier that called from above.

"Sir." He scrambled down the ladder and crossed to turnover a beaded nightgown to his superior, the man who had struck Adriana.

He shook it at the three members of the house. "What is this?"

"It was my grandmother's," Lea said quickly.

The man brought the satin to his face and inhaled, then closed his eyes. "Mmm. It does not smell like any old lady to me." His eyes flashed open, staring at Lea intently.

"That is because I keep honeysuckle in the clothes chest, to keep it from getting musty," Lea retorted without a hint of deception in her tone.

The fireplace logs shifted, and Seth glanced downward at the sound. His keen gaze noted a chunk of the princess's hair was not hidden by the crate. He planted his boot over it.

The leader rubbed the satin nightgown against his stubbly cheek, eyeing them distrustfully. "Very well," he said finally, "we will leave." He gestured toward the door and his men moved out ahead of them. He threw the nightgown in front of Adriana and into the fire disdainfully, and left without another word.

When the door closed behind them, Seth and Lea let out a sigh of relief, but Adriana fell to her knees amongst the broken dishes, her shoulders shaking. "Why did they do this to your beautiful dishes? They did not have to do this." She raked at the pieces scattered on the floor.

Lea bent in order to stop her. "Adriana, it does not matter."

"Nay, it does. They should not have done this. 'Tis all my fault."

"Nay, 'tis not," Lea replied soothingly, then, pointing to a smear of blood on the floor, she cried out, "You cut yourself."

"Nay. Nay, I did not." Adriana seemed a bit calmer. She held out her hands, which were red and raw in places. "'Tis only from the rope. I must have rubbed some of the skin off when I was trying to gather this mess."

Seth bent to assess her injuries. "You did this on the rope? Why did you not say anything?"

"I do not know." She shrugged. "I guess I did not think about it."

Lea and Seth exchanged a look of disbelief over her head.

She turned from where she still squatted amidst the pieces of broken pottery. "I will pay for this all. As soon as I get to the castle."

"Nay, 'tis fine."

"Nay, 'tis not. I insist."

"Fine, then, if it will make you feel better," Lea acquiesced. "But let me bandage your wounds," she added gently.

"Nay. They are not that bad."

"Let me clean them, at least."

She moved Adriana to the table, going to get a cloth wet. Seth sat, catching Lea's eye when she returned. The concern he felt for Adriana, along with the sheer wonder over her actions, he saw mirrored in Lea's face. He could not miss the fact she trembled as she sat beside him and appeared dazed.

Lea tended to her injuries tenderly. "There, that is better."

"Thank you," the princess murmured, staring at the bandages as if numb. She peered at Lea after a couple of seconds. "I am s-so sorry...if I had known...well, I should have known...if I had stopped to think..."

Lea slid an arm around her and gazed over at Seth helplessly.

He could tell she was overwhelmed by what had transpired. "Princess, we cannot take you to Ramport tonight. ...I know these kinds of accommodations are not what you are used to, but—"

"Nay. 'Tis I who am sorry to put you out."

"Do not be absurd," Lea said cheerfully. "It would be our honor to have you. You can have Tristan's bed, since he is not here." She stood, leading the way to the loft, but throwing a backward glance at her brother.

Seth leaned on the mantle and stared into the dying embers of the fire. A few minutes later Seth heard her descending the ladder.

"What were you thinking?" she began, laying the extra quilt she had brought on the table, but he raised a hand to interrupt her.

"Lea, you are not saying anything I have not been telling myself over and over again tonight." He pivoted to regard her earnestly. "I am sorry I have brought this trouble to your home."

She sighed. "'Tis hard to stay mad at you when you are being so contrite. Tell me how all of this happened."

He paced, rubbing his forehead. "I do not know! I went to thank her for saving my neck. I knew they would never let me in for a proper audience. If I even get near the place that Derrick is bound to trump up some charge against me. And...I guess I frightened her."

"You frightened her?" She frowned. "How did you get in to see her?"

"I was pacing around outside the castle, and...there she was, out on her balcony..." He stared off, remembering.

"And?"

"And, I...climbed a rope to her room. She had drifted to sleep."

Lea plopped down at the table, her mouth hanging open. "And so you traipsed into her bedchamber?"

Seth thought about how he was drawn there by the sight of Adriana's still body behind the filmy curtains surrounding her bed, her chest rising and falling gently beneath the lightweight covers. She had been incredibly beautiful, her hair splayed on the pillow, her lips parted, cheeks flushed. He had not meant to frighten her.

He began pacing again, his words spilling out now. "She screamed, and the guards came, and—" He gestured wildly. "Look, I know it was stupid. It was as if I could not help myself, do you not understand?" Irritation colored his words. "And then she was ...coming with me, telling me I needed a hostage. It was insane! Neither of us was thinking clearly."

"Fine. Fine." Lea took a breath. "What are we going to do now?"

He stopped and peered at her steadily. "We will get some sleep, and in the morning, I will take her back."

Lea sighed. "Aye." She lifted the quilt. "I brought an extra blanket for your bed. It has turned cooler." Seth followed her as she moved in the direction of his bedroom at the front of the house. She tilted her chin, lowering her voice. "She is odd, is she not?"

"Aye." Seth glanced overhead as if he could see her. "How did she fare when you showed her to the loft?"

"I do not know. Poor thing was trembling from tip to toe. I am sure she has never seen such drama within Ramport's walls, and I am certain she has never been struck that way."

"Aye." His jaw clenched. "I wanted to kill the bastard." He caught the disapproval in Lea's eyes. "I am sorry, but I did."

"Me, too," she said begrudgingly. She mused. "I like her. I never thought I would say that about a royal, but I really like her. She is sweet."

"You are only saying that because she said you were beautiful," he teased.

She snatched the pillow from the bed and hit him with it. "So she has good taste."

He laughed and grabbed the edge of the quilt to help her spread it over the bed. As it dropped, suspended in midair briefly, he wondered out loud. "She let you cut her hair. ...And you butchered it."

"Seth!" Lea pleaded. "I did my best. I was under some pressure, if you recall."

"I know, I know," he chuckled. "But she let you cut her hair." He thought about the tears in Adriana's eyes and how the princess had not made a sound while she had, undoubtedly, been in pain, while the knife struggled through layers of her hair.

"I know," Lea responded, equally flabbergasted. "The feel of that silky hair...do you know how many women would love to have hair like that?"

He grunted in reply.

After she left, he lay under the quilt, his arms crossed behind his head, reviewing every utterance, and every nuance of the evening, trying to make sense of it all. All he knew for certain was Adriana had a way of making him feel unsettled, and he did not like it. It was a long while before he finally fell asleep, thinking again about how she looked as he climbed onto her balcony; as ethereal as a fairy, as alluring as a siren. That image, and the image of her jumping angrily at the man who was destroying his sister's dishes, did not seem to go together. The princess was a mystery, this was certain. But did he really want to discover who she truly was?

Would it be worth the headache?

CHAPTER FOUR

Seth decided to give up on sleep when he could see the light outside his window becoming a shade or two lighter. He rose and stoked the fire, hoping to take a little chill out of the air before the women woke. As he did, though, he heard the creak of the ladder behind him.

"Ahh...you got her off early then. I had hoped to say goodbye," Lea said, her voice laced with disappointment.

"What are you talking about? Is she not there with you?"

"Nay."

He peered beyond her, out the window, where in the gathering pink of the dawn he could now make out a figure strolling around down by the pond. He crossed the floor quickly and headed out the door.

As he got closer he slowed his pace, watching Adriana carefully. She seemed absorbed in her thoughts at first. She rubbed her arms as she stared out over the pond. Perhaps the dress was not enough to keep out the chill.

"So, you were going to run off without saying goodbye, then?" he asked gruffly, not sure where the accusation came from.

She jumped, startled, and whirled around. He could see she was troubled. Seeming to react to the set of his jaw, she snapped. "Nay. Of course not. Why would I do that?"

Seth shrugged. "Perhaps you thought you did not need to speak to us lowly villagers."

Fire flickered behind her eyes and she opened her mouth to say something, but then clapped it shut, twisting away from him, perhaps thinking better of it. "I do not think of you that way," she said, her voice shaky. "I'm grateful for all you have done for me."

"Why did you come here?" he snarled, aggravated with himself, as much as with her.

Adriana turned and searched his face. He shifted his weight. "I do not know," she answered at last. The breeze blew his shirt against his chest and her eyes followed the motion and lingered there, perhaps a bit too long. Her mouth hung open a little when she lifted her gaze to his. Her cheeks colored and she glanced away. "Why do you always have your shirt undone?" she asked irritably.

Seth, recognizing the look in her eyes, smiled, feeling pleased. "Why? Does it bother you?"

"Nay, I..." Her focus flitted everywhere.

He moved to tighten the strings of his shirt, feeling bad for barking at her and not wishing to provoke her further. "It is just, when it is tight, it rubs against my back and it is painful."

Adriana winced and stopped him from tying it. "Oh! Do not then." She stared at her hands on him and withdrew them.

He lightly held her elbows, keeping her near for a second, and she froze, eyeing him with what he sensed was both fear and desire. When he touched her, a charge ran through him. He was conscious of the rhythm of her breathing, and of her scent, light and sweet, like a meadow full of flowers in the sun. He had already come to recognize the way her eyes would appear bluer when they sparked with anger, more grey when she was serious. Now they danced with the rising sun setting them off like stars in the night sky. He longed to taste her lips and it took all of his strength not to bend his head toward hers.

All at once, she stepped away from him and spun in the opposite direction. "I...should not have done that...I..."

He took a step forward, intending to find out what her feelings were, but she rounded on him fiercely.

"My father is not the man you think he is."

Her sudden change caught him off-balance at first, but then his eyes narrowed. "Did that slap in the face not teach you anything?"

She flushed and touched her cheek. "H-he would not approve of that behavior."

He laughed dryly. The ardent desire swimming through his veins moments ago was replaced with a bitter anger. He had seen too much of the king's cruelty. "Would not approve? He encourages it."

"Nay. You are wrong."

"You think so? Well, you should stick around here and find out for your-self. You would know better in a day's time."

"Perhaps I should," she replied defiantly, with a tilt of her chin.

She looked so damned cute as she stood up to him. It both angered and warmed him. He fought another urge to kiss her. He shook his head, clearing away the emotion that always seemed to be there when they talked. "Now, that is a ridiculous idea."

"Nay, 'tis not. You suggested it yourself."

He kicked the ground, raising a cloud of dirt. He spun away from her, gripping his hips, unhappy she had used his words against him. So the princess wanted to see how the other half lived. She had no real interest in justice, he was sure; after all, she was the king's daughter. It must be a game to her. But it was no game to him, it was his life. "Nay," he said finally. "You do not belong out here." He rotated to stare at her coolly. "You belong behind your perfect walls." He gestured toward the Castle Ramport. He could tell he had hit his mark, only it pained him as much as it pained her.

"I see..." she said, her voice wavering. "Well, I guess you have made it clear how you feel about me. You think I am a spoiled ninny." Her hands fisted at her sides, and tears sprang to her eyes. She closed them for a moment. She sighed, opening her eyes to study him. "Perhaps you are right. You are good, honest, and intelligent. And, I admit, I have never worked a day in my life, never wanted for anything, except perhaps..." She peered off for a moment at the rest of the village. He followed her line of vision. Smoke was rising from many of the chimneys now and lights could be seen through the windows. The houses appeared cheerful and comforting, like a gathering of old friends sitting around a campfire. "Perhaps you are right," she said again, her voice a mere whisper. She started off in the direction of the castle. "I will see myself home, then." She walked several feet, then, broke into a run.

Seth hesitated only a second before sprinting after her. "Wait. Wait. Dammit, Adriana! Wait!"

"Leave me alone!" she screamed, running faster.

"Nay, please. Wait." With the last, he finally caught her at the edge of the field and grabbed her arm. She shook him off but stopped, reaching out to lean on a tree's wide trunk to steady herself. For several minutes, all that could be heard was the sound of their heavy breathing and some birds tweeting mindlessly in the nearby trees. "I am sorry, Adriana," he said, finally. "Do not...leave this way."

"Why does it matter to you how I leave?" she spat, facing him, tears in her eyes.

He took a step forward, and she backed into the tree's trunk. He grasped a branch above her head, then, squinted down at her.

"I do not know," he said softly, the words escaping from him before he even had time to think about his response. He chuckled as he observed her. "You are a mess," he murmured. He reached over to brush the hair across her forehead. Then he caressed her smooth cheek, which had become smudged when she had tried to wipe away her tears as she ran. His held her shoulder loosely. "Come and at least have breakfast with me...with us," he corrected quickly.

She gazed into his face, seeming unsure at first, but then nodded slowly. They turned and walked to the house in tandem, silently.

When they entered the kitchen Seth got the feeling Lea had been watching them from the window. She was working a little too hard and her, "Good morning, Adriana!" when they stepped through the door was a little too cheery.

Adriana smiled shyly. "Good morning, Lea. Can I help with breakfast?"

"Do you know anything about cooking?" she asked uncertainly.

"Nay," Adriana admitted, "but I am willing to learn."

"Good, then. Let us get to work."

Lea was surprised to find Adriana to be a good listener and a willing helper. She chuckled a little bit when the princess mistook the flour for sugar, and when she was confused about what a "pinch" of salt was, but, all-in-all, both Lea and Adi enjoyed it immensely. Seth bustled around doing various chores, but he was perfectly aware of everything going on in the kitchen.

After they finished breakfast, he rose, reluctantly, and announced he had to leave to do some work on the king's new bridge. All of the healthy men, and even boys, had been enlisted for the heavy labor.

"This early?" Adriana asked. "'Tis barely light."

"I am actually late. I work the same hours as the sun."

"Oh," she said, clearly disappointed he was leaving so soon.

"I need to take this bread to the ducks," Lea said, rising to give him a peck on the cheek. He knew she was making up an excuse to leave the two of them alone. He did not mind.

"Seth, I am sorry about earlier..."

"That is the first time you have said my name."

"It is? 'Tis a good name, simple, solid."

The use of the word "simple" set him on edge. He had been called simple before, "just a simple commoner" he thought were the words the nobleman had used. "Aye. Makes it easy when I have to sign my mark." Feeling like his intelligence had been called into question, he referred to the illiterate people who could not even sign their own names.

Adriana seemed confused by his change in mood. "Did I say something wrong?"

"Nay," he answered curtly, "of course not." He yanked his vest on. "Well, it was nice meeting you," he called over his shoulder, and left, closing the door loudly behind him.

From the back, Lea heard the slam of the door and glanced toward the front of the house. She saw Seth, with his shoulders squared, marching along the road at a rapid rate, and guessed the pair had some sort of argument. Her suspicions were confirmed when she returned to the kitchen and found Adriana furiously scrubbing a pot.

"Hello," she said tentatively.

"Hello," Adriana replied, without looking at her. She sniffled, and Lea knew on top of making her angry, Seth had hurt the girl's feelings. "I want to thank you, Lea, for having me." She stopped, appearing to not trust her voice further.

"Adriana," Lea said gently. "Did you and Seth have an argument?"

She peered down, and after a brief pause, nodded. She started to cry, and Lea grabbed a towel and patted her hands dry. Her arms around the princess, Lea escorted her over to the table. "Whatever the big lout said, I am sure he did not mean it."

"Nay. That is the thing, I am sure he does. He thinks I think of him poorly because I am..." She struggled with the word.

"A princess?"

"Aye. But I do not care about that. I think he is wonderful. But every time we are together, things become heated. We shout at each other and say awful things."

Lea recognized the signs, remembering how she and her husband, Hayden, had bumbled through their first years of courtship. Oh, if she could only have that time again to spend it a better way.

"I told him I wanted to stay, and find out more about my father, from *his* side. And he told me I belonged behind my 'perfect' walls."

"How dare he." Lea pushed to her feet. "How *dare* he! You are not like that."

Adriana smiled through her tears. "You see that?"

"Of course. If you were some snobby princess would you have allowed me to cut your hair to save his hide? Would you have offered to help me cook breakfast? Would you have been upset about my stupid dishes?"

Adriana sprang up and ran to give her a hug. "Oh, thank you. Thank you!" But a shadow crossed her face again and she pulled back. "I only wish Seth could see me like you see me."

"He is an idiot sometimes, but eventually he will face his mistakes." Lea thought about it. "Why do you not spend the day with me? In a little while I will leave to take water to the men at the bridge. Seth and Tristan will be there."

Adriana smiled and squeezed her.

"Thank you, truly."

CHAPTER FIVE

The banks of the River Astri, though usually quiet, were bustling with life today. The king had decided a bridge would increase commerce between the kingdom of Hamiltonia and the neighboring kingdom of Dunneston and had sent his soldiers to organize the effort to build the bridge. Every healthy male in the village had been conscripted, and so it was that the shopkeeper worked shoulder to shoulder with the farmer. Clergymen hefted logs bolstered on the other end by tailors. Men led horses pulling huge timbers, or crawled like ants over the planks of the bridge with hammers. Several squads of the king's soldiers were seen here and there, juxtaposed to the villagers' staid browns and grays with their tight, white pants and bright red jackets. It was quite an undertaking as the span of the river was wide and it cut deep into the landscape. The bridge was elaborately designed with criss-crossing supports beneath an arching base and promised to be lovely, as well as functional.

Adriana breathed a sigh of relief when she noted the king's men gathered at the bridge were not the same ones usually posted at the castle. There was less of a chance of being recognized. Lea had timed things perfectly; they had arrived with the water just as the men were taking to the shade of the trees for a break. When Seth saw them coming, he was resting on the ground and scrambled to his feet. Adriana stopped to offer some men water, and he took the opportunity to accost his sister.

"What did you bring her here for?" he scowled.

"I do not know what you are griping for," Lea said innocently. "She wanted to come, so she came. It is her prerogative, you know."

"Her…? Of course I know it is her prerogative," he snapped, never taking his focus from Adriana, "but she is going to get in trouble, or she is going to get me in trouble, somehow. Good Lord, the woman had me kidnapping her last night, for heaven's sake."

"I am sorry, Seth," she said with a sweet smile, "but there are a lot of thirsty men here. I need to go."

"What about me? I am thirsty." But she ignored him, moving off to a group of men gathered under a big oak. He was annoyed with her transparent efforts at matchmaking. Sure, the princess was attractive, any man could see that. But a woman from such a lofty upbringing would have no interest in him, of that he was sure. And, besides, she would be too much of a pain for him to deal with.

Still, he stood watching Adriana from a distance. He did not like the way the men were looking at her. He crossed to her, finally, and grabbed her elbow. "I want to talk to you."

"Ouch!" she exclaimed as he hustled her off to the side. "You are hurting me."

"Sorry." He relaxed his grip a little. "What are you doing here?"

"I came to see how my father's men worked, remember?"

"And *I* told you it was not a good idea." His angry words were drawing attention, so he lowered his voice. "You need to go."

"Rachel!" A man motioned to her from the trees.

"Rachel?"

"Well, I cannot exactly go by Adriana, can I? I have to go."

"Nay, do not. I am thirsty." He grabbed the ladle from her bucket to detain her and started slurping up water. His gaze slid sideways. "See the way he is eyeing you," he muttered angrily.

"What are you talking about?" she retorted, snatching the ladle from him. "At least *he* is polite."

"Are you jesting? All he wants is to..."

"Is to what?"

"Come. Even you cannot be that naïve." Seeing her confused face, he corrected, "Well, perhaps you can." Seth took her shoulders and turned her so she was facing the man in question, who leered at her, raising his brow suggestively. "All he wants to do is to get you by yourself," Seth whispered in her ear, and, hearing the quickening of her breath and knowing his voice was arousing her, he finished meanly "—and have his way with you."

Adriana gasped, and stiffened under his fingers. She twisted and smiled at him, and then lifted the ladle of water and poured it over his head, before storming off. Several men laughed, but he ignored them, watching Adriana's back with a sour feeling in his stomach. Aye, he was hard on her, but she needed somebody to be hard on her. She was pampered too much, he told himself. But, his words were little comfort as he watched her walk away from him—yet again.

Lea walked over and spoke to him casually as she searched for another man in need of a drink. "Charming as ever, brother."

HE WAS SURPRISED TO see Adriana during the afternoon break. After watching her cater to other men's needs for a while, he rose and approached her.

"Adriana?"

"Leave me alone, Seth."

"Adriana," he said softly, "come, now. I am sorry."

She spun to peer him. He was tired and dirty, and his hair was damp with sweat. He must look a sight, he thought.

After a moment's hesitation, she held the ladle high to offer him a drink. She grasped the handle and cupped the bowl to hold it steady for him. He deliberately put his hand over hers on the bottom, staring into her eyes the whole time he drank the cool water she gave him. He was happy to see this affected her...and was surprised by how much it affected him.

She returned late in the afternoon, sitting on the hill and watching him work with those intensely grey eyes that seemed to miss nothing.

Knowing she was observing him, Seth hefted heavier than usual loads, glad she was there so he could show off a little. Perhaps she was not that bad, this princess. She had worked hard giving the men water, and those thoughtful, simmering eyes of hers about undid him when she would catch his eye.

His thoughts and emotions when she was around were confusing, the anger and possessiveness he felt were born from his strong need for her. Could it be possible she was the one he had been waiting for?

By the time the sun set, he was thoroughly exhausted. He climbed the hill toward her, his smile broad. "Hello."

"Hello," she replied with a smile of her own, getting to her feet and brushing off her dress. They walked down the road together contentedly.

"So...your hair is nice."

She patted it, blushing. "Lea made it appear as if I am wearing it up, rather than live with that whole chopped-off fashion."

He stopped and touched her hair. "It's pretty." He smiled. And then, laughed, as his stomach rumbled. "I am starving."

"Well, Lea and I made you a fantastic dinner."

He took her hand boldly as they walked, a gesture that would have given the impression of being casual to any onlooker. "Really?"

She smiled, and glanced at him shyly in a way he found immensely alluring. "Well, I was more like a helper, but I did learn a few things," she added thoughtfully. "Lea's really wonderful."

"Aye, I know. She is a fantastic mother to young Tristan, too." He surveyed her out of the corner of his eye, gauging her response. "Did you get a chance to meet him?"

"Nay. He was still at his friend's."

Seth was disappointed. He was proud of his nephew. "Well, you will meet him at dinner for certain."

"Actually...I am not going to be at dinner."

He stopped to regard her in the increasingly dim light. "Why?"

"I am going to the castle."

He stared at her for a minute, expressionless, and then pivoted and began walking rapidly along the road, her words like a slap in the face.

She ran to catch him. "Seth, please. I need to tell my father I am well and safe. I do not want him to worry about me."

He slowed his pace some, but he did not try to hold her hand as before. He was thinking about Adriana's hair. He had been stupid enough to think she had done it for him, but he could see now this was not true. She had done it for someone else. "Who was that man with you yesterday in the courtyard?"

Her already fair face paled. "W-well..."

He turned on her. "Who *is* he, Adriana?"

"H-his name is Garin."

Seth started walking again and she strove to keep up with his lengthy strides. "Garin," he repeated snidely. Again, he stopped. "And who is this Garin to you, *exactly*?" he asked, drawing out the last word.

"We have known each other since we were young." To avoid making eye contact with him, Adriana busied herself smoothing the line of her dress, although nothing had mussed it.

He shouted at her, "Who is he?"

She took a step backward, cowering a little. "He-he..." she sputtered.

"Is he your lover?"

"Nay!" she screamed, eyes widening.

"Your betrothed, then?"

She tried to speak, but managed only a small noise in her throat.

"Are you pledged to another man, Adriana?" he asked her, his voice mocking.

Her voice was barely audible. "Aye, but—"

"Go home to your castle, princess, and to your valiant prince."

The rage that filled him made him feel out of control. He heard what he was saying, but was unable to do anything to stop it. He stepped toward her, and she backed away from him as his venom spilled forth.

"Have you had enough of your commoner? Got dirty enough? Relieved your boredom? Go on home to your man with his fine clothes and clean fingernails." He took a few steps but then spun. "Does a pledge mean nothing to you?"

She shook her head, confused, and a sob escaped.

He wheeled around and walked off.

"Goodbye, princess."

CHAPTER SIX

Seth walked into the house, hours later, slamming the door behind him. Lea and Tristan exchanged a look.

Lea spoke up tentatively. "Seth—"

"I do not want to talk about it."

"Is this about Adriana?"

"I said I do not want to talk about it." He gripped the mantle as if he would rip it off of the wall, but then turned to ask her, "Did you help her do her hair?"

She could see by his manner he felt this was some kind of betrayal. Her own fury began to simmer. "Tristan, could you please go outside for a minute?" she said carefully.

Tristan moved toward the door. "Nay, Tristan. You are fourteen now, perhaps it is time you learned about the deceptive nature of women—"

"Do not spew that garbage at him. Go, Tristan!" she roared, pointing to the door. Tristan scurried out, seeming grateful to escape.

Seth straddled the bench and put his head in his hands and did something she was not expecting so soon. He sighed, his voice filled with self-loathing. "I am sorry, Lea. I should not have said that. I do not know what has gotten into me lately. I am usually so calm and rational."

Her anger melted in an instant and she went to him and clasped his shoulder gently. "What is wrong, Seth?"

"She is betrothed. She is going to him now." He stood abruptly, tromping around the room. "Ugh. I was a fool to think someone like her—"

"Why? What did she say to you?"

"Nothing. What could she say? She made a pledge to another man, and I was a case of a privileged girl's boredom."

"What?" she shrieked. "What did you say to her?"

38

Seth took a step away, staring at her. "What does it matter?"

"What does it matter, you...little fool! She was going back tonight to tell Garin she could not marry him."

"Sh-she told you about him?"

"Aye, she told me about him. *Everything* about him, as I am sure you did not give her the chance to do, you...you...jackass!"

He appeared as stunned as he would have been had she reached out and slapped him. She never cursed, but this obviously made her mad enough to.

"*She* did not make any pledge to Garin, her father did. They have been betrothed since she drew her first breath. Ugh!" she screamed, tugging on her hair in frustration and taking her own stroll around the room. "She was going to tell him she could not do it, because she did not have the feelings for him she ought to. Feelings she was beginning to have for you."

Seth's face paled. "But, why did she do her hair for him?"

"She did not do it for Garin, she did it for you. She did it so no one would question her about last night, to protect us, to protect you. That is why she waited to sneak in after dark. So it would be less likely that they would recognize her as the woman who posed as a villager last night."

"What have I done?"

"You have ruined everything. That's what you've done, Seth." She stormed out the door, slamming it behind her.

ADRIANA HAD NOT EXPECTED the castle gates to be closed. During the day they were left open and she had never had an opportunity to see them at night. She banged on the gates to awaken the guard in the guardhouse. How strange it was to be on the other side.

What do you want, Miss?" the guard asked roughly.

"I need to speak to Sir Garin."

"What are ye? His little village mistress? Well, you will have to wait until he returns to the bridge tomorrow." He spun from her to head back to his nap. "It must be nice to have a tart like you to cozy up to at nights."

"I am Princess Adriana."

Perhaps it was the tone of her voice that had the guard spinning on his heel, and hurrying to the gate to take another glimpse of her. Noting the resemblance to the princess, whom he had only seen from afar, he began to bumble with the lock. "Oh, Your Highness. Forgive me. I did not know it was you. Your dress is so...plain. If I had known I would have never..."

Adriana sighed. "Just open the gate, please. I need to speak to Garin immediately."

The guard bowed and let the heavy metal chain fall with a loud clank as she passed. She heard his sigh and the sound of his securing the gate as she climbed the slope toward the castle.

Adriana found Garin in front of the large, marble fireplace in the empty ballroom, sitting in a straight-backed chair. His fingers were steepled as he sat and watched the flames roaring. When he glanced over and saw her, he stared at first, as if she had stepped out of his dreams.

"Adriana! Oh, Adriana!" He stood and ran to her, embracing her tightly. "Are you okay, darling?" He pulled away to examine her face.

She nodded slightly. If he was going to be kind, she thought, this was going to be a lot harder.

"Has your father seen you yet?"

"Nay. I wanted to come to talk to you first."

"Well, I am honored." His tone took on a hint of snappishness. "Where, on earth, have you been, my dear? I have been worried sick about you. I've sent men across the countryside in search of you."

"I am sorry for that, Garin, I truly am. But I have been thinking about things."

"Aye," he replied hesitantly. "About what exactly?"

"Well, Garin...you know I love you..."

Her hesitation had his face becoming cold. "As I love you, aye."

"But, I am not sure if marriage is the best course for us."

"Who is he?" he cried out harshly, unintentionally mirroring Seth's words to her. Adriana gaped in shock, slow to formulate an answer. "I do not know what you are talking about."

"Oh, indeed you do. Who is the young stud you have forsaken me for?" He grabbed her, giving her a shake. "Have you let him take you, Adriana? Has it gone that far yet?"

"Garin!" she said, aghast. "Of course not."

"So there is someone."

"Nay. Well, in a way—" Seeing the fire in his eyes, she tried to backtrack. "Nay, there is no one."

"Adriana," he hissed menacingly, his face inches from hers, "you are a bad liar."

She gawked at him, trying to find the man she once loved in his inflexible features. She jerked her arm out of his grip and stumbled backward a step or two. "I am still the princess, Garin. You have no right—"

"Do not talk to me about rights, Adriana. What about my right to you, eh? What about that right? Were we not pledged to one another?"

"Aye, but...I have come to ask you...to release me from that pledge."

He huffed loudly and turned from her.

"Can you not see, Garin? I love you, just not in that way anymore."

"Ahh! And what, or *who*, has changed that for you?"

"There is no one," she repeated, and in truth, after the earlier argument with Seth, she was not sure if there was anyone. "I wish only to be fair to you...to both of us. This..." she gestured from herself to him, "...is not what...I want. I am sorry."

He strode away from her again, pacing in front of the fire. Then he came to a halt. "Fine. If that is what you want, then." He paused. "But I cannot just release you from your pledge. As the pledge was made for you, as a child, it will need to be broken by you as an adult. Until you become twenty-one, Adriana, you belong to me."

She thought about this. "But you will let me go? As long as I promise to stay true to my pledge until my twenty-first birthday, you will let me go?"

"Of course," he sighed. "All I want is for you to be happy. 'Tis all I have ever wanted."

She rushed forward, throwing her arms around him. "Thank you, Garin. Oh, thank you! I am so grateful to you."

Garin pulled her close, stroking her hair. "I do love you, Adriana."

She sighed. "Aye. And I love you, too." She held him close. "I am sorry, Garin, truly I am."

"Aye, I know. I know..."

CHAPTER SEVEN

Seth did not sleep. He sat at the kitchen table, gazing into the fire, or out the window. Or, from time to time, he rose to peer out the window and to the pond. Somewhere around five, he saw her walk out of the wheat field. He blinked his eyes. Was this an illusion? He opened the door and ran in that direction. Twenty feet away he stopped, his ragged breathing a match for the jagged pieces of his heart that were stuck inside him. He watched her.

Still in the simple dress she had borrowed from Lea, she stood with her arms crossed, rocking a little. Had she come to tell him goodbye forever?

"I could not sleep," she said finally, spinning to face him.

"Nor could I," he admitted. He took a step forward and she stilled, her gaze flashing to him warily. "I...I am sorry, Adriana. I know you have heard it before. It probably sounds meaningless—" he exhaled, "—but I *do* mean it. I have never been sorrier. I acted wretchedly toward you."

"Aye, you did."

"And, the sad thing is, I will probably act wretchedly toward you again."

"Probably," she agreed, her voice catching. She hesitated, but then, without looking at him, she took several quick steps toward him and threw her arms around his waist, sobbing into his chest.

"Shh-shh." He embraced her and stroked her hair. "I am sorry, Adi, I did not mean any of it." He kissed the top of her head and laid his cheek on it. Holding on to her while time seemed to stand still. "Is it still possible you would forgive me?" His words were choked, and it was not as if he was addressing her at all, merely wondering out loud.

She leaned back to study his face. She retreated, holding his hands for a minute and admiring them. "There is more I need to tell you." Her voice was almost a whisper.

He nodded.

"I went to Garin last night. I told him I loved him, that I had loved him for as long as I could remember, but I could not love him as a wife should. I asked him to release me from my pledge."

Seth stared off somewhere over her head for a second, sighed, then gazed at her again. "How did he take it?"

"He reminded me the pledge was not mine to break...as the decision to wed had been made while I was yet a child, the decision to break it would have to wait until I was an adult, when I turn twenty-one."

His stomach fell. "A year," Seth said bleakly.

"I know. I—"

"We will wait then."

She blinked. "You would wait for me?"

He swept her hair from her face. "Aye."

Tears sprang to her eyes. "But Seth, that means I still belong to someone else for a whole year, and we cannot hold hands anymore." Slowly, she released his hands and they fell, useless, to his sides. "We cannot touch anymore." She stroked his face and he closed his eyes, savoring the moment. She laced her fingers behind his head, and drew him to her. "And we could never...ever...kiss." She brushed her lips torturously over his, closing her eyes, and then laying her forehead on his, gathering her strength. She opened her eyes, searching his face. "Can you do that?"

He swallowed. "A year?"

She nodded.

"I could wait a lifetime for the right woman."

Her gaze shifted between his eyes. "I want to be that woman," she said fervently, almost as if it were a prayer.

He smiled, and then tried to put on a brave face. "A year, then. It will go fast."

She shook her head. "It will seem like a lifetime."

Already he burned to touch her, but he resolutely pushed the urge down. "You look tired."

"I am."

"Let us go inside." He motioned for her to go ahead of him, demonstrating he would not take her hand, as he desired to, but keep true to her pledge.

She glanced at the dark window on the second floor. "Do you think Lea will mind having me stay, for a while?"

Seth laughed. "Are you jesting? She will be thrilled. She about killed me when she found out about...what I did, last night. And you can meet Tristan," he added.

"I am nervous about that," she admitted, after a second.

"You are?"

She nodded, peeking up at the window again, as they reached the house. "Tristan means so much to you. What if he does not like me?"

"Adi," he said with a mock frown. "He is going to *love* you." He stopped suddenly. "You told Lea about your plans to go see Garin, and about your feelings about...things. Why did you not tell me?"

She dropped her gaze. "I guess it is because what you think matters a lot to me."

Seth crooked a finger under her chin and lifted her face. "I want you to tell me about how you are feeling."

"Sometimes you do not give me a chance to."

"Ahh! Touché."

Her brow wrinkled. "What does that mean? Touché?"

"Touch. It is a French word, a fencing term. If your opponent touches you with his sword tip, you say touché to admit he has scored a point. And you have a point, sometimes I tend to act before I think."

She peered at him admirably. "You are intelligent," she teased.

"I have my moments," he countered, feeling pleased. Seth followed Adi into the house, appearing thoughtful. "You can lie in my room."

"I would rather stay with you, and not sleep," she replied in a whisper, not wanting to wake Tristan or Lea, as she observed Seth from the corner of her eye.

"We will compromise, you will sleep, and I will stay with you. Just not in the bedroom," he said in hushed voice, anticipating her objection, "but here. We will sit near the hearth, and I will not touch you, I promise."

She smiled. "Agreed."

They lowered themselves to the hearth, their backs to the warm stones surrounding the fireplace. They sat as close together as possible, touching, without really touching. "I could get you a blanket to lie on."

"Nay," she said quickly. "Do not leave."

The room was silent, but for the occasional shift of the logs in the fireplace. The heat cocooned them, and Adriana fell asleep.

The sound of the ladder creaking intruded into Seth's dreams and he struggled out of his sleep. He opened his eyes to Lea's heartfelt, "Praise the heavens."

She stood, with her hands clasped in front of her, at the base of the ladder, and beamed at the sight before her. The logs were burnt down to mere embers and Seth was resting his head on Adriana's, who was resting her head on his shoulder.

By the time Tristan had reached the bottom of the ladder behind Lea, the pair had started and sprung apart. Seth helped Adriana to her feet.

"Oh! Good morning, Lea." She turned to consider the newcomer. "And you must be Tristan?"

"Aye." He offered to shake in gallant fashion.

It took only minutes for it to become obvious that Tristan was besotted by Adriana. Even Seth recognized it. He was both amused and strangely annoyed by it. For her part, Adriana seemed quite smitten with Tristan. He felt slightly better when she whispered to him, "He is a smaller version of you."

At breakfast, they explained to Tristan the need to keep Adriana's identity a secret, and he agreed to be very careful.

Lea and Adriana cleaned the dishes and began to take care of some of the other household chores. Before long, it was time for the menfolk to leave for their day's work. While Tristan ran ahead, Seth lingered at the door, smiling at Adriana. "Come here," he ordered, his voice soft.

Lea smiled, but looked the other way.

Adi walked over hesitantly.

"Closer," he whispered, glancing over her shoulder to make sure Lea was occupied, or at least pretending to be.

Adriana moved a little closer, her heart beating faster. What was he doing? Did he expect her to break her vow and kiss him now?

He stood on the other side of the threshold, clutching the edge of the door, elbow bent, leaning toward her, with a huge grin. For some reason, she relaxed, leaning toward him, too.

"Will I see you later, then?"

"Aye," she said, biting her lip and gazing into his eyes. She grasped the doorframe just below his hand, close enough to feel the heat from his skin.

He shifted and rubbed his finger up and down the edge, watching it as it came perilously close to her, and then glided away. He leaned in closer—so close she was sure he could hear the thumping of her heart.

"I will see you later then, Princess." His voice was deep with emotion.

He spun around to leave, and she watched him as he walked away, her heart in her throat. He turned after a minute and smiled at her, waving.

She clutched the wood behind her as she leaned against the doorframe, thinking a year was an awfully long time to wait.

CHAPTER EIGHT

Adriana searched through the crowd of men for the man who had so recently won her heart. Her gaze lighted on him on the partially finished bridge and her heart began the skipping beat he inspired. But then she heard a familiar voice bark out an order. Garin.

Adi spun toward the sound. Before she could move, he lifted his head and saw her. Though he was yards away, and a half dozen people stood around them, their eyes locked. His lips turned up in a sneer which sent a chill creeping over her skin. She felt like her hair was standing on end. So his words last night had been a lie. She wondered when he seemed so willing to release her. He had no intention of letting her off easily. He was here to spy on her and find out what, or who, had changed her mind about marrying him. There was no other reason for her father's royal commander to be personally overseeing a project like this. Feeling panicked, she set off across the hilltop, scanning faces until she spotted Tristan.

She hurried to him. "Hello." She smiled at the boy, not wanting to alarm him.

"Hello." He grinned back.

"Tristan, I need you to take a message to your uncle. Can you do that?"

He nodded.

"Tell him to be careful...and to stay away from me. Tell him *Garin is watching*. This is important. Do you understand what to say?" Tristan nodded and then scampered off. Adriana glanced over her shoulder, and Garin was following Tristan's progress downhill toward the bridge.

Feeling unnerved, she tried to divert Garin's attention away from Tristan by approaching a group of men.

"And how are ye gentlemen, today?" she asked flirtatiously, making sure she spoke at a volume that the commander would hear. It had the desired effect; his focus was once again riveted on her and those she was addressing. He searched their faces, presumably for some kind of tell-tale sign that they were the one who took her away from him.

"Mmmm...a lot better now," one said, touching her arm. "Could you give me a drink of that water?" He stared at her with an intensity that communicated he was interested in more than water.

Absentmindedly she held the ladle out for him, trying to find Tristan or Seth in the throng on the bridge as she did so.

"You are shaking, beautiful. Am I making you nervous?"

It was true; water was slopping on the ground from her ladle. The men in the shade behind him followed the exchange between the pair with interest. The worker chuckled low in his throat, then grabbed the hand that supported the ladle with a suddenness that made her jump and they all laughed.

"You there!"

The man raised his head, ready to glare at the speaker, but then his expression changed to one of fear.

"Go about your business."

"Aye, sir."

Garin spurred his beautiful, white horse forward, not looking down at Adriana.

She continued to pass out water to the thirsty men around her. Seth glanced in her direction from time to time, but thankfully, kept his distance.

When she returned later on in the afternoon, Seth warmed her heart with a glowing smile, but continued working. She drifted from one cluster of men to another, thinking about him the whole time.

Garin always seemed to be milling around, on horseback, or on foot, constantly observing. At one point, she saw him speaking quietly to Derrick, and shortly afterwards, she saw the big beast of a man and two other soldiers in an exchange with Tristan. She moved closer.

"Come, you little runt. Pick it up!"

Tristan glared at him, but bent again to try to heft a heavy, wooden crate, much too large for one person to lift. As he struggled, barely able to raise the heavy weight off the ground, they heckled him.

"What is the matter, sonny? Ain't ya got enough muscles for that?"

"Come, we haven't got all day."

One of them whacked him on the shoulder with the flat side of his sword. "Your Momma not got enough food to keep you strong, boy?"

Tristan became flushed. His muscles strained and sweat rolled along his hairline. His eyes were tense as he became increasingly embarrassed by the number of people who had become aware of his predicament.

At the bottom of the hill, Seth was engrossed with his work, unaware of what was going on just yards away.

Adriana pushed through the crowd. Her face was red with ire and showed no fear of the three men who towered over her. "Cease that this instant! Have you nothing better to do than to force this boy to take on a burden the three of you together could not lift?"

At first Tristan was afraid for her, and thought to go get his uncle, but then, he saw, with amusement, she seemed to have the situation under control—for the moment. In the blink of an eye, though, things changed.

Derrick stepped threateningly toward Adriana, and the two others circled around behind her. Derrick spat on the ground in front of her. "Who are you, young miss, to question me? Perhaps you need to be shown the consequences of speaking insolently to your betters?"

Her jaw tight, she snapped, "Show me where they are, sir, so I can apologize to them, for I see no one here who fits that description."

There was a ripple of low laughter through the crowd around them. The big guard's jaw tightened and with a nod Adriana's arms were grabbed from behind.

Tristan struggled with indecision. Should he go to get his uncle's help? Or stay so he, himself, could help her? As she fought with her captors, appearing truly fearful now, Derrick removed his white gloves while never breaking eye contact with her. It was clear he wished to not soil them when hitting her.

The officer raised his hand and a voice cried out, "Halt, soldier!"

Garin urged his horse through the crowd to Adriana's side. "Woman," he said, peering down his nose at her. "You will come with me."

The two men reluctantly released her. Adriana turned, straightened her dress, and trailed after Garin. When he reached the little makeshift hut that served as his office, he dismounted, passed the horse's reins to a sentry, and walked through the door without looking back. Hesitantly, she joined him in the dim interior of the building.

Tristan hastened to follow, moving to the side of the building where the ground sloped to the river. He listened below the open window.

"Adriana," Garin said with impatience, strolling around to stand behind his desk in the cramped quarters. "I cannot keep bailing you out every time you get yourself into trouble."

"But Garin, Derrick and his thugs were picking on the boy."

"Who is the boy to you?" he asked sharply.

"No one. He is no one," she answered too quickly. "'Tis just...he could not be more than sixteen. And they were three grown men."

"I am not going to argue with you, Adi. If you are going to play your little games at being a commoner, then you will be treated like one." He sighed, coming around to her side of the desk. Tristan ducked, measuring the sound of his footsteps, trying to imagine the scene inside. When Garin spoke next, his voice was soft. "I miss you, Adi."

A lengthy silence descended, and Tristan's insides squirmed, wondering what was going on in the building. He heard Adriana's quiet voice, and it surprised him to hear how full of emotion it was. "I miss you, too, Garin. But, I have made a choice." There was a pause. The next time she spoke, her voice was higher. "Do not touch me!" There was the sound of a scuffle.

"Come, Adi. Surely you miss the way I used to kiss you. I am not so blind I could not see how I aroused you."

"Leave me be!" Her voice shook, and again it sounded like furniture was being bumped into.

Tristan pulled himself up to peek in the window. She was retreating from him and bumped into a huge, red velvet chair that toppled behind her. He encircled her waist and had her wrists trapped behind her.

"You are still mine, Adi!" his voice rang out, his face inches from hers.

"Only by the pledge, Garin." She stared into his eyes, fire dancing in hers. "My heart is someone else's."

"Who does it belong to then, Princess?" he asked through gritted teeth, squeezing her wrists mercilessly and shaking her so violently her teeth clattered together. "Eh?" He grabbed ahold of the front of her dress and tore it a little. "Your heart may be taken by someone else, but your body is still mine, Adi."

Still, she showed no fear. "Would you take me by force then, Garin?" she asked evenly.

He drove her backward, kicking a chair out of the way as he did so and pinning her against the door. "If that is the only way you will have me, then aye." He kissed the flesh exposed at her neck where the dress had ripped. She grappled with the sides of his head, trying to push him away. Realizing she was in trouble, Tristan was about to run for his uncle, but suddenly, Garin stilled. He pushed off her and turned, leaving her standing, catching her breath. He spun and yanked the door open as she scurried out of his way.

He grabbed her elbow and dragged her outside, pushing her into the middle of the dirt road in front of his office. He took off his coat, laying it on the railing of the shallow porch in front of the building. He undid his cuffs, as a crowd began to circle around them, leaving only the area on the side of the hill vacant. Adriana stood looking at him with her chin high as he paced in front of her, jerking at his sleeves as he rolled them. He rotated to slip a riding crop from his horse's saddle. In an instant, two men appeared and seized Adriana, thrusting her arms out.

Tristan had raced to the front of the building when Garin opened the door of his office, but the crowd had already become too thick for him to make his way to Adriana in time. With a whistling noise the crop struck her hands. Tristan, who had been pushing through the crowd, froze in horror. Adriana caught his eye and silently begged him to stay afar as tears covered her cheeks. *Thwap*! The crop bit into her a second time, making him jump and waking him from his stupor. He began to change course and make for an opening in the circle. Sliding across the hillside, he screamed out for Seth.

Hearing him now, Seth whirled and took in the confrontation between Garin and Adriana at the top of the embankment. From his distance, he could not hear the sound of the protesting crowd, or the crack as the crop again ripped into her, but he did see her knees finally buckle and the soldiers drag her to her feet again. He jumped from the bridge to the ground before Tristan even made it down the hill. He scrambled up the slope, but was hindered by the loose rock.

At the top of the hill, Garin stared at Adriana. The fourth time he cracked the crop, she did not even cry out, though her hands were bloodied by now. Her eyes had become dead. In a fury, he raised the crop as if to hit her in the face. She shrunk against her captors, but, with a roar, he threw the crop over the edge of the embankment. Placing his back to the crowd, he pinched the bridge of his nose then rubbed his eyes.

"Release her." When the soldiers did not move, he repeated loudly, "Damn it, I said, release her!" Reluctantly, they let her go.

Her muscles shook from the pain and the strain of struggling against the soldiers. With one last glare, Adriana spun and walked through the crowd that parted around her, her head held high.

When Seth finally crested the top of the hill, four soldiers stood with swords crossed in front of them, guarding the building Garin had disappeared into. Many of the workers had gathered before the soldiers, maddened by what they had seen, shouting and gesturing.

Seth squinted in the opposite direction and spotted Adriana walking along the dirt road, Lea beside her, with an arm around her. With one last look in Garin's direction, Seth sprinted off, cutting through a copse of trees, to reach the road. Running, breaking through small branches, he shouted her name.

When she heard him, she wheeled about. He ran forward as if to embrace her, but she held out her hands to ward him off, remembering her pledge.

Seeing her bloodied palms, Seth's jaw tightened. "I will kill him!" He reversed course.

"Nay, Seth! Nay." She ran after him and grabbed his shoulders to stop him, but with a sharp cry of pain, she let go.

He twisted and tried to pull her close to comfort her, but she shrunk away.

"Nay! You cannot. I cannot!" she cried out, sinking to her knees in misery.

He gestured to her bloody prints, which slid down his sleeves. "Would you honor the pledge given to a man who did this to you?" he shouted, his voice cracking.

She covered her face, forgetting about the blood.

Lea bent to lift her. "Help me!"

But Seth was still half-turned toward the construction site.

"We need to get her home." Lea pleaded a second time.

As if fighting the force of magnets, he came back. He bent to lift Adriana to her feet. Burying his murderous thoughts in his heart for the time being, he helped her home.

CHAPTER NINE

"She is asleep now," Lea said with a sigh. "The mead finally helped to calm her."

Seth did not comment as he straddled the kitchen table bench, staring into the fire. She crossed to his side. "How are *you*?"

"She will not even let me touch her. Do you know how hard it is to not be able to comfort her when I can see what he...did to her?" His voice was full of disgust. He bent, his elbows resting on his knees, and covered his face. Lea rubbed his shoulder in an effort to soothe him.

Lea and Seth lifted their gazes as Tristan timidly opened the front door and paused on the threshold. Lea extended her arms and he ran into them. Seth patted Tristan's back.

Tristan sniffled. "How is she?"

"Sleeping," Lea answered.

But then they all heard the creak of a door opening. Tristan broke free from his mother and rushed to Adriana.

"Are ye hurt badly?" he asked, his words muffled by her body as she embraced hi, careful of her wounds.

"I am faring well, Tristan. Do not worry." Concerned that her reassurance was not enough for Tristan, she looked to Seth for help.

"This is all because of me."

"Nay, Tristan," she scolded lightly. She put her fingertips under his chin to tilt his head up and peer at him. "I would like to explain what happened, if your mother approves."

Lea nodded, and Adriana walked with Tristan over to the bench Seth had occupied. When they sat, facing each other, Seth returned to his seat, sitting closely behind Adriana. Her attempts to hold Tristan's hands in hers were made clumsy by her bandages.

"What happened today happened because Garin was angry with me, and it truly did not have anything at all to do with you."

"Why would he be angry enough to hurt you so much?" Tristan asked, incredulous.

"Well... You see, ages ago, before I was even born, my father and Garin's father were the best of friends. They fought alongside each other in battles before either of them became kings, because their fathers had been friends, too. When Garin was born, my father promised Garin's father if he ever had a girl of his own, she would wed Garin, and I was my father's first daughter, and so have been pledged to Garin since even before I was born."

"That is strange."

She chuckled. "Aye. In a way, it is. But that is sometimes how things are done." She glanced at Seth. "So...lately I have been starting to think, like you do, this was kind of strange, and not what I wanted. But, you see, for my entire childhood, he and I were best friends. Do you have a best friend?"

Tristan nodded. "Demetri."

"And you and Demtri have been friends for a while?"

Tristan checked with his mom. "Oh, yes. For a long time...."

"They moved next door when Tristan was about four, I guess."

"Well, like you and Demetri, Garin and I were childhood friends. We would play hide-and-go-seek in the castle, or chase each other through the dark hallways. In fact, I cannot remember a time when he was not my constant companion. But...I told Garin last night I did not want to marry him. So he is a bit angry, and a bit hurt and...sometimes when people are miserable, they want everyone else to be miserable, too. So Garin wanted me to feel bad. Do you understand?"

"Aye. He is a big bully."

Seth snorted and Adriana elbowed him. He tried to cover the sound with a cough, but Tristan grinned at him.

"He can be a bully, at times. But you have to understand, like me, he has always gotten whatever it is he wanted, and to lose me...proved...difficult for him. And, I know this sounds strange, but I still love him. I always will, that is just how it is." She doubted she had explained it to the boy properly, but could not think of anything more to say.

"So...enough of this talk. I am starving. How about you?"

"I could eat a stag."

Lea ruffled his hair playfully, and gave Adriana a smile. "Well, let us see what we can do about that."

Throughout dinner, Adriana continued to join in the conversation joyfully, although Seth did catch her wincing frequently when she touched something. He marveled at her strength and wanted to hold her so badly he ached. After dinner, he grabbed a towel and began to dry the dishes she was washing. He nodded at the water.

"Does it not pain you?"

She shook her head. "Nay. Actually, it feels good. Removes the sting a bit."

He observed her with a smile.

"What?" she asked self-consciously.

"You are amazing."

"Washing the dishes is not that hard," she said confused. "Oh, you are jesting because I did not know how before."

"Nay, not at all. I was talking about your capacity to forgive that man."

"Oh, come, Seth. It is like...I am sure you and Lea got in fights when you were younger..."

"Of course."

"And, there was probably some bloodshed from time to time?"

"Aye. She gave me a bloody nose once."

She laughed at the idea, but then said, "That is what it was like for Garin and me."

"Adi, she gave me a bloody nose. She did not beat me, in front of a group of bystanders, with a riding crop. And she felt bad about it afterwards. Awful, really."

"Well, I am certain Garin feels bad, too."

He rolled his eyes, dropping the subject as he saw Tristan approaching.

"Good night, Uncle Seth. I am heading to bed. Good night, Princess Adriana."

She enveloped him in a hug, and then, after they both had wished him good night, they watched him climb the ladder to his room.

"He is so sweet."

"Aye. He is a good boy."

There was a soft rap on the door. "Who would that be at this hour?" He questioned with a frown. He crossed to the door, and Adriana took the dish water to the back door to throw it out.

When Seth saw the man on the doorstep, every muscle in his body went suddenly rigid. He changed his focus to search the dark areas behind the man. Gripping the edge of the door, he leaned aggressively forward.

"How foolish of you to show up here all by yourself. Where are your men, commander?" he asked through gritted teeth.

Garin ignored his question. "Can I speak to Adriana?"

Seth tried to block his view as she came in from outside. "What makes you think she is here?"

But Garin could see her.

"Adriana!"

Seth half-turned to take in her reaction and Garin pushed past him. She spun, but then froze, assessing him coolly.

"May we speak alone?"

"You are insane if you think I am going to leave you alone with her for one second."

"Nay. I want to hear what the man has to say."

"He is no man," Seth muttered, but he walked past him to the ladder. "I will be right upstairs if you need me," he said pointedly, more for Garin's benefit than for hers.

A heavy silence followed his departure. Garin's gaze darted around the small place, but then focused on Adriana. He took a tentative step forward.

"Can I see your hands?"

She did not move. Emotion swirled inside her, but she let her eyes remain cold and hard as steel.

"I need to see what I have done."

She had unrolled the bandages while she washed the dishes. She held out her arms so he could see the angry, red welts he had raised on her palms, along with further evidence of the skin being broken.

"Oh, Adi," he breathed out, crossing to her. "I am *so* sorry." He fell to his knees at her feet, overwrought. "I do not know what possessed me. It is only...I was so angry I could not see straight. The thought of another man... I am sorry, though. Believe me, Adi," he pleaded, peering at her miserably, with tears in his eyes. "Can you ever forgive me?"

Her heart melted and she pulled his head into her skirt. "Aye, I forgive you, Garin." Her voice came out choked. No matter what he had done to her, she could not bear to see him in such distress.

Garin looked up. "Will you come home with me, then?"

She stepped back. "Nay. I thought I had made myself clear."

"Oh, come on, Adi. You cannot possibly think to stay in this squalor?" He gestured at the surroundings. As he rose from his knees he added, "We both know you will not be happy here."

"This is a lovely home!" she cried out in shock and disbelief. "It is warm, and full of love—"

"Do not be foolish," he retorted, anger seeping into his voice. "You know you are used to far better."

"Nay!" she shouted. "We both know nothing of the sort." She stared at him. "I thought I knew you."

"Perhaps we were both wrong about that!" he snapped. He grabbed her. "You come here to humiliate me, letting that young buck ride you."

Her anger made her strong, and she tore free from his grip and struck him across the face. She cried out in pain. The slap hurt her far worse than it did Garin. She clutched her wrist, having reopened her damaged skin.

Seth was halfway down the ladder ready to thrash Garin, but her cry made Seth change courses. He held her elbows and steered her to the sink where her bandages were.

"Get your filthy hands off of her!" Garin screamed, seizing Seth.

In a flash Seth had laid Garin out, sending him crashing into the table. Fists clenched, he stood over him. "I should have killed you this afternoon!" he roared, kicking a pot that had fallen from the table out of his way as he advanced.

"Seth. Stop!" Adriana cried, trying to restrain him. The attempt caused another stab of pain to course through her. She knew all Garin needed was an excuse to arrest him. "Leave me alone, Garin. I'm happy here. Can you not be happy for me?"

"You are *pledged* to me!" Garin spat, his voice shaking with anger, as he got to his feet.

"And I have kept that pledge," she returned icily. "Though it has cost me." Silence filled the room.

"You have made your choice then?"

"I have made my choice." Her answer was unequivocal.

Garin stared at her for a moment, then, spun and left without another word, shutting the door quietly behind him.

"Ooh! That man!" she steamed. She shook with anger and pain.

"Here, let me help you," Seth said quietly. He guided her to the sink, pumping cold water over her palms to wash away the blood. Adriana started sobbing.

Lea was there in an instant. "Oh, honey," she cried out sympathetically. Seth stepped aside, feeling useless, as Adriana laid her head on Lea's shoulder and cried.

"I thought I loved him. How could I have been so wrong?"

Lea let her cry for a while, then calmed her, and re-bandaged her injury. She started to lead her to the front bedroom. "You need your sleep."

"But...where will Seth sleep?"

"I will sleep here, by the fire. I will be fine."

She stepped closer to him, peering at him earnestly, her eyes red from crying. "I am sorry, Seth. I am sorry I let this into your home."

He had to stop himself from touching her. "This is not your fault."

"Oh, but it is. I have made a lot of poor choices that led to this."

"Adi, the choices were made for you." Despite his promise to her, he put his hands on her waist; she did not resist. Gazing into her tired and distraught eyes, he said, "You need to get some sleep. We will talk about things tomorrow."

"Seth...there are things I want to say to you." She looked down. "But my vow prevents it."

"Shhh, Adi." He gave the top of her head a quick kiss. "Get some sleep."

When Lea returned to the kitchen, after seeing Adriana to bed, Seth was deep in thought. "We need to leave here. He will not stop until he gets her back, one way or another."

"How do ye know that?"

"Because it is what I would do," he stated simply.

She sighed. "Fine, then. We will go wherever you want us to go."

Seth blinked. "You would go, too?"

"Of course. You do not think I would let you leave without me?"

"I do not know if I can ask you and Tristan to do that. He makes enough money now to feed the two of you."

"It is not something I'll debate," she said firmly. "Where you go, we go."

He smiled at the set of her chin.

"Now, if we are going to be moving, you should get some sleep." She tossed a quilt at him. "Good night." Without another word, she was up the ladder.

Seth made a makeshift bed out of the quilt in front of the hearth. He watched the fire burn low and thought about his course of action.

Eventually the warmth lulled him to sleep.

CHAPTER TEN

The night exploded. Seth was on his feet before he was even fully awake. He saw the two soldiers enter the front bedroom where Adriana slept, but there were four more between him and the door. The piece of wood that barred the door was jaggedly broken in two, its brackets torn loose from the wall.

In the loft above, Lea and Tristan both sprang from their beds and crept to the edge to take in the action below. Two men were hauling a kicking Adriana through the bedroom door. Seth was already being restrained by two soldiers, but when Adriana's terrified gaze met his, it was all they could do to contain him. Adriana screamed as the soldiers half-dragged, half-carried her to the door.

Tristan made a move toward the ladder.

"What are ye doing?" Lea hissed, grabbing on to his nightshirt.

"I have to help."

"The best thing that you can do for your uncle is to stay quiet."

Tristan knew by her tone there was no point in arguing with her. He returned to her side, both of them lying on their stomachs and straining to hear and see what was going on below.

"Leave her alone!" Seth broke free from his captors, and landed a crushing blow to the nearest man's jaw. In an instant, he fell amid a shower of soldiers' blows.

"Seth!" Adriana's horrified cry rang out above the rest of the voices shouting, her eyes wide as she stared at the spot where he disappeared.

The last thing Lea and Tristan saw of Adriana was her hands on the door frame as she clutched at it desperately, trying to break free. Her fingers slipped and she was ripped away.

The remaining soldiers gave Seth's semi-conscious body one last kick on the way out. He groaned and lay still.

Lea rushed to the ladder. When she got to Seth, he had managed to flip onto his back, but lay there panting and grimacing in pain. Tristan was on her heels, his eyes wide with concern. "Follow them," Lea ordered. "But *stay out of sight.*"

Tristan flew out the rear door, paralleling the soldiers' path along the front of the house. They took Adriana, gagged now, to the Parishes' house next door. Silently he shimmied up a tree he and Demetri had often slid down together when sneaking out of the boy's room. He found the window unlatched, and was able to push it open and crawl through. To his surprise, Demetri was not in his bed. The house was arranged in almost an identical style to his, so it was easy for Tristan to creep to the edge of the loft in the dark to see what was going on. Below, he saw the Parishes huddled in one corner with two soldiers standing in front of them, barring their way into the room. A rocking chair was pulled to the fireplace, and the man the princess called Garin was sitting in it with his sword in front of him balanced on the arms of the chair. A large group of soldiers brought in a thrashing Adriana, dressed only in the thin, linen dressing gown.

Noting she was gagged, Garin shouted, "Unbind her! She is still the king's daughter." They did as instructed and deposited her on the braided rug at Garin's feet.

"What is the meaning of this?" Adriana spat out regally.

"I have come to get you," Garin replied, as if the question were utterly ridiculous.

"Well, as you can see, I do *not* wish to come with you."

Garin glared at her. "Leave us!" he shouted. "All of you, out!" The soldiers started to retreat out the door. "Take them with you." Garin gestured to the Parishes, who were then hustled out ahead of the remaining soldiers. The only three left in the house were Garin, Adriana, and the hidden Tristan.

When Garin spoke next, although Tristan strained to hear, he could not make out the words, but hoped watching would be enough.

"Adriana, I hate to have to be the one to inform you, but your father is gravely ill."

"Wh-what?" she cried out, appearing stunned by this twist.

Garin laid his sword aside and stood. "He was ill before you left, but things have gone steadily downhill the last couple of days." He sighed, peering at the fire briefly then returning his gaze to her with a grimace. "They were not certain if he would make it through the night," he added tenderly. "I thought you would want to know."

It was too much, after her emotional day and lack of sleep. She swayed forward and he caught her. He brushed her face. "I am sorry, Adi."

It was all Tristan needed to see. He belly-crawled backward and hastened out the window to his home. When he came in the door, Seth was sitting at the table and Lea was wrapping his ribs tightly with long strips of cloth.

Seth looked up. There was a cut open on his forehead above one eye, but he appeared more alert than Tristan had expected him to.

"Where did they take her?" he asked.

"To the Parishes," Tristan responded guardedly.

"How does she fare?"

Tristan's mind flashed to the image of Garin and Adriana in front of the fireplace; Garin stroking her face, and she not withdrawing. "Well, I suppose."

Seth read something in Tristan's face. He sprang from the bench, grabbed his shirt and shot out the door before Lea could stop him.

In front of the Parishes' house, Holt Parish, Demetri's father, was shouting at the soldiers about his rights. It gave Seth enough of a distraction to sneak around to the side of the house and peek in the window. Garin's held Adriana's waist. Seth tried to read their lips, but the light was too dim and the angle was not right.

"Is there nothing the doctor can do?"

Garin shook his head solemnly and drew her into an embrace. "That is why I have been taking over some of his duties. He put me in charge of the bridgework, as well as my other commands."

Adriana thought of something. She separated from him, studying Garin's eyes. "This is not some sort of trick, is it? To get me home?"

"Adi," he said, as if hurt. Again, he stroked her face. "You know I would never do that to you."

She scrutinized him. Would he? She did not know if she knew him well anymore. The man she had loved never would have struck her, especially in the vicious way he had that afternoon. She was so lost in her thoughts she did not notice him leaning closer. Suddenly his lips were pressed to hers, his hands slid possessively around her, yanking her in, allowing her no room for escape.

Outside, at the window, Seth felt as if he had been punched in the stomach. This is what Tristan had not wanted him to know. She had forgiven Garin. She had more than forgiven him.

But, wait. I have jumped to the wrong conclusions about Adriana before. I will put off guessing what this is about until she explains things to me herself. I will not be overly hasty and blow things out of proportion this time. Unhappily, he retreated to his house to wait for her.

Adriana pushed away from his embrace. "You are a liar. Father is not sick. You are trying to play on my emotions to win me back. But it will not work, Garin. I love Seth. And *nothing* will change that." She spun to leave, but Garin grabbed her arm to detain her.

"Nay, Adriana. I am not lying. Your father is sick," he cried. "I am sorry I kissed you, I could not help myself. But I would not lie to you about your father's health. Even I am not that cruel. But we must go to him now."

She examined his face again. "I have to talk to Seth first."

"There is no time for that." Garin led her out the door. "I think I may have tarried too long as it is."

Once outside, he called out, "You there!"

A soldier who had been threatening the Parish family came forward. Garin gestured to another soldier to bring two horses. "Tell those next door the princess has gone to see her father, who is fatally ill. She will return, or send a message to them, by tomorrow."

He looked at her, and she nodded.

"I brought two of my fastest steeds."

He helped her to mount her horse. He mounted the other himself and they tore off into the night.

The soldier who had been asked to deliver the message helped the others to get the Parishes inside. He knew his true orders were *not* to deliver any message. Garin had made that clear before they had even stepped foot out of Ramport that evening.

CHAPTER ELEVEN

Adriana rushed into the outer chambers of her father's bedroom. "Doctor," she said with relief, as he entered from an opposite door. "How is he?" She had known the older gentleman for as long as she had been alive.

The doctor smiled. "He is fair, Adriana. Quite fair. He is finally sleeping now, so it would be best not to disturb him."

"But you will get me if he takes a turn for the worse? I need to tell him I love him in case he..." A small sob escaped.

"Oh, princess! Princess. There is no need to get this upset. 'Tis a cold. Albeit, he is tired, but he will be right as rain soon."

"A cold?" Her gaze slid to Garin's. He smiled at her smugly as he had on the ridge above the River Astri, making her skin crawl. He had lied after all. "I won't stay here with you another minute." She whirled to leave, but a pair of soldiers was blocking her way. She spun back. "You lied to me! You cannot keep me trapped here like a prisoner. If my father knew..."

"I do know." Adriana's father opened the inner door and stepped through, looking as robust as ever. He was a big man, with a full head of dark hair and a beard. "*I* sent Garin after you. I will not have my daughter slipping between the sheets with some filthy commoner."

"Father!" Adriana breathed, shocked. "You cannot approve of Garin's actions."

"Not only do I approve of *them,* but I approve of him, as a son-in-law. And I think we should wed you speedily, before you make a mistake."

Out of the corner of her eye, she saw Garin bow to her father deferentially, but with a wicked smile. So they were in cahoots. Adriana gaped at them.

"You would not demand that I marry him against my will. You would not do anything that heinous!" Her voice rose hysterically. "Surely I know ye that well. Do I not? You will not...make me...?" She began to cry.

The king was moved. He took her hands, glanced at the bandages a moment, and addressed her.

"You are right, Adriana. As much as I love you, and as much as I think it would be right for me to compel you to marry him, for your own good... I could not do that. But neither can I approve of a match between my daughter and some villager."

"But sire—"

"I will not force her, Garin," the king said adamantly. "However...you have a year to convince her marrying you is the right course for her. That is as much as I can do for you." He gave Adriana's fingers a gentle squeeze to soften the blow. "Now, off to bed, everyone. It is late." With that, the king disappeared again behind the door.

Adriana glared with utter contempt at Garin, who ignored her.

"See Princess Adriana to her bedroom," he ordered the soldiers present.

"Adi, do not dream of trying to escape this time. You will be kept under constant guard."

She shot him a withering glance, and left the chambers. Once behind the doors of her own bedroom, she fumed. Crossing the room to her balcony, she went outdoors. Below her, in the courtyard, she spotted four sentinels: two stationary, and two patrolling the grounds. Beyond the walls of Ramport, she could see Seth's house. Lights still flickered inside. She sighed. What a little fool she had been, believing Garin. She prayed Seth was safe. She wished she was in the comforting warmth of his home, instead of within the chilly, stone walls of the castle. She wondered what he must be thinking. Had he gotten her message? Had the message been sent at all? She vowed to herself she would find a way out and return to the man she loved.

"ADRIANA, EAT SOMETHING," Garin ordered, annoyed with her.

The princess slammed her fork down. "I am not hungry," she said distinctly. She rose from the table and went to stare out the window for the hundredth time, leaning on the stone wall along its side. She had been trapped inside the castle for nearly three months.

He got to his feet and came to stand behind her. "He is not there," he whispered meanly in her ear.

"I know he is not there," she replied, fighting back the tears that were building behind her eyelids. "I have watched every night and I have seen no light..." Her voice trailed off.

So much had changed. Garin and her father were not the men she had thought they were, and she felt increasingly unstable these days. She longed to hear Seth's voice, to see his face...and Lea's and Tristan's. A thought occurred to her, a strange and horrifying thought. She spun around. "Garin, you did not harm them, did you? You did not... Because, if I found out that was true, I would have nothing to live for. I swear."

"Quit being so melodramatic, Adi." He sighed. "He is gone, is all. He became tired of you. You know, the appeal of good looks only lasts so long, and then he discovered the two of you had nothing in common, and made a decision to leave. It gets no more complicated than that." He sidled up to her again. "But you and I, we have a lot in common." He slid his hands around her waist, but she immediately pulled away.

"I thought that was true once, but you and I have *nothing* in common anymore." Her teeth were gritted in anger. "*Nothing*!" She spun on her heel and left, hurrying to her room.

She closed the door behind her, feeling relieved to be alone. She crossed to her balcony, where she had spent a lot of her time lately. The night before last, in fact, she had slept on its warmth-robbing stones, miserable, sickened by her plight. It was the only place in the castle she felt remotely close to Seth. She remembered the night they met there. She was thinking of herself as the fairy tale princess locked in the tower, but she never imagined, in such a short time, that would come true. Yet here she was, locked away, under guard, without any way of getting a message through to Seth. With no way of telling him she loved him and she wished, with all her might, they could be together.

SETH WANDERED THROUGH the orchard at dusk, his head hanging low, as he thought of Adriana. This had become his habit, meandering among the trees by himself in the growing dark, and allowing his musings to drift to the princess. Not that his mind did not go there during the day, but he did, at times, have to concentrate on his blacksmithing, and so would have to push memories of her away. But at night, his thoughts were so often with her, it was as if she walked by his side beneath the laden branches of the trees.

This evening, he marveled anew at the constant loneliness he felt. Before she came into his life, he was perfectly content living with Lea and Tristan, and watching the boy mature. Now it felt like he was never content; there was always something missing. Adriana.

It infuriated him she had waltzed into his world for such a brief time, had, in fact, waltzed into his heart, and then left him so out-of-sorts. He tried to hate her for leaving him, but whenever he did, sweet images of her would crowd his brain and drive all unpleasant thoughts of her away from him. He would often see her determined face when Lea had cut her beautiful hair; or the sleeping princess who had first stirred his heart when he had climbed on her balcony. Who was he fooling? His heart had first awoken when his gaze caught hers across the courtyard when he had been brought in for hitting Derrick. It was not until later, when he had gotten to know her better, that he understood what had drawn him to her like a hummingbird to nectar. It was her simple, sweet strength.

Again and again he tried to reconcile this side of the princess he had come to know, with the woman who had disappeared from his house in the middle of the night, never to be and never returned. Holt Parish had told him she left with the commander of her own free will; the two of them galloping off in the night side-by-side. Had she then decided her pledge meant more to her than she had thought? But if that were the case, he was sure she would have come to him to explain her feelings to him. What, then, would have caused her to leave without any explanation?

Perhaps he had been wrong to leave Hamiltonia so soon. Perhaps she would have come to him to give him an account of her actions. But the house seemed like a cage after she left, and he was haunted by memories of her wherever he went. He could not work on the bridge, he could not take a walk by the pond, without her presence torturing him. And now, ironically, after he had traveled so far to get away from memories of her, she was still ever-present.

Seth's feet stopped their heavy, purposeless trodding, and he leaned against a tree and gazed up at the moon snagged, as it seemed, in the branches of the trees above him. How long would it be, he wondered, before his heart would cease to ache for her with every breath he took? How long would misery be his bedmate? How long would it take for him to forget how to love her?

CHAPTER TWELVE

A driana sat listlessly on the wall of her balcony, her bare feet drawn beneath her as she clutched her knees to her chest. She had run out of plans to escape from her prison. Each of the previous plans had failed her, and she had been dragged back to her room and, each time, even heavier restrictions were placed on her. Even now, when Garin's attention seemed to be focused elsewhere, she was continually stymied by those whom he had left in charge during his absences. They had come to know her too well and trust her too little.

The sound of orders being shouted on the grounds below drew her out of her stupor. She glanced over the edge, longing for a distraction from her thoughts of Seth. To her surprise, she saw a large gathering of horsemen in the eastern courtyard. The horsemen were sitting at attention on their mounts in regular rows—dozens of them— and, in the front, one held a banner with her family crest. As she mused over this odd assembly of men, her maidservant, Clarise, brought in a tray of food, though she had barely touched food in days.

"Clarise?"

She jumped. "Oh! You scared me, my mistress. You usually sit there in a daze and I wonder if you even know when I come and go."

"What is happening below?"

"Oh. I believe it is the first wave of the attack on Dunneston, miss." Adriana had insisted no one call her 'princess' anymore, nor any other royal title.

"Attack on Dunneston?" she repeated. Her face drained of what little blood was there these days. She straightened. "But they are our allies. We have been friends with the royal family there for...forever."

"Aye, miss, but, from what I gather—not that I eavesdrop while serving, but sometimes I cannot help but hear—Dunneston has a great deal of wealth. Wealth which *some* would seek to acquire."

"Some? As in my father and Sir Garin?" Adriana asked with an edge to her voice.

Clarise hesitated, but then gave a noncommittal shrug.

"Preparing for a war, then. Is that what has been occupying Sir Garin's time?"

"Aye, miss."

"I see." She grabbed a piece of bread from the waiting tray and sank her teeth into it.

A smile broke out on Clarise's face. "Anything else, miss?"

"Mmm..." Adriana murmured, chewing her food, "Nay, thank you, Clarise."

ADRIANA SAT ON THE edge of her bed fidgeting with the ties on her long traveling cloak. She waited for the knock on the door that may mean her chance at freedom. Where was Clarise?

Three sharp raps sounded and she jumped up. Had she been less anxious, she may have noticed the knock did not sound right; it was too confident, too commanding. She opened the door to find Garin on her threshold.

"Adi," he breathed, and she sensed some sort of relief on his part to see her. He stepped in the door immediately. "I am—" For the first time, he took in her garb. "Why are you wearing a traveling cloak? 'Tis nearly midnight."

"Oh, I was going to take a stroll around the grounds. I could not sleep."

"Hmm...well, I am glad I caught you then."

She was grateful for his distracted state. Surely any other time he would have questioned her extensively about her intentions, but tonight he seemed to take them at face value.

He grasped her arms, but then seemed disturbed by the barrier of the fabric.

"Take this thing off," he grumbled, pulling it from her shoulders. "I wanted to come to you tonight...to be with you. Adi, tomorrow I must go away,

and I do not know how long I will be gone." He gazed at her intently in the
waning candlelight.

She could tell he was worried.

"Where are you going, Garin?" She searched his eyes for answers.

He walked away, turning his back to her, silent for a moment. "We are at
war, Adi, with the kingdom of Dunneston. Or at least we will be soon. I have
to lead my troops."

"War?" She feigned shock. "But I do not understand. We have always
been friends with the royal family of Dunneston. You and I used to play with
Lawrence for fortnights at a time, surely that alliance has not changed."

"I remember those times, too," he said with what sounded like a twinge
of regret. "But our lives have changed. Dunneston is a very wealthy kingdom.
They have great stores of gold, and a well-fortified position, on the hill."

"Have they attacked us?"

"Nay. But do not worry about it, Adi," he added, not understanding the
accusation in her words. "I will protect you." He moved to her. "But...some-
times things can be so unsure. I wanted to spend the night with you before
I left, in case..." He trailed off, but they both understood what he meant. In
case he did not make it home. "I am sorry for the way things have become
between us, Adi. I love you. I do. And I do not always show it properly, but I
want to make up for that tonight."

He bent close and coaxed her lips into a kiss. For a moment, she gave in.
His lips felt wonderfully good after so long without being kissed. And he felt
so comfortingly familiar; it was easy to convince herself this was right—for a
second. But then, suddenly, she knew it was abundantly wrong. He may seem
familiar, but he was not the man she once knew, and he was *not* the man she
loved.

She pushed away. "Garin—" her voice contained a warning "—you told
me you would wait. You promised me."

"Aye, Adi, I did. But...dammit! Things have changed. I ride tomorrow,
Adi, and I may not be returning."

That was it. He was frightened.

"Garin, it will be fine. You will be safe," she tried to reassure him. "Who
else would torture me if you were not here?" she teased, but he would not be
swayed. His gripped her more tightly. His gaze was penetrating.

"I *will* be with you tonight."

She sucked in her breath. He was determined, then. She would have to do something to keep him at bay.

"Aye," she said at last. She let her face relax into a smile. "But I am nervous, Garin. Can we not have some wine first?" she asked him, coyly.

He let out a big breath and smiled, making his face appear lighter, younger. It was amazing how much his added responsibilities had aged him.

"You want wine? We shall have wine." He walked over to a cabinet where he knew it was stored.

"Nay. Let me pour it. It will help to calm my nerves some."

"Of course."

He was only too agreeable. He took off his jacket and laid it over the foot of the bed and started wrestling with the thick, tied collar of his shirt, babbling on as he did so. "I am glad you have finally come to see things my way, my dear Adriana."

She checked over her shoulder to make sure he was still by the bed as she passed by her dresser and snatched a vial of medicine the doctor had given her to help her to sleep.

"I knew, given some time to cool your heels and think about things—"

With her back toward him, she hesitated with the vial over the cup of wine she had poured. What if she gave him too much? What if she accidentally killed him? "—you would come to realize what a mistake it would be to get involved with that filthy blacksmith."

His aristocratic speech was his undoing. With a flourish, she emptied the entire vial into his cup, shaking out every last drop. Who cared if it killed him? It would serve him right.

"Here you go," she said merrily, offering him his glass.

"Oh, nay. I do not need any mead to get me in the mood. I want to be able to remember every single second of tonight."

He held by the nape of her neck and drew her in for a kiss.

As before, his mouth was pleasant. His kisses tugged at her, and again, part of her wanted to respond to him because of the boy she once knew, the boy who was still inside of him and was afraid now, as he had been afraid of the rats in the dungeon so many years ago. But then his exceedingly haughty comment about Seth filled her nostrils again, like the odor of the pungent darkness of the cellars, and his kiss turned sour.

He lowered his head, his lips trailing along her ivory throat.

"Oh, Adi!" he moaned. "I have been waiting for this for a *lifetime*." With the last word his ardor came to a fevered pitch. He heaved the top of her dress open, the tiny buttons giving way without protest to his prying. He seized her breasts roughly and she gasped. "I will not be gentle with you, Adriana," he said edgily. "You lost that favor when you went to *him*."

"Wait!" she all but screamed. "I need a drink. I want to do this right." She peered into his eyes and tried to place the right emotion in hers. She must lie like never before. "I want to *please* you, Garin. I want for it to be incredible." She reached between his thighs and found him hard and hot. She felt repulsed, but he stilled, and she could see that he was enjoying the sensations she was creating. She slipped out from between him and the bed, going to her drink, which she had left on the liquor cabinet. She gulped at it, her hands shaking.

Then he was grabbing her breasts from behind, knocking her wine glass from her grasp. The metal goblet bounced loudly across the floor, the red wine splashing like blood across her white dress. But Garin was out of his head with passion. Oblivious to everything but her, he spun her violently in his arms and began to kiss her chest again.

"Oh, Adi, the taste of the wine on your skin." Now his tongue was gliding over her, lower and lower as he sunk to his knees, forcing her to the floor with him. "We will do it here. You, on the stones, naked. Get undressed," he commanded, his tone again harsh. "Now, Adi!"

She was trembling as she fumbled with the buttons yet undone, and her heart was pounding in her chest.

His eyes were filled with lust as he watched her. The fabric opened to reveal the top of her corset and the fullness of her breasts. But he could not wait for her. "Oh, aye," he rasped.

He was on top of her again, his mouth on her flesh, teeth piercing her painfully. He fought through satin and tulle, yanking the fabric higher on her hip, until he finally found the skin of her thigh.

"Garin…" she breathed.

He pushed himself up on his elbows and rested above her for a minute.

She looked him in the eyes. "Let me show you how willing I am to be your servant. How much I want to please you." She arched her under him as she closed her eyes, and, licked her top lip with what she hoped was a seductive moan. It did not take much to fool him; he wanted her desire to be the truth so badly.

"Oh, Adi, aye. Anything you want. I knew you would be good at this, I just knew it," he said triumphantly.

"I want you to drink your mead. I have never told you this," she said playfully, "but I love the way it tastes on your lips." She pulled one of his fingers into her mouth and ran her tongue along it, nipping at it as she removed it.

Garin moaned as if he was in pain. He spotted the goblet on her bedside table then returned his gaze to her, staring at her breasts which were heaving as she breathed heavily.

Adi caught the candlelight glinting off the moist line where he had licked her. Her stomach revolted and she covered it.

"Aye," he agreed quickly. He rose and crossed to the bed in two impatient strides. She hastily got to her feet, too, watching him as he lifted the cup to his lips, tipped his head and drained it. He threw the goblet and it crashed into the wall like thunder, and then he lunged for her.

She dodged his groping, and darted to the opposite side of the bed, clutching the gleaming wooden post there. "Nay, nay," she teased with a wicked grin. "You will have to catch me first." She hoped the activity would increase his heart-rate and send the drug pulsing through his blood.

He laughed, and lunged again.

She swung around that pole to the other, at the head of the bed. But before she could flit away the next time, his strong fingers dug into her hips.

"There is no getting away this time, Adi," he murmured in her ear.

For a minute panic seized her. Did he know her intentions?

He seized her hair, which had grown to nearly shoulder-length, and jerked her head, forcing a sharp cry to escape from her. "Tell me you want me, Adi." He released her hair and grabbed her wrist, neatly twisting her arm behind her as he hauled her against his hard body. "Tell me you want me!" he shouted, shaking her.

"I want you! I want you!" She was frightened by the brutality she now knew he was capable of.

He lessened his hold on her, pulled her hand from behind her back, and forced it open. He examined the scars there, the ones he had created. He shifted his gaze to focus on her eyes as he ran his tongue across the longest one. His intentions were clear, his actions speaking louder than words. He wanted to have her, and part of him wanted it to be extremely painful for her, to punish her again and again for choosing another over him. He lifted her easily and tossed her on the bed, yanking on her dress and ducking his head underneath its thick layers.

Adriana searched through the material to find him and push him away as he advanced, making his way along her thighs, his breath hot and moist.

"You are splendid, Adi. Absolutely splendid." Again, he bit and clawed at the tender flesh of her inner thighs.

She writhed, trying to squirm to the far side of the bed, away from him and his steadily progressing mouth. She cried out.

"Aye, Adi. Scream. With my life, I love it!"

Tears squeezed from her eyes as he finally arrived at her center. Would he win after all? Why was the drug not working? Half of what she had given him, a fourth of it, would have knocked her out. Was she to lose her virginity to a man she now loathed?

And then, his head fell to one side and he was still. The room that had been filled with the sound of the rustling of fabric and her cries became stone quiet. Adi let the hot tears roll down her cheek. But now relief squeezed her chest almost as painfully as the fear had, since she knew how close she had come to oblivion. She pushed on the top of Garin's head and squirmed upwards, but his body's weight pinned her dress. Finally getting high enough on the bed to plant her feet, she got free of him and tumbled off the opposite side without even an ounce of grace. She sobbed for a minute, staring at his comatose figure on the bed and clutching her dress to her.

A knock on the door startled her, and her head snapped in that direction, but then she heard Clarise's voice. She hurried to let the girl in.

In one glance, Clarise took in her mistress's tearstained cheeks and disarrayed clothing and the form lying lifeless on the bed. "Did you kill him?" she asked, her eyes wide.

"Nay! Of course I did not kill him." Adi was horrified at the thought, but as she looked at him, she became worried and crept to the bed. Fearful at first, she tugged her skirt up to crawl across the bed next to him and check his pulse. As soon as she felt a heartbeat she dropped his wrist disdainfully. "I have to get away from here."

Clarise retrieved the princess's cape from the floor. "Let us go. We have not much time."

"Wait." Adi walked over to an urn, removing the moneybag she had hidden there. She nodded to Clarise and the young maiden led her out and through the dark corridor.

"How did you get rid of the guards?" Adriana whispered.

"I did not need to," she answered with a smile. "Sir Garin dismissed them himself. Said he could more than handle you. I guess he was wrong about that."

Adriana shivered and gave the girl a half-smile, knowing how close she had come to complete failure. They heard footsteps approaching. Clarise shoved Adriana into the cover of a recessed doorway and began to scream.

Two guards rushed to her. "What is it? What is it?"

"A rat! As big as your head, he was. Ahh!" She screamed and danced about, clutching at them, and then waving Adriana on behind her back.

"Which way did it go?"

"Further up the hallway, I think. It was huge! It could have eaten one of the castle cats."

The commotion faded away as Adi hurried on. She reached a dark winding staircase and made her way down using the wall as a guide, totally blind to her surroundings. The lurking darkness became a little lighter, and that is when she finally heard the footsteps ascending. She hastily tried to backtrack, but had to hold still as the figure got close enough to hear her. She could see the shadow on the wall now. A shadow that big could only be Derrick. As she held her breath, he turned and exited the stairwell through a low door. She let out the air in her lungs, gulping in the stale air of the stairwell for a moment and covering her heart before continuing her descent.

Several minutes later, she began to recognize the way the steps became narrower and more tightly-curved and she knew she was near the end. Finally, she bumped into the solid oak door at the bottom, and pushing it open, stepped out into the fresh, chill air. She said a silent prayer of thanksgiving for having gotten this far, but she knew she had a long way to go before she was free. And she knew she would either live in freedom tonight, or die; either at Garin's hands, or as his wife, either was death to her. She slinked in the shade of the trees that ringed Ramport until she drew close to the area below her own bedroom. She froze, hearing the low rumble of men's voices. Through the murky light, she could make out four guards standing in a tight circle below her balcony, looking upwards.

"Aye. Sir Garin told Jakes and Embry he would take care of the princess tonight, if ye know what I mean." Their deep, bass chuckles carried on the air to where she was hiding.

"Aye. I wish I could be there to watch. Or even just listen." This was followed by more lusty laughter at her expense.

For the briefest moment, she thought about stepping out of her concealment to chastise the four men for their unclean thoughts. But then she realized, even if she were not hauled off in chains, there were some men who were completely beyond redemption, and these were some of them. As they stood, making their nasty jokes, she crept around the base of the castle wall to the gate. To her dismay, she found it locked.

She retraced her steps to a tall tree she had seen and began to scale its branches. She climbed higher and higher, cringing with each creak of a branch, but a brisk breeze was rattling through the trees anyway and it, thankfully, covered her noise. When she came level to the wall's top, she stretched to grab it, but it was just beyond her fingertips. She lay on the branch, and inched her way across until she could touch it. As she did, the branch gave way and plunged toward the ground below her, before getting caught on a lower branch. She grasped the top of the wall, breathless, trying to peek over her shoulder at the guards below. But no matter how hard she craned her neck, she could not see them. She swung her legs and straddled the top of the wall. She listened intently but heard no shouts of alarm, no footfalls.

She studied the situation. The problem now was how to manage the other side of the wall. This was not something she had thought about; she had only figured out how to scale it in the first place. She lay flat on the cold stones and inched her body along the top of the wall, until she discovered what she was searching for, a tree, tall enough, and near enough on the other side to be her escape route. In the hundreds of years of peace in the kingdom, the tree had been allowed to grow. She knew, because of Garin's war, in the coming weeks it would be felled to prevent enemies from gaining the castle walls. But for now, it was her way out.

Hearing voices again, she twisted her head and saw she had come even, again, with her own balcony and the voices were those of the guards, still murmuring crudely amongst themselves and staring up at the light from her bedroom. She was totally exposed. Should one decide, for any reason, to glance her way, she would be caught—without question. She lay still, her legs straddling the wall, her face pressed along its top, and sighed, wondering for a minute how she had gotten there in the first place. Of course she remembered, literally how she had gotten there, but what had happened to her that she had abandoned her home, risking her life to leave it behind?

And then she thought of Seth.

Her life had seemed full enough before him, but he had made her see it for all its emptiness and drivel, and now she could never go back to it. She wanted to work at something important, to love, to live, with all its pain and drudgery. She longed for the world outside the castle walls. She was tired of going through life with blinders on. She wanted to live her life, and she longed for that life to be lived by Seth's side. But even if not, she could not bear to continue on with Garin as before, at the very least.

Okay, Miss Adi. 'Tis time for you to make your choice. Slowly, she stretched toward the branches of the oak on the edge of the wheat field, the tree where Seth had stood before her, unsure of why he wanted her to stay with him. The branch felt smooth, and solid. She grasped the branch tightly and swung her leg over, swinging out into space. Her heart racing, she walked her hands carefully in until her legs could wrap around the thick tree trunk. Her muscles shook with relief as she shifted the weight lower. Fairly quickly, she made her way to the ground.

She was close to him now. They could be together, if she could only make it through the wheat field to his house. She ran. The sheaves of wheat tugged at her cloak and at the edges of her dress, but she kept running. At last she reached his house, panting, her sides searing with pain. She wrapped her arms across her middle, trying to squeeze the hurt away. She caught her reflection in the window by his door. Her hair was wild, her dress torn, and stained with wine, but she had never felt so alive.

But the house was dark, as she thought it had been from her room. She knocked on the door anyway, hoping they were simply in bed. After all, it was well after midnight and Seth had to work so early in the morning. But no one came. Her heart sank. She trudged around to the front of the house, and knocked again. Receiving no response, she stood still, her head lowered, defeated. She knew anyone could spot her here on the doorstep in the bright light of the new moon, but she did not care. Part of her had known he was gone; part of her had still hoped.

"You there!"

She tensed, poised to flee, then turned and recognized Seth's neighbor, Holt Parish.

"Mr. Parish!"

"Princess?" He stepped forward and took in her stained and tattered dress, and her generally disheveled appearance.

"Aye, 'tis Adriana." Her voice held a note of hope. "Do you know where Seth is?"

His face fell. "Gone, I am afraid."

So Garin had not lied to her, at least on this one score. "Where?" she asked weakly.

"I have no idea," he replied, watching her deflate before his eyes. "Why do we not go inside?" The kindly man escorted her into his house. As she warmed by the fire, he studied her.

She glanced down again, noting in the light, the torn and dirty clothes and cuts and scratches from tree branches, stone walls, and one over-ardent lover. She must present quite a sight.

"Are ye well?"

She shook her head a little, and then asked again. "Do you have any idea where he went?"

"None whatsoever, I am afraid. All I know is I walked with them as far as the new bridge. *He* did not even know where he was going, princess. He just knew he needed to leave."

"Because of me."

"Well... You rode off without sending word, and he thought you had returned to your other life. He needed to be, as he put it...somewhere you were not."

She nodded, hanging her head for a second, but then raising it with a look of fierce determination.

"I have to find him. If only to tell him the truth about what happened. Garin tricked me. He told me my father was ill, to get me to go to the castle, and then he kept me prisoner against my will. Not a day has gone by, not a moment has gone by, I have not dreamed of escaping and coming back to Seth. Tell me," she queried after a second, "if I were to find him...would he listen to me? Would he believe me?"

Holt thought about it. "I do not know, princess," he answered truthfully.

Again she nodded. "I have to try," she said solemnly. "Thank you for your time. You have been more than kind." She moved toward the door, but he called after her.

"Wait. Wait, please." When she stopped and faced him, he explained. "You cannot go searching for him dressed like that. It is not wise for a woman to travel alone at all, but it would be especially unwise to go out dressed in your finery, even if it is a bit torn. Let me get you one of my wife's dresses."

Before she could protest, he left, returning shortly with a bundle. "I will leave, so you can change." He held her hands. "Good luck."

She pressed some coins into his fist.

"Nay, I will not take this. I am doing this for Seth."

"Thank you," she whispered, her heart clutching.

Before she left Adriana put money on his kitchen table, enough to pay for a dozen over of his wife's dresses.

CHAPTER THIRTEEN

Adriana stood at the middle of the bridge, uncertain. She gazed on her home one last time, and then continued on her way. Her shoes echoed dreadfully on the planks of the bridge, and it was all she could do not to remember Seth had laid some of these very same boards.

She had already decided her first course of action was to warn King Lawrence, her former playmate and friend, of her father's pending attack.

When she reached the castle gates of Dunneston at dawn a sentry accosted her. "Halt! Who are you?"

"I am Princess Adriana of Hamiltonia. I have a message for Lawrence...King Lawrence."

He studied her suspiciously. "Please forgive me, miss, but you are not dressed like any princess I have known."

Adriana glanced at her attire. "You are right, of course. But still, that is who I am." She thought about this. "I know. Give this message to the king, and he will know it is I. Tell him Adi wants to know if Lawry has ever made his way out of the wardrobe in his great aunt's room." She giggled at the memory, and the guard took off, perhaps questioning her sense of reason.

She sat on the dirt path to wait, worn out from her travels. When the guard returned, he was not alone.

"Adi!" The king shook the gate. "Open this immediately. How good of you to come."

"Let us hope you think so after I give you my message." The young king burst from the gate as soon as it was opened and caught Adi up in a bear hug, swinging her around gleefully.

"It has been so long. You look wonderful. Except for this dress. Where did you get this thing?" he asked, tugging on the rough fabric. "No offense, but it is hideous."

She laughed. "I see your sense of diplomacy has not left you. It must serve you well as king."

"Oh, hush and come in here."

"Actually, Lawry, I cannot stay, and you have a lot to prepare for."

But the king did not seem to hear her. He was chuckling as he appeared to be remembering times they had shared together in the past. "So," he held his arms out from his sides, "as you can see, I finally did get out of that wardrobe. No thanks to you."

She smiled, patting his shoulder. "I am sorry. That was not nice of me."

"Nay. If I had been you, I would have locked me in there and thrown away the key. I was a little scoundrel then. Speaking of which, how is Garin?"

"I am afraid he is still a scoundrel. That is actually why I am here."

"You have run out on Garin?" he asked, shocked.

"Aye."

He shook his head. "Too bad I am an old married man—" he raised her knuckles to his lips, "—or I would snatch you for myself, Adi. That is why I was such a pinhead, you know. I was head over heels for you."

She felt her cheeks warm. "Do not let Sariah hear you say that, or you will find yourself locked inside that wardrobe again."

He laughed loud and hard. "Oh. Sariah will be glad to see you."

"Lawrence, I cannot stay. I only came to warn you. Garin and my father are planning to attack you. I am so sorry. The bridge was a pretext to give them easy access to you."

He shook his head. "I suspected as much," he responded sadly. "Well, thanks to your warning, we will be ready for them. And perhaps we can avoid bloodshed altogether." He considered this a moment, rubbing his chin, but then peered at her. "Where will you go, then?"

"I do not know, exactly."

The king was moved by the sadness he saw in her eyes. "Adi—" he ran the back of his hand down her face tenderly "—I hope you find someone to love you as you deserve."

She gazed at the dirt beneath her feet, and said quietly, "I thought I had."

"That is who you are chasing after?"

She lifted her head, surprised that he had guessed, but then nodded.

"Good luck," he said sincerely. "Please take one of my carriages. I cannot stand to see you on foot."

"Oh, I could not. I do not know if I will ever return this way."

"Then at least take a horse." He snapped his fingers and a servant who had been hanging in the shade of the trees stepped forward. "Bring me Lancer, and make sure he is fully supplied." The servant took off at a run. "What else do you need?" He led her over to a bench to sit. "I am at your disposal. Your warning will save many Dunnestonian lives."

"I am fine, Lawrence, truly. I brought money with me. I can purchase any provisions I need."

He sighed. "Tell me about this man you seek then. What is he like?"

Now it was Adriana's turn to sigh. "He is handsome." She smiled.

"Of course," he teased with a fake groan.

"Honorable...headstrong," she added, with an exasperated sigh.

"Oh, then, you two are a match made in heaven." He laughed.

She laughed with him. "He is from Hamiltonia," she continued. "He is a blacksmith. He lives with his sister and a nephew."

"You are not talking about Seth Hobbes?"

Her mouth dropped open.

"I met him a few months ago. And Lea and Tristan. Such a nice boy, that Tristan."

"You m-met Seth?" she sputtered. "Where?"

"Here. In my court. He came to ask permission to settle in my kingdom."

"How was he?"

"How was he?" Lawrence repeated. "I do not know. I am a member of the male species, Adriana, I do not notice that kind of thing. He seemed well, I guess."

"Did he say where he was going?"

"Nay. I am afraid not. But to the west, I think."

"Did he say why..." she hesitated, "...why he had left his home in the first place?"

"He said there were too many memories in Hamiltonia." He watched her face. "Are you part of those memories?"

"I am afraid so. Oh, Lawry. He thinks I left him of my own accord, but Garin tricked me. He told me Father was ill…" Her voice faded out. "Do you think Seth will forgive me if I tell him the truth?" she asked him quietly.

He took her arms. "I am sure of it, Adi. He would be a fool not to."

She kissed his cheek tenderly, a single tear getting past her guard and slipping down her cheek. "I had almost forgotten how sweet you could be." She smiled at him.

They spun at the clip-clop of a horse's hooves on the rock pathway. The servant was arriving with the most magnificent stallion she had ever seen. He was white, dappled with tiny, black spots and bore a glistening, black mane. Decorative silk triangles cut from a vibrant red cloth hung from his reins and a matching blanket was draped under a black saddle.

"Oh, my," she breathed. "He is beautiful." She reached out, and the horse nuzzled her with his velvety nose and then snorted.

The king laughed. "I think he returns the compliment."

"Oh, Lawry. I cannot take him. He is far too—"

"I insist." When he saw her getting ready to protest again, he spoke over her. "Please, Adi. It will make me feel better to know you are in Lancer's hands, or hooves, as the case may be. Please, Adi," he pleaded.

She patted the stallion's neck, saying finally. "I will bring him back to you. I promise."

"As far as I am concerned, he is yours," the king replied simply. "But I will hold you to that promise to visit again."

The princess caressed his face. "You will be safe, Lawry, will you not?"

He put his hand on top of hers, twisting his head to kiss her palm. "Aye. And you?"

"I will."

King Lawrence helped her to mount Lancer. The horse swung his head to look at his master curiously.

Lawry stroked Lancer's muzzle. "Take good care of her now, Lance." He laid his forehead on the horse's head and they both closed their eyes for a moment. When Lawry straightened, Lancer snorted and pranced. The king chuckled heartily. "Okay, boy. You will be out of here in a few seconds." He moved to Adriana's side once more. "Fair ye well, sweet Adi."

She bent and gave him a peck on the cheek. "Fair ye well, my Lawrence."

He gave the horse a slap on the flank and watched her ride away with a sigh. "What a girl."

She turned and waved, the stallion's hooves raising small clouds of dust on the roadway. She saw Lawry wave, and then the gates close with him on the other side. She continued to watch as he got smaller, and then a bend in the road took him out of her sight for good.

CHAPTER FOURTEEN

Seth shrugged deeper into his coat. This far away from his fire, the chill air, as it blew in the open sides of the smithy, cut to the bone. He squinted at the leaden sky as the first big snowflakes of winter began to float to the ground. Retrieving his hammer, he returned to the fire, drawing out the sword he had been heating in the depths of its flames. He pounded steadily on the sword as it lay on the anvil, the ringing of metal on metal shattering the stillness, but going practically unnoticed by him.

He had been making quite a few of these swords of late. The King of Dunneston and his army had been under siege for several long months by the Hamiltonians.

He worried about his friends on both sides. The men he had worked alongside in the village, and the good King Lawrence, who had received him and his family most graciously when they first left home.

He worried, too, about Adi. She seemed to show no concern for her own personal safety at times. Would she be foolhardy enough to get into the middle of something like this? But then, he thought, she had another man to take care of her now; she was not his concern. That thought made his blood boil hotter than the molten iron he had made arrowheads from earlier. He swung his hammer down so hard the handle split and the head fell into the stone pit that housed his fire.

"Damn!"

"Seth?" He heard Lea's voice calling from a distance.

"Aye. I am in my shop."

She trudged up, tugging her shawl closer. "It is snowing," she stated, scanning her brother's face intently. "Did you rise early again? And late to bed, I have no doubt." He did not comment. She sighed. "Are ye hungry?"

"Nay, not yet. I broke another hammer," he growled. She peered at the splintered piece of wood he held. "I broke my spare last week and did not make myself a new one. Foolish. Now I will have to pay for something I could have forged myself. I'll go into Morriston in a few weeks to get one."

"Aye. Trist and I will go, too. I could use a few things they do not have at the Smithson's store. But we are going there now for some goods. Is there anything you need from town?"

"Nay," he answered her absentmindedly, frowning into his forge. "Save news on the fighting. I do not like making my living from death." He sighed. "Give me a good hoe or a plow to forge, any day."

"Do not think of it as earning your money from others' wrongdoing, baby brother," she said, stretching to kiss his cheek. "Think of all of the innocent people who will be able to protect themselves and their families because of something you created and made strong with your sweat."

He wiped the sweat from his brow as she said it and bent to kindly kiss the top of her head. "Thanks, sis. I am sorry I am grumpy. I did not sleep well."

"I heard that from somebody. Anything on your mind?"

You mean anyone? he thought dryly. He shrugged. "Just worried about keeping you and Tristan safe if the fighting comes this far." While it was not all together the truth, it was not all together a lie either. He was worried about his family, and the one he could no longer protect.

"We will face that together, when the time comes." She smiled. "I will be off, then, before this little storm gets any meaner."

But by the time Lea and Tristan arrived at the little general store in town, the wind had increased enough to literally blow them in the door. Together they strained to close it behind them.

"Oh, ho, ho! 'Tis getting wicked out there, is it not?"

"Aye, Mr. Smithson." Lea answered, shaking the snow from her cape. "How fare you today?" she asked with a bright smile.

"Never been better, Mistress Tanner. And how is young Tristan today?"

The boy's eyes shone; Mr. Smithson was one of his favorite adults.

"Well, Mr. Smithson, well, thank you."

"Good, good. Now then, why not bring that list over here and I can help you fill it while your mother checks out the new fabric that just came in."

As Lea fingered the pretty blue fabric, trying to decide whether or not it was sturdy enough for everyday wear, a new customer blew in the door, setting the bells above it jingling. When the bundled figure turned around and pulled the shawl that was covering her hair down, Lea gave a little shout of joy.

"Olivia Parish! What are you doing here?"

The two women rushed into each other's arms, exclaiming in delight.

"Oh, Lea! How good to see you. I have missed you so."

"Oh, me too, Livvy. Is Demetri with you?" she tried to search through the chilly, frosted windows at the front of the shop.

"Nay. He is home helping his father." Hearing the commotion, Tristan looked up and then hurried over to receive a hug from the new arrival. He had spent so much time at her house, Mrs. Parish was like a second mother.

"Oh, Tristan. You have grown. Demetri will be thrilled to see you."

"Are you here visiting someone?" Lea asked.

"Nay. We have left Hamiltonia for good," she answered darkly. "Things are not the same anymore." She glanced at Tristan hesitantly.

"Trist, finish filling our order, like a good lad, and add another pound of beef...that is, if you can all join us for dinner tonight, Livvy."

"Oh, that would be fantastic, anything that will save me from cooking." The two women watched Tristan's back as he walked away.

"Is it that bad, then?" Lea whispered.

"Aye. And worse. They commandeered your place, made it into a sort of garrison. And when Holt protested..." She shuddered. "They beat him, Lea. Beat him senseless. He is blind in one eye now."

She gasped, "Nay."

"'Tis the God's honest truth. That Sir Garin. What I would say about him if I were not a lady."

"What about Adriana? Is she well?"

"Adriana? Have you not heard?" Reading Lea's blank expression, she continued. "The princess escaped from him. Garin tricked her that night she left. The loathsome toad told her that her father, the king, was dying."

"I knew she would never have left Seth of her own free will." Lea spoke so loudly Mr. Smithson and Tristan peered over from their list. "Trist, hurry.

I need to get home to your uncle." She bent her head to Olivia's again. "You say she escaped?"

The older woman nodded. "Sir Garin had the poor thing under lock and key. She was a sight when Holt saw her...I guess it was about six months ago now...thin as a rail, and heartbroken to find you all gone, Holt said."

Lea smiled, clasping her friend's hands in glee. "Where is she now?"

"I could not say." Lea's face fell. "She went off in search of you. Holt walked her as far as the bridge, but we did not leave, ourselves, for another month. Have not seen hide nor hair of her on our travels."

"Searching for us," Lea repeated, distraught. "On her own?" Olivia nodded. "You have to give that girl credit. She is one courageous princess."

"Indeed. But you have to keep in mind, she is rather inspired. Anyone could see the girl was head over heels for your Seth."

"Well, he has been miserable without her," Lea confided. "Ugh! This is so frustrating. She could be anywhere."

"Aye."

Lea gave Olivia directions to the pair of cottages they were living in and set off, after a few moments, with Tristan, for home. When they neared their cottage, Lea ran the last several yards, desperate to share the good news about Adriana with Seth. She stepped through the door, shaking off the snow that had settled on her cloak on the way home. She heard hammering in the loft. She hastily set her groceries down and hustled to find Seth, who had taken apart Tristan's bed and was replacing one of the side slats with a longer piece to accommodate Tristan's growing frame.

"Seth!"

"What is wrong?" Seth asked, surveying her from where he was sitting on the loft floor working.

Lea was flushed and breathless.

"Adriana," she gasped out between breaths.

"What about her?" Seth growled. The name had remained unspoken between them for many months.

"She did not leave you. She did not!"

He bolted to his feet. "What are you talking about?"

"Garin tricked her. He told her the king was dying to get Adriana to go back, then, locked her in. She had no intention of leaving you."

His face paled. "How do you know this?"

"Olivia Parish. The Parishes have moved in by the Mill Pond. Holt saw Adriana. She escaped. She is searching for you."

"Searching for... Where? Where is she?"

"They do not know," she responded, losing her enthusiasm. Tristan had climbed behind her but did not interrupt. "They saw her several months ago. She is looking for you," she repeated feebly. "The Parishes are coming over for dinner. You can talk to Holt then."

Seth sat, appearing stunned, on the side of the frame he had extended. He glanced up at Lea. "He lied to her?"

"Aye," she answered, wanting to tell him more, but not in front of Tristan.

"But, she will never find me," he cried out forlornly. "No one knows where I am."

Lea took a few more steps into the room. "She will find you, Seth. She escaped from Garin...she will find you."

He shook his head, lowering it to hold it mournfully. "I should never have left. I should have believed in her."

"Seth," she said softly, coming to squat in front of him. "Do not torture yourself. I am telling you, *she will find you*. You two were meant to be together. It will work out."

He grinned weakly. "Always the eternal optimist, eh, Sis?"

"Aye." She grinned. "Now—" she slapped her palms on her thighs and rose, "—I have a roast to make."

Tristan followed her to pelt her with questions about Adriana and Demetri while she cooked.

Seth could hear their voices as he rose to stare out the window. The wind was blowing the snow across the lawn to where it had begun to form drifts against the low stone wall separating the yard from the orchard. Adriana was out there somewhere, searching for him. The idea swamped him with emotions, chief among them, guilt. He hung his head again. He had found it so easy to believe Adriana had chosen Garin over him, and now he had lost her. *Still*, he raised his head and peered through the swirling snow, *she is out there somewhere hunting for me.*

For the first time in a long time, he felt a glimmer of hope.

CHAPTER FIFTEEN

Adriana put her sewing on the table and rose to light a candle. She rubbed her eyes wearily. She should have quit working an hour ago, instead of struggling in the dimming light. Stiff from sitting in her rocking chair for so long, she put her hands on her back and stretched and shivered a little. The temperature had dropped some; she would have to stoke the fire. She walked over to peer out the tiny window of her little cottage and was surprised to see it was snowing, and must have been for some time, as the snow had gathered around the yard and stables. Plucking her cape from the hook beside the door, she hurried to bed Lancer down.

She bent her head against the wind and listened to its lonely howling. It suited the grayness of the day, and the bleakness of her spirit. She had searched for Seth for months, and finally left off, realizing it was useless. The man could be anywhere. Sometimes she wondered if she would become an old spinster woman here, alone in this cottage, sewing clothes for others to support herself, her heart always heavy.

A few of the bachelors in Morriston had taken a shine to her when she first came to live in the old abandoned cottage. Some had even come out to help her make repairs, but all had found her melancholy and beyond their reach. She was kind, and pleasant, but it was obvious to all her heart had taken up residency somewhere else. One or two of the more persistent suitors would still stop by, from time to time, to chat with her, but never found her open to their advances. In fact, a few times she was distracted enough to be oblivious to their attempts to seduce her. So, they had left frustrated, but told her they continued to be drawn to her fair appearance and honest heart.

Adi pushed on the stable door, which scraped against the ground hindering her progress. She laid a hip against it and shoved. When she had gotten it open a crack, she squeezed inside and felt around for the candle and matches always left in a holder attached to the wall. Lancer snorted impatiently in his stall.

"I am coming, Lance."

She lit the candle and found the soulful eyes of the stallion watching her lovingly.

"Hey, there, big boy."

The horse raised his head and put it over her shoulder. She rested against the stall door and stroked his muzzle, finally resting her cheek against it and closing her eyes. Lancer was her only friend these days, the only comfort in her loneliness. It was just the two of them now, and while the horse had no complaints, Adriana longed for the company of others, namely Lea, Tristan, and Seth. Sometimes, when she was particularly lonely, she would talk about them with Lance, describing them in detail as her singular friend mutely looked on.

"Are ye hungry?" she finally asked, giving him a pat, and moving to fill his bucket with oats. She opened his stall door, and placed his feed before him, currying his coat idly. "It is to be a cold one tonight, boy." She glanced at the high, cracked window that still let in a little of the waning light. "I wish it was a little less drafty in here for you."

She pulled an old blanket from where it hung over the side of the stall wall, and stretched it over Lancer, smoothing it as she talked. "Not quite the fancy livery you are used to, eh, Lance? Oh how the mighty have fallen." She laughed. "Well, the hay will keep you warm, fella." She patted his flank before leaving, but spun after closing the stall door behind her. "Tomorrow we will go for a ride, boy." The thought of getting out of the depressing confines of her house for a while cheered her.

She still would occasionally take these trips, riding out for a day to search for Seth, but always returning home in the twilight. Tomorrow she would head north, and see what she could find. Though she knew it was futile, she could not altogether cease her pursuit of him.

SETH CLOSED THE JANGLING door of the Morriston general store, shutting out the wind and the rain.

"I am sorry, Lea. I picked quite a day to go out for a ride."

Lea peeled off her soaked shawl. "You could hardly predict the weather, Seth. Besides, I would rather be out in this than be sitting at home with nothing to do. Let me see your coat."

Seth twisted so Lea could examine the tear in his jacket. His eyes had been restlessly searching the woods along the road for any signs of Adriana, and he had not seen the branch that had snagged his sleeve.

"Well, hello there," thundered a jovial voice from the rear of the store. "Oh, that is too bad. Such a nice jacket. I am Utey Deadlow, proprietor." The balding man unlaced the fingers he had entwined in front of his round stomach and held out his hand.

"Seth Hobbes. This is my sister, Lea Tanner, and my nephew, Tristan."

The store owner shook with all of them in turn. "Nice of you to help your mother and uncle out today, son," he said in a friendly way to Tristan. He took measure of Seth, then hooked his arm through Seth's and led him aside, saying confidentially, "There is a really *incredible* seamstress—" he raised his eyebrows "—who could furnish what you need. She is a real princess—"

Lea hooked Seth's other elbow and dragging him away from the shop owner forcefully. "He already has his own princess, thank you," she said with a polite smile.

Seth looked at her with amused surprise.

Utey cleared his throat apologetically. "Well, let us see about filling your list then."

He switched tactics and escorted Lea through the store, pointing out various items he thought might interest her.

Meanwhile, Seth drifted toward the door. He stared out the window through the driving rain. The blacksmith's shop across the street was about twice the size of his. He thought, for a minute, about crossing the street and striking up a conversation with the smith, but the steadily-falling rain deterred him. He noted the beautiful horse the man was busy shoeing. It was white, with black speckles. It had silk triangles draping from the reins, unusual for a horse out in the country. Sure, Morriston was larger than the village they lived in, but still, it was hardly big enough to have someone so wealthy in town. *Perhaps passing through*, he thought idly.

The lady who appeared to own the horse stood, with her back to him, shivering visibly despite her proximity to the fire. Her hooded cape drooped from her shoulders. *Poor thing is drenched! Too bad her fine horse threw a shoe in this horrible weather.* He studied her again. She wore a work dress, similar to any of the dresses in Lea's trunk at home. *I wonder why someone so plainly dressed has such a smartly dressed horse?* He mused, again feeling pulled across the street.

"Seth! Are you listening?"

"Huh? Oh, umm...I guess not."

"Is this the kind of hammer you need?" Lea lifted a mallet about half the size of the one he was on the hunt for.

"Nay," he answered, crossing to aid her with the rest of the purchases.

Before long, the shopping was taken care of, and the goods stored on his horse. Seth tightened the strap of the saddlebag, then rested his hands on the pommel, standing with the rain dripping from the rim of his hat. He squinted between raindrops at the girl at the blacksmith's shop for a second. Then Lea walked out on the porch of the shop.

"Ready?"

"Huh? Aye."

He walked around his horse to offer Lea help in mounting hers. Once aboard, she turned her horse's head and waited for Seth to mount. She peered in the direction that he had been focused on and caught sight of the woman in the cape.

"She seems vaguely familiar."

He shrugged. With one more glance across the road, he spurred his horse forward.

"Hyah!"

Lea followed him, but her gaze also lingered on the blacksmith's shop.

Seth scanned the road ahead, and the lines of trees on each side, keeping his eyes open for the princess who so frequently haunted his dreams.

No sign of her.

ADRIANA WAS OUT FOR her usual ride with Lancer. Today, she had chosen to go east, toward Dunneston proper, where she had come from so many months ago. Perhaps there was a chance she had missed Seth the first time around. She had exhausted all other directions, in any case, so it was east she headed.

It was one of those days when the weather was so fine and perfect the soft, white clouds stood out in crystal-clear relief. It looked like someone tacked them in the sky. She could not help but feel cheerful as she trotted about on Lance, even though her day had started out in stark contrast to the one she was having now.

She had awoken from a dream about Seth so real she had broken down sobbing for fifteen minutes or more. It had been a long time since she had cried like that, excluding the nights she fell asleep softly weeping. Perhaps it had been the catharsis needed to drive the dark clouds away and replace them with the billowy, wildly white ones that floated above her head now.

In her dream she was getting some supplies she needed at Deadlow's General Store. She found just the right color thread she needed to hem a wealthy lady's ball gown and was ecstatic, having searched for it everywhere in her dream. She opened the door of the store and stepped out. It had been raining, a cleansing, untroublesome mist. But then she had peered across the street at the blacksmith shop, and instead of William Cox, who had shoed her horse the other day, it was Seth. In her dream, she had dropped her packages in her surprise, even the lady's fine dress, and it had fallen into the muddy street and been ruined. But she did not care. It was Seth. She called out his name and began to cross the street to him, but out of nowhere, a black carriage pulled by two fierce, black horses came careening along the street, out of control, headed straight toward her. She screamed, and Seth wheeled around and recognized her. He said, his voice hollow, his eyes full of disdain for her, "I do not want you anymore, Adi. You are nothing to me. Less than nothing." He slowly turned from her. She stared at the carriage as it approached to trample her. The horses reared, their hooves rising over her, thrashing through the air threateningly. A head appeared out of the window of the carriage. The passenger had been all dressed in black. It was Garin. He laughed hellishly, the sound cutting through her even as the horses' hooves came crashing onto her.

It was not the pain of the sharp edges of the horses' hooves that had made her cry out and wake from the nightmare, it was Seth's words. What if, after all this time, thinking of him day and night—wondering what he was doing, praying for his safety and happiness—what if, when she found him, he did not love her anymore?

Thankfully, the pain of his imagined rejection was hard to remember on the brilliant day. She was riding through woods, more dense than most of the ones she had been in, when she realized she had lost track of both time and location. It was much later than it generally was when she chose to make her way home, the light was already starting to become murky. And she had wandered from the path. As she sat, trying to figure out which course to take, she heard the sound of men's voices. She twisted, and it was as if time had slowed for a second. They were there, three soldiers on horseback, her family crest on their uniforms. Her eyes met the steely eyes of the biggest one, Derrick.

Things sped up. He shouted, "It is the princess!" at the same time as she jerked on the reins and pointed Lancer in the opposite direction.

In panic she dug her heels into Lancer's sides and urged him into a gallop. At first she could hear shouted threats behind her, and calls to stop, but soon it became only the sound of the horses' beating hooves on the ground, and the occasional branch snapping past. Lancer flew, his speed born of sheer terror as three horses bore down on him. She was able to keep a healthy distance between them at first, but their mounts were fresher and they soon closed the gap. Derrick's horse pulled alongside hers and he gazed at her with menace. An evil smile cracked his face as he reached over and snatched the reins from her, bringing their horses up short.

"Nice to see you again, Princess Adriana." He sneered. "Sir Garin was not happy about you leaving. But I am sure he is going to be thrilled to see you tonight." He looked at his companions and laughed with them at the prospect of their leader's response to seeing her again. "You will be coming with us now."

Adi watched his hands with the reins. He made a move to tie hers to his horse's saddle horn, laying his on his horse's neck for a beat.

"The hell I will!" she spat, noticing he had relaxed his grip as he began to loop Lancer's reins to tie them.

She made a "che-che" noise in her throat and spurred him on, but her stallion needed no more coaxing. In a flash, the pair was racing through the forest as Lancer wove expertly in and out of the trees, like thread through a loom. She bent low over his neck, whispering words of encouragement. Ahead she saw the banks of a river they had forded earlier in the day.

"Come, Lance. Hah-hah!" Lance breasted the river, and without hesitation, leapt into the water. Behind her, Adi heard the other horses shying as they hit the cold water.

She whirled to check, rising from her saddle a little, and heard the *wwh-hizzz* of the arrow a half-second before the sharp pain pierced her shoulder.

The momentum of the arrow, shot at such short range, nearly propelled her off the horse, but she clung to Lancer's neck. Going back meant hell, the only way was forward.

She collapsed over Lance's neck, mostly dead weight as he sped onward, hitting the bank on the other side and not breaking stride.

It seemed like they rode forever.

Her legs were too weak to grip the horse's sides or even to stay in the stirrups, so with each hoof fall, Adi's helpless body bounced in the saddle, sending teeth-gnashing flashes of pain burning through her.

Her eyes were open wide now, her breathing raspy. She did not think she could hear any riders chasing her, but she couldn't be sure because it seemed like the excruciating searing sensation of her wound was blocking out all other senses.

Lance continued to pound out a rhythm, a rhythm of jarring, mind-wrenching agony. Her sight bleary, the blur of the passing trees became a smear of color. All she could hear was the horse's hooves, and then...nothing.

CHAPTER SIXTEEN

Seth stood warming himself by the dying embers of his forge. The night was well on its way to becoming dark. He should have finished work a while ago but had lost track of time as Lea and Tristan were not there to remind him to come in for dinner, as the two of them had gone to the Parishes' for dinner. Seth had opted out, claiming that he had too much work to do before they took their goods into Morriston in the morning. That was only partially true. He had really begged off because he was just not in the mood for socializing.

It had been over a month since he had learned Adi was searching for him. Numerous discussions with Lea and Holt always came back to the same conclusion; it was best for him to stay put, rather than trying to find her. If they both were on the move, they could go around and around forever. Someone needed to stay still, and that someone was him.

But waiting went against Seth's nature, chafing him unbearably. He had never been a patient man. He was a man of action. He would make a decision, and, good or bad, act on it.

Tonight, while he was working, he decided to place notices for her—telling her where he lived—in all the surrounding areas. He should be inside right now, making copies, in the hope of having extras to give Mr. Deadlow to give out to travelers, who could then post them far and wide.

But something was enticing him to be outside of the house. It could have been that the glorious day had become an equally-glorious evening. It could have been that he dreaded returning to his little one-room cottage alone.

In any case, he stepped out of his shop and gazed up at the thousands of stars that illuminated the night sky. To his left, a half-moon hung so clearly he could make out the entire dark side of the moon as well. It seemed as if he had only to stretch to hang his coat on the end.

He pivoted to go in, but heard the sound of a horse whinnying. It was not coming from his own stables. To his surprise, a riderless horse stomped slowly through the trees, its head down. As it drew closer, he recognized it as the white, dappled horse he saw in Morriston.

"Hey there, fella," he murmured, approaching cautiously so as not to drive it away. "You're a long way from home, there, Charlie."

Making small motions he came within feet, and the horse stopped, watching him. It snorted and twitched but did not take flight. Slowly Seth reached out and grabbed the dangling reins. He patted the stallion's neck and was surprised to find it wet with sweat. The horse shook its head.

"Hey. Hey. It's okay, big guy. What spooked you?" Seth scratched behind its ear. "You take off on your mistress, did you?"

As he contemplated what to do, he heard the *pit-pat* of something hitting the dry leaves below. He bent his head and was surprised to see, even in the pale light of the moon, a blood-red droplet standing out on the spine of a brown leaf.

"Are you hurt, boy?" Seth asked sympathetically. He ran his hands over the horse's flank. He could find no injury, or evidence of blood, so he ducked under its great head to examine the other side. There the horse's beautiful white coat was awash in moonlight. Only it wasn't white. Blood was thick and fresh on his neck, and dripped occasionally to the ground. Again Seth felt for an injury, but found none.

Comprehension sank in. It was not the horse's blood. It was the rider's.

"Oh, Sweet Lord!" he exclaimed. "Where is she, boy?" he asked, not expecting an answer.

Seth turned to head deeper into the orchard, searching the ground to the left and right. The horse circled around with him and started walking ahead. At first Seth ignored it, and continued to sweep the ground in front of him with his eyes. But the horse snorted impatiently, twisting to observe him. It trotted forward a few yards, then, again swiveled its head to check on him. He followed, advancing more quickly now, putting his faith in the steed.

Ahead, the horse came to a halt. This time it didn't retreat when Seth drew near. He scrutinized the vicinity.

If the horse hadn't stopped, surely he would have walked right passed her. Crumpled on the ground was a woman.

It was too dark to make out her features, but the moonlight glinted off the arrow stuck in her shoulder.

"Oh, dear God," he breathed, bending to gently scoop her up. She wasn't much of a burden to him, a tiny thing really. He rushed with her, secure in his arms, to his cottage. She did not stir and he wondered if she was already dead, but the heat of her body as she lay against his chest seemed to deny that.

As he lay her on the bed, her hood fell back, revealing a tumble of brown hair. The light was still too low for him to see her face or examine her wound, so he went to the fireplace and lit a candle that sat on the mantle, and stoked the fire to life.

When he spun around, he froze.

It could not be.

His eyes must be playing tricks on him, seeing her there simply because he wanted to see her there. The woman just looked like Adi, that was all.

He forced his feet to move, and as he got closer, he realized the woman in his bed was actually Adriana.

He fell to his knees by the side of the bed, setting the candle on the floor where the holder almost tipped before rocking into place. Her face was ashen as he gazed on it. Her hair had grown to beyond shoulder-length, and she wore a plain, brown dress...but it was her.

Before he could do anything, even take another breath, her eyes fluttered open. She stared at him oddly, as if trying to identify a new species, then groaned and squeezed her eyes shut.

"Oh, Lord, you are too cruel." She opened her eyes again. "Good God in heaven! Is that really you, Seth, or is this just another damned dream?"

He laughed, as much from relief and surprise as from joy. She sounded much stronger than she appeared.

"It is me, Adi. It is me." His voice shook. Her voice brought tears to his eyes; he recognized the warmth and texture of it as it wrapped about him comfortingly, like an old, familiar blanket. He brushed the hair from her face, gazing at her.

Tears poured down her cheeks. "Oh, Seth!" She reached to touch him, but cried out in anguish.

Alarmed, he tried to calm her. "Nay, Adi. Be still. You are hurt." He inspected her wound. It still oozed a fair amount of blood; he needed to bind it. "Adi...I have to break the arrow off so that I can bind it and make it stop bleeding. But it will hurt, do you understand?"

She nodded feebly, the pain seeming to increase with every minute, as if her body was waking to it by bits and pieces.

He straighten, steeling himself, and took hold of the shaft of the arrow at the base. He hesitated, peering into her face once more. "Are ye ready?"

She didn't respond, awash in a flood of agony, already steeped in pain too far to comprehend more. He closed his eyes for a moment, and then, with a jerk, snapped the wood in two.

She cried out sharply. Her body gave one huge spasm, and then went limp.

He wanted to weep...for fear, for love...but he knew he had to work quickly to save her. He shrugged out of his coat and drew his shirt off over his head. Grabbing the fabric, he began to rip it into long strips. He glanced at her face from time to time. She was still; her chest barely rising as she breathed. "Hold on, Adi. Hold on," he whispered hoarsely.

Her dress was so saturated with blood that it was cold and heavy on her. He rose and brought some towels back with him, along with a bowl of water and a knife. He unbuttoned her dress to the waist and, being careful not to get the knife caught in her corset strings, diligently cut it away.

He pulled her to a sitting position, trying to be careful of her shoulder, and laid several of the strips across the bed before gently lowering her. He wondered if he should clean the wound before sealing it. There was blood everywhere. He wondered how there could be any left in her. Even though he was trying to move her as little as possible, he worried that he shouldn't have lifted her at all.

All the while, she did not make a sound or twitch a muscle. He dampened a towel with water and worked to clear away the blood, but found it to be an impossible task, since as fast as he worked, more would come out. He prayed it would be an adequate cleaning job. He braced himself. He knew this next part would hurt her. He folded the towel and laid it over the wound, and then loosely tied it to her chest before getting a better grip. With a whispered prayer he yanked it tightly to put pressure on the wound.

She yelped and shook her head from side to side, moaning, her face creased with pain. Her hands at her sides clenched and unclenched spastically. He snatched the next tie, and did the same, hurrying through them to get the procedure over with.

She whimpered, breathing heavily, and tears pooled on the pillow beneath her. Her hair was damp with sweat.

I wish I had something to give her for the pain. Or something to knock her out, to get her through the worst of this. But he knew the village doctor had gone to her in-laws for a visit, warning them all to not get hurt in her absence. In any case, she was really no more than a wise, old lady who had seen more of life and death than most.

He remembered a flagon of mead that a friend gave him instead of payment for repairing his farm equipment. He rummaged through a small, wooden chest at the foot of his bed, and exclaimed happily when he discovered it there. He lifted her slowly and brought the bottle to her lips. The odor made her turn her head although her eyes stayed closed.

"Adi…drink some, honey. It may help with the pain."

She fought him at first, like a child taking their medicine but, finally, let a little pass her lips, and then more, until he was satisfied.

"There," he said soothingly. He lowered her and she appeared to relax a little. Since there was nothing more he could do, he set the bottle on the floor, and curled up around her on his side, curving his body over the top of her head, and kissing her hair. "Rest, now, Adi…rest." He sighed, closing his eyes and praying she would make it through to the morning light.

He was surprised a while later when she spoke.

"Seth?"

He lifted his head. "Aye, I'm here."

Her eyes were still closed. "You seem worried about me," she started tentatively, with a note of curiosity in her voice.

"Aye. I am. But you are going to be fine. I will take care of you."

Her voice was breathy and her lips lifted a bit at the corners. "Do you love me, then?"

His heart swelled in his chest, and for a minute he did not think he was going to be able to speak at all. "Aye, ye little twit." He laughed, kissing her hair again, "I do."

"So you are not just taking care of me to be nice?"

He felt the pain of the last several months lift from him. "Go to sleep, Adi," he scolded with a grin, but he curled his body even closer to her.

"I wish I would have known that before." She sighed, and then drifted off to sleep.

CHAPTER SEVENTEEN

Three quick knocks on his door shattered the stillness of the morning. Seth rose, careful to not jostle the bed, and went to the door to stop whoever it was before they woke Adriana.

"Seth," Lea said almost immediately. "There is this strange horse out here covered in blood. I tried to drag him to the stables to wash him off and assess his injuries, but he refuses to go."

She watched in confusion as he stepped out and patted the stallion's neck. "It is all right, boy. I took care of her."

"Care of who?" Lea's brow furrowed. "And I thought you wanted to get off to Morriston early this morning, why were you not up?"

Instead of answering, he stepped aside and opened the door to let the morning light fall on his bed. Lea staggered forward, using the door frame to right herself. "Seth," she breathed. "It is Adriana!"

"I figured that out." He laughed, gripping his sister's shoulder and kissing her head.

She broke away and hurried to the bed, sitting near her friend. "She is hurt!" She pulled the blanket down a bit to examine her and saw Adriana was only in her corset. "Did you...?"

He nodded, a little embarrassed. "I needed to put pressure on the wound, it wouldn't stop bleeding."

"I can see that," she said matter-of-factly, gazing at the blood that seeped through the goose-feather mattress and pooled on the floor. "My Lord, is she going to be all right?" She choked back a sob.

Seth held her shoulder to steady her.

"We'll get through this. You told me yourself we were meant to be together."

She covered her mouth. "I did, didn't I?" She looked at her brother. "How did this happen?"

"I don't know. I found her on the ground in the orchard with an arrow sticking out of her."

He bent and scooped the broken arrow shaft from the floor to examine it. The blood drained from his face and his stomach dipped.

"What's wrong?"

"'Tis one of mine," he murmured, his voice flat.

She rose. "Oh, Seth."

"'Tis one of mine, Lea!" he roared. "They used one of my own weapons to shoot her."

"Seth?"

They both whirled at the sound of her voice. Seth rushed to the bed and crouched beside her.

"Good morning," he said softly, brushing the hair from her forehead. She smiled weakly in response. "How do you fare, love?"

"I've been better." She tried to adjust her stiff muscles and winced.

"Lie still, now," Lea cautioned.

"Lea," she said gaily, her smile returning. She grabbed her hand, grimacing again. "How have you been?"

Lea laughed with relief. "Well I am a whole lot better now that you are here."

"Mmm..." Adriana murmured, closing her eyes. "I'm glad to be with you." Her voice was weak. "I am sorry...I am..." She drifted off to sleep without completing her thought.

Lea's creased her forehead. "Do you think we should have the doctor?"

"I do not know. I have been thinking about that, and if Adriana was shot not too far from here, I am not sure if it would be wise to send Trist, and I do not want to leave her." He glanced at the princess again. "And, in any case, she's at her in-laws', remember?"

She nodded. "I am sure that you have done all that can be done for her," Lea reassured him, touching his arm. He hugged her.

"You were right!" he exclaimed, his voice choked. "She came back to me."

"I am always right," she teased. "Oh! I need to go tell Tristan. He will be so excited." She turned at the door as if remembering something. "Why, pray tell, do you have your shirt off?"

Seth's face heated like metal in his forge. "I used it to make bandages." When he saw his sister's teasing grin, he wanted to throw something at her. "Get out of here!"

Adriana slept most of that day, and the next. By the third day, she was much stronger and was impatient to get out of bed.

Lea had ousted Seth to her cottage with Tristan and taken over Adriana's care for the most part, which was a form of torture for both her patient and her brother. Adi finally let her unhappiness with the situation get the best of her, multiplied by the fact that she could hear Seth's hammer ringing, but not see him, and complained crossly, "Lea, when *do* you think I can get up and move around? I have spent months searching for Seth, and now that I have found him, I cannot even enjoy his company. I swear that hurts worse than any arrow ever did."

"Patience, Adriana," Lea scolded as she folded laundry and piled it on Seth's tiny kitchen table. But she studied Adi's eyes and added, "I was thinking we could all have dinner together, here, tonight."

Her expression brightened. "Truly? Oh, that would be wonderful, Lea. I swear I will not complain for the rest of the day. I do appreciate all you have done for me. You have been sweet to help," she finished, feeling a little remorseful.

Lea had helped clothe her and wash her, which had been uncomfortable for them both, at first, but had brought them closer in the end. Adi had a new-found respect for a woman who could so selflessly serve others.

"Well, Princess," Lea said, coming over with a fresh quilt for her, "you have been a fantastic patient. I have never known anyone with such strength and determination. And I know how hard it is for the two of you to be apart. I remember when Hayden and I could not get enough of each other..." She trailed off, lost in memory, and Adi watched her. Lea was smiling to herself, and then when she caught Adi observing her, she blushed and they both laughed.

When Seth came in later, Adi and Lea shared a secret smile. "Our patient wants to try sitting." He spun to look at Adi and Lea gave her a wink. "Do you think you could help her?"

He smiled broadly. "Aye." He went to her side and bent over her. "Now, you let me know if anything I am doing hurts, or if you want to stop."

"Aye." She grimaced and braced for a wave of pain, but found when she gritted her teeth, the pain was quite bearable. Still, she was breathing heavily when she was finally upright, sitting across the bed, with her back resting against the wall.

"Are you well?" Seth asked anxiously.

"Quite well. Quite well." She was pleasantly surprised. "Lea said that you all are going to eat dinner in here with me tonight," she added, hardly able to contain her excitement.

Seth seemed equally pleased. "Well, that is progress."

Dinner was extremely pleasant, everyone catching Adriana's enthusiasm. When it was over, Lea started gathering the plates to take them to her cottage. Seth rose to assist her. "That's okay, Trist can help me. You just keep Adriana company."

"Really?" he said with a silly smile.

"Really," she returned, batting him with a dish towel. She closed the door behind her, glancing over her shoulder with a smile. Seth stood awkwardly in the middle of the room.

"Can I come sit by you?" he asked tentatively.

"Oh, please do. I've missed you, Seth."

He quickly climbed beside her. "Me, too." They sat as close as they possibly could, shoulders and arms touching, as well as hips and legs.

Seth sighed. "Oh, Adi. I wish I could just hold your hand."

"Seth," she said quietly, "last week was my birthday."

"Oh. And I missed it."

"Seth—" she looked at him pointedly "—my *twenty-first* birthday."

He peered at her blankly for a moment, then repeated, "Your *twenty-first* birthday. Does that mean you are a free woman now?"

"That is exactly what that means."

"No pledge to another—absolutely free?"

"Absolutely."

"So, if I wanted to, I could—" he took her hand "—hold your hand, for instance."

"Exactly." They both sat, spellbound for a moment by the sensation of touching.

"Or," Seth said quietly, "I could stroke you, like this." He ran a finger along her skin, sending a pleasant shiver through her.

She had to clear her throat before responding. "Aye."

"Or—" he said, taking her chin to turn her toward him "—I could—" he ran his thumb over her lips, curling the rest of his fingers under her chin, "—kiss you." He leaned forward slowly, his eyes flickering over her face before touching his lips to hers.

Her heart leapt. This was nothing like it had been with Garin. Garin had been a good kisser, but Seth's kiss left her unable to tell which direction was up, like someone deep underwater.

He kissed her again and seemed to have to summon his will power to pull back.

She stretched her neck further and caught his retreating lips with hers, pleading with him to stay without saying a word. The heat between the two rose and he buried his hands in her hair, hauling her closer. She relished the feeling of the muscles that rippled beneath her fingertips when she touched him.

"Ooh!" she cried out, withdrawing and clutching at her injured shoulder. "Oh!"

"Oh, Adi. I am sorry."

"Nay. Nay," she cried in frustration, tears springing to her eyes. "I finally get to be near you, and I cannot even love you as I want to."

"Tsk, tsk, tsk," he murmured, wiping her tears with his thumb. "It is fine, my love. We have a lifetime." Gazing deep into her eyes, he became serious. "We have a *lifetime*."

"A lifetime," she repeated, in a daze. It was all just too good to be true. Her eyes strayed again to his lips, and, as if she commanded them, they moved in again to claim hers.

Lea cleared her throat from the doorway. "I think my patient has had enough *activity* for the day," she said, enunciating the word for emphasis.

Now Seth had to clear his throat. "Aye," he said, smiling conspiratorially at Adriana, "I guess she has." He left the bed, but lifted her knuckles to his lips. "Good night, then. I will see you in the morning."

"Aye," was all she could manage.

Lea smiled at Seth as he slid past her with a triumphant grin. She closed the door, peering at Adriana with her eyebrows raised.

"Oh! He is so *incredible.*"

"Hush! That is my little brother you are talking about," Lea said with feigned indignation. But then she ran over and hopped on the bed next to her.

"Tell me all about it."

Their giggles ran well into the night.

CHAPTER EIGHTEEN

Each passing day found Adi's strength returning, but Seth still seemed surprised to see her walking, unaided, to his workshop one fine morning.

"Hello," Adi said coyly.

Seth set his hammer on a stone and took off his gloves. "Hello," he replied, his smile wide. "What are you doing here?"

Adi leaned on one of the workshop's support posts. "I wanted to come and see you." He looked so good. Dark brown pants, with one of the lightweight beige shirts he often wore. He appeared fresh and attractive, and since she could make out his broad chest below the thin layer of cloth, her heart was hammering as violently as he had been minutes before.

He smiled, moving toward her. "Did you, now?"

She shuffled her feet in the dirt. "Your sister—" then peered at him "—went to the store."

He came to grasp the pole above her head. "Did she, now?" He bent and kissed her long and tenderly, making her tingle throughout. When he drew back, her eyes opened slowly, and she gave him a petulant pout. He laughed. "Are you well enough to take a stroll through the orchard?"

A smile eased across her face again. "That sounds nice."

They strolled through the trees, holding hands and talking about this and that.

"So," Adi said after a bit, "I understand you met my friend, Lawry?"

"Lawry?"

"Oh, I mean, King Lawrence."

"Oh, aye. He was very nice. Down-to-earth."

"He liked you, too." Adi was pleased her two friends had gotten along so well. "You know, I grew up with Lawry." She giggled. "In fact, when we were...about fourteen, I think, we used to sneak over to the pond, just out-side the Castle Glindimore, and go swimming. If his dad had ever found out, he would have skinned us both. He felt that kind of activity was 'beneath us'. How silly." She laughed again.

Seth liked to imagine her, young and happy, doing everyday things all children did. He listened attentively to her talking, having never really seen this side of her.

"If we had listened to the king, Lawry's father, we would have missed out on an awful lot of fun." She paused, reflecting, but then the corners of her lips twitched again. "One day, Lawry decided to hang a rope from a tree so we could swing out and jump off into the pond. He challenged Garin to try it, and Garin made excuses, and while they were arguing the point, I took hold of the rope and swung out myself, letting go, and drenching them. You should have seen their faces. At first, they just stood there with their mouths hanging open. Then...Garin was furious. And Lawry...Lawry was so proud of me."

The orchard opened into a meadow full of wildflowers.

"Oh, how lovely. I do not remember coming through this."

"That is probably because you were barely conscious. I still can't believe Derrick shot you. You are still the princess."

"Not to them. I am just a runaway. Do you mind if we sit and rest a bit?"

"Not at all." He helped her to settle under a tree.

She had on a lighter-weight dress today as the weather had turned warm. He gazed at her out of the corner of his eye, admiring how the fabric hugged her body. He picked a daisy and gave it to her.

"You look especially pretty today."

She blushed. "Thank you." She sighed. "It feels so good to be out here in the fresh air and sunshine. And to be alone with you," she added, boldly.

"Aye," he said softly, as he had spoken to her in the workshop. He slid his hand underneath her hair, rubbing her neck. Then he leaned in and stole another kiss. "Mmm..." he moaned when he withdrew. "Lean on me for a minute." She did what she was told, leaning so that her back was against his chest, and he nestle her into him comfortably. He sighed. "I love you, Adri-ana," he murmured in her ear.

"I love you, too, Seth," she whispered, and they sat, Adriana locked in his embrace, for a long moment, not speaking. They did not seem to need words.

"I cannot believe how lucky we were," she said finally, "to have found each other after all this time. It almost seems not fair. But I am not going to let it bother me," she added.

He laughed, kissing her hair. "Me, either. I think we have been through enough to deserve it." It was quiet again, and Seth realized she was leaning more heavily against him. "Adriana?"

"Hmm?" she mumbled drowsily.

He knew by her rhythmic breathing a few minutes later she had drifted off in his arms, and the idea secretly thrilled him. He sat still as long as he could, but when his stiffness became painful, he shifted to lay her in the grass. He changed positions so he could lie on his side, stretching out his sore legs, and watched her sleep. She was incredibly beautiful when she slept; her lips separated slightly, her cheeks flushed, her eyelashes in stark contrast to her porcelain skin. He was reminded of when they met, in her room.

When her breathing broke rhythm and she opened her eyes a few hours later, he was sitting next to her with his knees pulled in, his palms on the ground. "Oh!" she exclaimed, "I fell asleep."

"That you did."

She scrambled to her feet. "Oh! We have to go. Lea will be furious."

He stood, too. Grabbing her hips, he pressed her against the tree trunk. "Lea," he said, tasting her lips, "will get over it."

He held his body against her, careful of her shoulder, and felt her give in to him completely. Their kisses became heated, and he greedily caressed her skin. She clutched at him, her fingers exploring the definition of his muscles.

Although he knew it was wrong, he was filled with the desire to have all of her. He had waited so long, and now she was so near and the smell of her, the taste of her, was driving him insane.

Her brain screamed, "Stop!" But the rest of her was saying, "More, more, more!" A lady would stop this before it went much further. Problem is, I am not feeling like much of a lady. Did she not deserve him? She climbed a castle wall. She lived by herself for months, sewing until her neck ached and her eyes were red. She took an arrow, for goodness sakes.

Simultaneously they parted, staring at each other and breathing heavily.

He rubbed his mouth and chin. "We-e-e should head in now."

"Aye," she agreed, still feeling the urge to be clasped against him, their hearts pounding as one, like perfectly-choreographed dancers.

He smiled slowly, and she laughed. He held out his hand, and she placed hers in it. They walked home together in the waning light to face Lea's ire.

"YOU ARE NOT GOING TO Morriston by yourself, and that is it."

Adriana stood with her hands on her hips. "I promised that I would finish this lady's dress, and I'm going to finish it."

"And end up with another arrow in your shoulder? Or dragged back to him? It is out of the question."

"Those people at the store said they have not seen any of my father's men in a week."

"So perhaps that just means they are due to return. You are not going, Adriana, and that is final."

Seth and Adi had been arguing the point all morning and Seth found Adi to be very stubborn on the point.

"Ugh!" she stomped her foot and stormed out the door, slamming it behind her.

"You could have handled that better, you know," Lea commented as she finished sweeping.

Seth glared at her and snatched his hat. "I have to go into town. Keep your eye on her." He, too, slammed his way out of the house – by the front door.

Fifteen minutes later, Lea heard the sound of galloping hooves, and caught the blur that was Adriana and Lancer heading toward Morriston.

"Oh! She did not." Lea grabbed her shawl, and set off after Seth.

From the neighboring cottage, Tristan also heard hoofbeats, and glanced out the window to see his mother take off after his uncle. After a moment's hesitation, he headed for the stables and saddled up his uncle's horse, Champion.

ADI GATHERED HER THINGS and stuffed them into her satchel. As she took one last scan around her ramshackle cottage, she heard a knock. At first she was startled. Who knew she was home? But then she realized her father's men would, no doubt, not bother with knocking. Still, she opened the door cautiously.

"Tristan!"

He bowed. "My Lady Adi."

"What are you doing here? Do you realize how dangerous it is?"

Tristan stuck out his chin. "Do you? Besides, I am not the one they are after."

Good point. She took another peek at Tristan. He had grown a lot since the first day she met him, and was beginning to appear very mature.

"You are right. I was so mad at your uncle for telling me what to do. If he had told me how he felt instead of ordering me."

"He was concerned. Uncle Seth often does that. He yells when he is worried about someone. I should know, he has yelled at me plenty."

"Perhaps," Adi agreed. "I should not have flown off the handle like I did. I do not take to being bossed." She put her arm over the youth's shoulder. "In any case, I need to get you home. Your mother will be worried sick."

"Aye," Tristan said apprehensively. "I wonder which one of them will yell the most."

"I will just tell her I kidnapped you."

"Aye," Tristan said with a grin. "As if she will believe that."

For the first half of the journey back, they kept a torrid pace, but by the time they forded the stream where she had lost her foes the last time, they felt it would be permissible to slow down. After watering the horses, Tristan asked, "Adriana, how do you know if a girl likes you?" He put his foot in the stirrup and swung on board Champion, a rich bronze-colored stallion with a coal-black mane.

Adi smiled as she mounted Lancer. "You have a girl sweet on you, Trist?"

"I do not know. Gwen Smithson seems to constantly be peering at me when we go into the store..."

Adriana gasped in surprise. "The Smithson's oldest daughter?"

Tristan nodded, his cheeks coloring slightly. "And when I gaze in her direction, she smiles and looks away. And she's given me an extra sweet or two a couple of times."

Adriana considered this for a second. She was so not the person to talk to for love advice, as was evident from that morning's interaction with Seth. "Well...it does sound like she likes you, Tristan. What do you think of her?"

"Well, she's pretty and all," Tristan said, squirming a little in his saddle, "and she's nice. But should I not know right from the start?"

"You mean like love at first sight?"

He nodded.

"Not necessarily."

"But that is what happened with you and Uncle Seth, right?"

Now it was her turn to blush, remembering that initial eye contact across the courtyard. "Aye. But that is not always the case. We were fortunate, I guess."

He watched her out of the corner of his eye. "You are not still mad at Uncle Seth, are you?"

"Well...perhaps a bit. But it will pass," she replied with a grin.

"Good. Because I like you. You make things interesting."

"Well, it is going to get really interesting when your Uncle Seth finds out I went to town against his wishes."

They both were quiet for a while, thinking about what lay ahead for them. Finally, Adi broke the silence by saying thoughtfully, "You know, you are a good lad, Tristan. You help your mom and your Uncle Seth without complaining. I have never once heard you be disrespectful..." She stretched to squeeze his hand. "And I like you, too." And it was true. Tristan had a certain calmness about him his uncle was definitely lacking.

When the pair arrived home and came trooping out of the orchard, Seth stood waiting for them outside. After seeing they were both fine, he stormed in the house. Tristan and Adriana glanced at each other knowingly and continued on to the stables. After they put their horses up, they headed out to face their consequences together.

Lea started in first. "Tristan Robert Tanner, I want to speak to you."

"He was only—" Adriana began.

"It is fine, Princess Adriana. I will face this like a man," he told her, though his face was pale.

"I guess I need to go face it like a woman," Adriana mumbled to herself.

When she walked into the house, Seth stood with his back to her, his hand on the mantle.

"Seth, I—"

"It is not bad enough you have to put your life in danger, but you drag my nephew into it, too," he raved. He had obviously been worried about them all day, and had now traded his concern for anger.

"I did not have anything to do with Tristan coming," Adriana began, her own ire rising.

"The hell you did not! You cannot see how smitten he is with you?"

"What?" She gasped. "Tristan?"

"Oh, come, Adriana. Even you can see...but then again, I forgot who I am talking to."

She fought the hot tears threatening to spill over her lashes. "You can be mad at me all you want for my leaving, Seth. But I did not even know Tristan was behind me until he showed up in Morriston."

"That just goes to show," he fumed, throwing a hand in the air dramatically. "One of his men could have been following you the whole time," they both knew that he was speaking of Garin, "and you would never have known it." He stepped forward and Adi shrank away. "Or maybe you want to get captured. Maybe you want to be with him." Seth seemed as surprised as she was by that statement. Where did that come from?

"Seth Hobbes, you are the most exasperating man I have ever—"

"Well, Princess," he spat meanly, "the same goes for you."

His words stung. She whirled to leave but he grabbed her arm.

"You are not going anywhere."

"Get your hands off me!" Her voice broke on the last part of her sentence, but she held it together, barely.

Seth released her, turning and running a hand through his hair roughly. After a moment of silence, he spun around. "Look, I'm sorry I said you were exasperating. Wait..." he paused, thinking, "nay, I am not. You said I was exasperating first."

Adriana thought about that. "You are right. I am sorry about that...sort of."

"You are sorry about that sort of? What the hell kind of apology is that?"

"The only kind of apology you are going to get from me," she retorted, the heat rising inside her once more. "You cannot just order me to...." Seeing a wildness in his eye, she stopped in mid-sentence.

He stepped forward and she retreated, but he grabbed her and pressed her against the wall, kissing her with a harsh fever. His hand was on her throat.

She wondered for a minute if he was going to strangle her, and then she thought, I don't care if he does, as long as he keeps kisses me like that. But his hand slid from her throat under the thin material of her dress to her upper chest. She froze.

He stopped, too, but did not pull away. "I was worried about you, Adi," he practically growled, his voice still raw with anger. He pressed his lips to hers, tilting his head to get a better angle. "I did not think that you were coming back." He peered from one of her eyes to the other, his voice still dangerous. "Do not ever do that to me again."

"I promise I will not," she replied in a breathless whisper, and she kissed him with equal passion.

His lips moved down to her throat greedily. Adi's palms were pressed flat on the wall, and she began to dig her nails into the wood, tipping her head up to expose more of her neck to him.

A knock sounded.

Lea, who had been waiting outside patiently, heard the yelling, and then the sound of Adi hitting the wall, and then little else. She had become concerned. She noted, with a smile, how they jumped guiltily apart when she entered, and how each was flushed and out of breath.

Without a word Seth marched out the open door. Adi straightened, running a quick hand over her dress. "Lea," Adriana managed, still a little breathless, "I am sorry about Tristan coming with me—"

"You need not say that," she said, still a tad irritated. "Tristan explained to me you had no idea he followed you. But let us get one thing straight—" she slapped her hand on the table, making Adi jump "—nobody rides out of here without all of us. Understand?"

"Aye, Lea, I understand."

"Good. Now that we have that all settled, we need to get some sleep."

Adi smiled with relief. "Aye."

CHAPTER NINETEEN

Weeks passed without any further excitement. The biggest goings-on had to do with the baby birds born under the eaves of Seth's cottage. Adi fell into a pleasant routine, sewing during the day, with a break to spend lunch with Seth, Lea, and Tristan, and walks in the mild evenings with Seth in the orchard.

Naturally Adi's thoughts began to focus on securing future walks for the two of them by being wed. They loved each other wholeheartedly, and there was no denying the intense passion that ignited each and every time they were alone together. It seemed like the next logical step.

But it would appear that Seth did not think so.

Days would pass where they had long discussions about their future together, but still, he did not ask for her hand. She, who had never been a patient woman, found it nearly impossible to wait for their life together to truly begin, as man and wife. But wait she did, on her seamstress pins and needles.

Therefore, she was looking forward to the family's trip into Morrison, as it provided a much-needed distraction, shifting her thoughts from when Seth was going to propose. Would it be today? Tomorrow? And how would he do it? She imagined her various verbose or pithy answers, depending on the moment, when he finally did ask the question. Where would he do it? The house? The barn? The orchard? She searched for any hints that would tell her he was thinking the same manner she was, but she suffered disappointment after disappointment as it turned out today was not the day, the stable was not the place, he only needed to find Champ's brush, and none of her carefully prepared answers were put to use as no question was ever forthcoming. It was enough to drive a girl insane. So, aye, distraction was indeed a Godsend.

Seth was pleasant enough on the trip; it was not until they were in Dead-low's General Store that he became edgy. He scrutinized and questioned every item Lea picked up until she finally told him to go bother Adriana.

Seth swung from the counter, where Lea was examining cuts of meat, and caught sight of Adriana as she stood in the light of the doorway. She had picked up a bolt of white, silk fabric and was draping it across her body. Her face was dreamy and wistful.

Seth began to panic. He had been against this trip into Morriston, but Adriana had a dress to deliver and he needed to sell some goods, so he had finally consented. But all they ever wound up doing in Morriston was spending far too much money, and how was he ever going to have enough money to buy Adriana an engagement ring if the money was going out hand over fist? When he had pulled out his mother's ring weeks ago, the one he had always liked, he began to think of the undoubtedly enormous ring Garin would have given Adi, and his ring seemed woefully inadequate. So, he had determined to buy a new one. He had saved quite a bit of money, but how much did it cost to buy an engagement ring fit for a princess?

And now, seeing Adriana mooning over the undeniably beautiful silk fabric, a muscle twitch along his jaw. Without even realizing he was doing it, Seth crossed to her side.

"Adi," he snapped, "if you think we can afford fabric that dear, then I am sorry to disappoint you." He saw the shocked look on her face, but couldn't stop himself. "We do not have an endless supply of money like 'our betters' do."

"But Seth, I—"

"No buts Adriana, put the fabric down. This is not any royal palace here and I am no prince with a weighty coin bag in every hand."

He saw the shock replaced by hurt and anger.

She looked over his shoulder now to where the people at the counter had twisted to gape at them, and swallowed. Tears stung her eyes and her bottom lip quivered. "Seth! I had no intention of asking you to pay for this fabric. I have money of my own."

"Oh, aye! I forgot. You can always go back to *Father* and he will give you anything you want." His sentence ended abruptly, as he caught the look of fire in her eyes.

Without a word, she shoved the bolt of fabric into his hands and spun on her heel to rush out the door. The jangle of the bells above the door was the only encore to Seth's harsh speech. After a second, Lea brushed past him; but as she went to open the door to follow the princess, Seth's big hand closed it.

"What are you doing?" she asked, eyes flashing. "I'm going out there to talk to her and you're not going to—"

"Nay, you're not," he responded, his voice still commanding. He looked up and out of the window to where Adriana was marching in the middle of the street. "I am going to talk to her." His voice was quiet now and filled with the remorse he felt.

He walked out of the store and hurried after Adriana. It did not take his longer legs much time to catch up with her. "Adi, wait!"

He did not have to convince her to stop, because she swung around, infuriated.

"How dare you say those things to me? How dare you! The money that I have, although 'tis none of your business, is mine because I worked for it. Worked long and hard over a tedious task into the waning hours of the day 'til my fingers bled with needle pricks and my eyes were so tired I could not focus."

She glanced up as the store's door bells rang again. A curious couple cast an inquisitive look their way. She paused until they were out of earshot.

"Do you have any idea how embarrassed I am right now?"

"I know, Adi, I—"

"And that is not even the worst part—" she interrupted. "The worst part is that it hurts to know *you* think of me like that."

He lowered his head, ashamed.

"Seth, I love you." Her voice became choked and she had to stop for a second. "But all you have ever seen me as is a princess. Well, take a look at me, Seth," she pleaded. "*Take a look at me!*" She was screaming now, her emotions appearing to drive her to the edge. "I am more than your damned princess!" She sobbed. "I am a friend. I am a daughter, a seamstress, a darn good one, for your information. And I am a woman. A woman who has been fool enough to fall in love with you," she ended, seeming worn out by her tirade.

She walked past him and mounted Lancer, turning him and spurring him on past where Seth stood, frozen by her words, in the street.

Eventually Seth's feet moved him back into the store. Everybody looked up when he entered.

Lea hustled up and hissed at him, low enough so no one could hear, "How could you do that to her, Seth? How?"

"I know, Lea. I—"

"I do not want to hear your excuses!" Her voice rose, causing a few people nearby to throw them a sidelong look. "Did it make you feel like a man to yell at her like that?"

"Nay, Lea," he answered, his voice almost pleading now.

Lea felt a little sympathy welling up inside, but then she thought of her friend's stricken face and squelched it.

But before she could speak again, he hurriedly told her, "I will apologize to her. And I apologize to you, for embarrassing you—"

She waved him off. "You better hope, Seth William Hobbes, that this is not one apology too many." She stared into his eyes for a minute, and then pushed past him and out of the store.

Seth wiped his face with his hand. Well, he really messed up this time. Why was it whenever he wanted the most to love Adriana, he always ended up hurting her? He looked up and saw the shop owner glaring at him. Seth walked toward the man uncertainly, his head humming, the feel of a headache hovering on the horizon of his brain. When he reached the counter, he spread his arms wide and leaned on it, sighing, and hung his head for a second. He finally lifted his head and asked, "Do you know where she went?"

"Who? Mistress Tanner?" Utey Deadlow asked coldly.

Seth could tell the man knew full well he was asking after Adriana. "Nay! Adriana," he snapped, bringing one hand up to rub at his temple distractedly.

The shop owner looked him over. "I am uncertain whether I should tell you that or not."

"Look either you can tell me, or I can walk across the street and ask the blacksmith—" he waved a hand in that direction "—or I will keep on asking people until I find out."

"Fine," the older man snarled. "I am guessing she went to her place." When Seth just looked at him blankly, he elaborated. "It is up the road apace. You will see two nice houses, and then be on the lookout. Her cottage is set back some, on the right. Not much of a cottage, more like a rundown shed with an even more rundown, one-horse stable beside it."

"Thank you," Seth grumbled.

He strode across the wooden floor and out the door. He glanced around once he hit the sidewalk, but did not see Lea. He figured she was in another shop, and, in the periphery of his mind he had been aware of Tristan shuffling out of Deadlow's behind her, so he was certain they were together. He swung aboard Champion, pointing the stallion's head to the road Lancer took, and set off.

Deadlow's was on the edge of town, so he only needed to cross a small meadow before he saw the first house, a sprawling white abode with a large lawn. Further along, he noted a similarly-sized stone monstrosity. He continued on, nervously reviewing what he would say when he saw her. He almost passed by her place without seeing it. Nestled between two huge sycamore trees, the shack looked like it was leaning drunkenly on one of them for protection. Pieces of stone that had once been part of the chimney were scattered off to one side of the house, and on the other teetered the dingy little stable Utey Deadlow had described. Tied to an iron ring in front of it was Lancer. He whinnied as they approached, but then seemed to recognize Champion and settled down.

Seth dismounted and tied his horse to the same ring, patting his flank as he hesitated, afraid, now that he was here, of speaking to Adriana, and messing up again.

He strode slowly toward the house, taking it in as he approached. It was part stone, part wood and may have, at one time, been quite a charming house. As it was, the stone was crumbling, the wood, scarred and dirty, the roof sagging with age and from being abused by the elements. The door was slightly ajar. He could tell from the crooked way it hung, it probably took some work to close it properly, and his guess was that Adriana hadn't taken the time to do that in her upset state.

He called her name softly, and then pushed on the door. It creaked in protest, but swung open. She stood across the room, gazing out a window with a jagged crack across a field of weeds. She must not have heard him call out, because she jumped at the creak of the door and whirled around. The brief glimpse he got of her distraught face convicted his heart before she turned around. Again, he had qualms about speaking, turning his dusty hat over and over in his big hands.

"Adi, I...I know you don't want to listen to me apologize again for running off at the mouth..." He stopped, unsure of how to continue. She did not come to his rescue either, just stood stone still with her back to him.

He glanced around the tiny house. Adi had somehow made it into a home. Despite all the time she had been gone, the room was neat as a pin. A sunny yellow and blue calico quilt...had she made it? he wondered...hung on one wall. There was a white rocker pulled up to the fireplace, her bed in one corner, a table, big enough for two, underneath the window, covered with evidence of her work, bits and pieces of cloth, scissors and thread, and half-finished projects.

He cleared his throat and his voice was low again when he continued, "You were right, Adi. I have not known you as I should. When I looked at you, I did think of you only as a princess...a beautiful, enchanting princess...but a princess all the same."

She did not turn, did not clear her throat, did not make a sound at all.

Seth shuffled his feet. This time his voice sounded hoarse as he addressed her.

"But Adi, it was only because I didn't feel worthy of you."

To his surprise, she turned at that, an unreadable expression on her face. He looked away for a second, but then gazed directly into her eyes.

"When I first saw you across the courtyard, I thought you were the most incredible woman I had ever laid eyes on. But then I saw you wore a crown, and realized you were the king's daughter. I know now it was not fair, but I judged you by my own experiences with royalty, and the king's men. Judged you harshly. But then you did something I never expected—" his voice rose in pitch, as he relived the surprise it had caused him "—you asked for my freedom." He paused, thinking about the wonder of it, and he could see now she was engaged, listening to him, and hope began to stir in his chest.

"I came to see you that night—I never told you why—but it was to thank you. And it was because I could not reconcile your actions with the person I thought you to be, and it bothered me. And, I guess, to be honest, part of the reason I was there was simply because I was drawn to you, almost against my will. And that night, when you let Lea cut your hair to save me...that was one of the bravest and most self-sacrificing gestures I have ever seen. So you see, Adi," he took a step closer, "you contradicted everything I had come to know about royalty, and you still confound me sometimes."

She smiled, a little, and he swallowed, overcome at once by his love for her. He dared to take her hand. It was cold, and she did not respond when he brushed his thumb over it, but she did not remove, either.

"And then I fell in love with you. Head over heels, irreparably in love with you...and you left." He did not try to hide the hurt this had caused. "I know now that was not your choice, but at the time..." He shook his head, looking at her small hand in his. "And then, you came back." His voice became too choked for a minute, and he couldn't speak.

Moved, she touched him consolingly.

He continued. "I have been trying to live up to that gift of having you in my life again. Trying, and failing miserably." He touched her cheek softly. "I love you, Adi, with all my heart."

It was too much, she retreated, wrapping her arms around her stomach. "B-but you don't even know me."

He stepped forward and drew her in. "Aye, I do, Adi. Aye, I do now."

"Nay. You said—"

"I know, I said some awful things, but it is only because..." He did not want to divulge his secret, but could see no way around it. "Dammit, Adi!" he blurted out. "I wanted to buy you a ring. A truly nice ring. The kind of ring fit for a princess. The kind of ring that you would be proud to wear as my wife."

A small noise came out of her throat, like the cooing of a dove, and her hand went to her mouth.

"But do you not know, I have no need of that."

"I do, now. I mean, a girl who could live in a place like this," he jested, gesturing widely. "I mean, 'tis nice enough, but 'tis no palace."

She laughed a little, glancing around as if assessing her surroundings anew. "True, it is not exactly a palace, but I like it."

"That's exactly what I'm talking about. That is a very unprincessy thing to say."

They chuckled, and he took a step closer, his tone turning serious.

"Adi, you never cease to amaze me. You are right, you are not just a princess. You are the woman who slid down a rope with me, dragged heavy buckets of water to quench men's thirst, climbed over a castle wall, and fought to find me, with an arrow imbedded in your shoulder. You are the woman who stands up to me when I am wrong, and who loves me despite my faults...at least I hope so. You are the woman whose kisses send me over the edge, and whose whispered, 'I love you's,' make my heart stop. Please, Adi...please find it in your heart to forgive me this one last time, and I'll spend a lifetime making it up to you, I promise."

"A lifetime?" she asked with a smile.

"A lifetime."

He waited with bated breath while she deliberated.

"Oh, Seth," she sighed, closing her eyes for a minute, but then opening them to look deeply into his. "I could not stay mad at you even if I wanted to. And I do not want to. I do not want to fight anymore."

She encircled his waist and he drew her into his chest, letting his air and anxiety out as he did so.

"Oh, Adi! What did I do to deserve you?"

She did not answer. She simply laid her head on his chest.

He placed his hands on either side of her face, lifting it so that he could look at her.

"Adi...I don't want to leave just yet. Do you think that we could stay here for just a moment or two together, before we go home?"

She nodded and he kissed her face.

"Can we just sit, on the bed together, for a minute?"

He led her over and sat across the bed, resting against the wall, and she scrambled up next to him. She laid her head on his shoulder. Time passed, and the sun started getting lower in the sky. They both knew they should be leaving soon if they wanted to make it back before dark.

Finally Adriana spoke, "Shouldn't we be leaving?"

"Yes, we should...but can we just lie together, I will not do anything improper," he added quickly, "I just want to lie beside you."

She nodded, and shifted so they could lie next to each other. She laid her head on his chest and he wrapped his arms around her, having to squeeze close in the narrow bed.

"Adi...I promise not to be a jackass like that again."

"Sh-sh-sh," she murmured, turning to him and putting a finger to his lips. She sat up on one elbow. "I will not have any talk like that about the man I love."

She leaned to kiss him, innocently.

The sun haloed her hair, setting it ablaze, and she looked like some fearsome angel. As she retreated, Seth's hand shot up to hold her close, cupping her neck fiercely. His kisses were feverish; he needed her to love him, now. He shifted so that he was out from under her, cradling her neck now as he laid her gently on the bed. He stared at her, his heart pounding in his chest, dreaming of what it would be like to be with her on their wedding night. He brought his lips to claim hers, tenderly at first, but then with a growing need for her. She kissed him, too, curling her fingers in his hair and moaning his name when he brushed his lips over her neck and nibbled her jaw. He shifted his weight so that he was mostly over her, his hands dropping to her sides, feeling the hint of her breasts, the indent of her waist, the smooth curve of her hips. Her heat radiated out through the thin material of her dress and it seemed like only an inconsequential veil over her body.

He buried his face in her hair, nuzzling her earlobe as he whispered desperately. "Adi, I cannot wait until our wedding night. I probably should not tell you that, but...mmm, I want *all* of you. Body and soul."

Seth kissed her neck and she thrilled at the desire she could feel pulsing through his body as he lay on her. He pushed up, resting on his left elbow on one side of her and on his right hand on the other.

She saw the haze of lust in his eyes.

He lifted his weight from her, but didn't move away. He unhurriedly ran his gaze over her body and she shivered. He trailed his eyes up the lines of her twisted dress, and then took a finger and skimmed it over the fabric, up her legs to her core, across her abdomen, and then lifted it to place it just above her breasts that rose and fell with her tense breathing. It finished its course upward along her neck. Involuntarily she arched, giving herself to him. As his finger met her chin, she brought it down and he traced the outline of her lips with his finger. She closed her eyes, her face contorted as her want for his touch grew, as the need became unbearable, and then his lips were there once more, hot and moist and terrifyingly skilled, awakening her, his tongue dangerous...and then he parted from her, shutting his eyes and steeling himself.

"We should leave. Immediately."

She almost laughed at the comically pained look on his face, would have, if she hadn't felt the same way.

He stood, but then smiled at her, offering her his hand. She let him tow her out of bed and into a quick embrace.

"Do you need anything from here?"

"Nay. I have all I want right here." She squeezed his fingers and he gave her that glorious smile of his again.

"Come, then. Let us go home."

CHAPTER TWENTY

A loud knock reverberated through Seth's tiny house. Both Lea and Adriana gasped, sitting up and drawing their covers around them tightly. Even in the dim light, with only the moon streaking through the windows to cut the blackness, they could see each other's wide eyes and feel each other's fear.

Were the men who had shot Adriana back for her?

"Lea. Lea! Open up! 'Tis me, Seth."

Lea flew to the door and opened it. "What's wrong?"

"'Tis Tristan. I heard him moaning in his sleep and I went over to check on him. He is as hot as my forge. The sweat is pouring off of him. I think you need to come look at him."

Without further questions, she rushed out the door. As Seth was starting to close it, Adriana called out. "Seth?"

"Adi, honey. Go to sleep now. We do not need you getting sick when you are just barely recovered. We will return shortly."

He left and Adi fell against her pillow. Tristan, sick? She shifted onto her side, and tried to sleep. But she could not recover from the heart-thumping shock of the unexpected knock on the door and the adrenaline still swirling through her system. In addition, she was concerned about Tristan.

She swung her feet out of bed and stood so quickly that she felt off-balance. Putting a hand on her forehead, she waited until the dizziness had passed, and then grabbed a robe and rushed out after Seth and Lea.

When she entered Lea's house, she heard worried murmurs from above in the loft. Knowing that this might be more of a family issue, she gave them their space. She went to the well and got water. Upon re-entering the house, she put it on to boil for tea. She had a feeling that somebody might need it. She looked around for something else to do and noticed that some mud had been tracked in earlier in the day, so she started to clean the floor. By the time Seth and Lea came down, she was halfway across the floor and had pushed all the furniture to the sides of the room to gain access to the middle of the room. They stared at her.

"What are you doing?"

"Uhh..." She looked around the floor as if she was just seeing it for the first time.

"Cleaning the floor?"

"'Tis the middle of the night," Seth pointed out, looking amused despite the seriousness of the situation with Tristan.

"I needed something to do," she answered crossly. "How is he?"

"Not very well, I'm afraid," Lea replied.

"Is there anything I can do?"

"You mean besides cleaning the floor?" Seth teased.

Adriana smiled, admitting to her own foolishness. "Maybe I could make you some tea, instead?"

"That sounds wonderful," Lea said with a tired sigh. She and Seth sat at the table, quietly discussing their observations of Tristan, and Adi brought them both a cup of tea. "That cold washrag seemed to make him more comfortable."

"Aye," Seth answered, staring into his tea but not drinking.

"You were right, he did seem worse than usual this time. Ugh! I hate it when he gets sick like this."

"I know," Seth responded, laying his hand over his sister's on the table. "Do you think I should go for the doctor?"

Adi was surprised by how upset Lea seemed to be. It wasn't like her. She always seemed to be the one with the cool head and steady hands in a crisis situation.

Lea thought about this. "Not yet. We'll check on him again in a little while."

"Well, it's not doing us any good to have all of us up tonight. I will sit him until morning, and then—"

Lea shook her head. "I will take the first watch. I could not sleep anyway."

Adriana spoke up. "I will take over in the morning, so Seth can go to work."

They both looked at her with surprise, and then Seth grinned. "Aye, that sounds like a plan. But if you are going to be up in the morning, you better get some sleep right now."

"Aye." She turned to leave and Lea grabbed her hand.

"Thank you."

Adi smiled and patted her hand. "'Tis nothing."

"I will walk with you."

Seth closed the door quietly behind them and then held her around her waist. They sauntered through the cool evening air, prolonging their time together.

"Lea seems like she is truly worried. Is it that bad?"

He stared off ahead of them for a minute, and she could tell he was trying to formulate an answer.

"Her husband, Hayden—he was a friend of mine—he got sick, horribly sick, without warning. One day he was this big, strapping man, the next...he was cold and in the ground." He paused, his voice hollow. "It was extremely hard on Lea. Tristan was eight. Old enough to feel it, but not yet old enough to understand it. And Lea and Hayden...they had a special relationship. They were best friends. Sometimes I would walk into the stable, and they would not know I was there, and I would hear them laughing and teasing each other..."

Without seeming to know it, he had stopped walking. "Hayden was a good friend to me, too. He farmed mostly, but he would help me out in the shop sometimes. He was one of those people who would do anything for you, if you needed him to. I still miss him, and I do not know how Lea got through it."

"She leaned on you, I imagine," Adriana said quietly.

"Aye. We leaned on each other. So—" he started forward again "—seeing Tristan sick always conjures up a host of bad memories for Lea, and fears."

She hugged her body tighter to Seth's side.

"Here we are, Miss Adi," he said more cheerfully, as they came to her door. He bent to kiss her sweetly. "Get some sleep."

She stretched up on her toes to play with the sandy-blond hair forever falling into his eyes. "Good night, Seth." She gave him one last kiss, then, squeezed his hand as they parted.

Seth stood outside for quite some time, staring at the moon, and losing himself in memories. Finally he crawled up to the loft that he shared with Tristan. A lone candle sat on the floor by Tristan's bed and Lea wiped his forehead with a damp cloth, not looking away from his face when Seth climbed into the bed on the opposite side of the room from Tristan.

"Good night, Seth," she whispered.

He watched her worried face in the candlelight. "Good night, sis," he returned softly.

ADI SLOWLY PUSHED OPEN the door to the cottage, being careful to not make noise. It was eerily quiet in the house as she crept in and stole up the ladder to the loft. Seth was asleep in one corner, his back to the room and his blanket wound tightly around him. Lea sat in a chair beside Tristan's bed, asleep, her head on her folded arms which rested near his waist.

Tristan, however, seemed restless. Still trying not to disturb the sleepers, Adi found the bowl of water Lea had been using, and reached for the rag folded on Tristan's forehead. She was amazed by the heat emanating from his skin; it almost hurt to touch him. She let out a small gasp, then, quickly checked to see if she had awoken Lea or Seth, but neither had stirred. She dipped the rag in the water, cooling it as it had picked up a lot of Tristan's heat. She hesitated a second, getting on her knees to dab the cool cloth on his face and glide it around to the nape of his neck.

He sighed, the muscles in his face relaxing, and became still.

She stared into his sweet face. He was such a little Seth. She glanced at Lea and wondered how she could have ever borne the pain of seeing the man she loved sick like this. Peering at Tristan, she took a stray lock of his hair and pushed it in place, running it between her fingers as she did so.

She was startled by the sound of a gruff voice behind her.

"Good morning," Seth said, his voice still hoarse from sleep.

She twisted. He was sitting, bare-chested, on the edge of his bed, stretching for his shirt, which hung on the bedpost of the footboard. His chest, shoulders, and biceps were muscular and well-toned from his work in the blacksmith shop, and as usual, she was struck speechless by the sight of him.

He pulled his shirt on, his hair tousled as his head cleared the neckline. The fabric slipped over him, robbing her of the view she had when she had first turned.

He smiled at her, crossing the room to stand next to her. "How is he?"

Her voice choked as she tried to answer, "He is so hot!"

"Aye." He frowned.

She gazed up, her eyes trusting. "Isn't there more we can do?"

"I am not certain."

His eyes swept from Tristan's face to Lea's and he moved over to his sister and crouched beside her, laying a hand on her. "Lea?" he whispered. "Lea?" He gave her a gentle shake.

She sprang up. "What?" she cried out in alarm. "What is it? Is he worse?" She blinked her tired eyes, trying to force them to focus.

"Nay. Nay, Leah. There has been no change. I just want you to get some sleep."

"Nay, I'm fine," she said dismissively. "I'm not leaving him."

Seth grimaced. He could remember her saying the same thing when they came to take Hayden's body away, and he found the only thing he could do now, was repeat the words he had told her then. "Lea, you need to rest." She didn't budge. "You will not be doing Tristan any good if you get sick, too."

"It is out of the question."

Adriana smiled. "She sounds like you."

"Listen..." he started forcefully.

"How about if you lie here, Lea? In Seth's bed. You will still be here with Tristan, but you can get some rest."

"Well..." Lea hesitated. "Maybe for a minute or two." She stumbled into bed and was asleep almost instantly. Seth covered her with his blanket.

He led Adi aside to the railing, where the loft overlooked the ground floor.

"You are brilliant," he murmured, kissing her forehead and rubbing her arms. She shrugged. "Will you be able to take care in here if I go down to my shop for a while?" He looked over at the bed, torn. "I have an order to fill."

"Of course. That was the idea."

He glanced wistfully at Tristan.

"Sometimes I cannot hear well when I am working, just keep calling though if you need me, and I will eventually hear. And I will come check on you from time to time—"

"We will be *fine*, Seth." She gave his hands a reassuring squeeze.

He cupped her chin and tilted her head back to see if she had any doubts. When he saw none, he brushed his lips over hers. "Adriana," he murmured, "I love you." He kissed her and was gone.

Minutes later, he returned carrying a tray with a fresh bowl of water and some biscuits with butter and jelly on them.

"It was all I could find," he said apologetically.

"They look delicious." She smiled. "How did you manage the ladder with your hands full like that?"

He shrugged and kissed her again on the forehead and headed to his shop.

CHAPTER TWENTY-ONE

Three days had passed, and Tristan was no better. He had never woken up, and they had barely been able to get water past his lips. Everyone was exhausted; partly from caring for the sick boy, but mostly from worry.

That evening, after the doctor left, Seth noticed that Adriana had been gone a long time fetching water. He stepped outside into the cooler night air and saw her bucket of water sitting, discarded, in the grass. He checked in his cottage, which had remained empty since Tristan became ill, but could not find her. Starting to become a little apprehensive, he decided to try the stables.

When he opened the door, the light fell on Adi. She was leaning her forehead on Lancer's nose and rubbing his muzzle as she wept.

"Adi!"

She jumped and Seth stepped over to her. She jabbed at the tears on her face.

"Honey."

"I am fine," she said determinedly. "I am fine." She tried to slide out of his arms, but he held her.

"Talk to me."

She stilled for several seconds, and then her shoulders began to shake.

"He's just so..." She sobbed, becoming inarticulate for a moment. "I never knew it could be this hard."

"What could?" he asked, confused.

"Loving someone. I cannot stand to see him like this. He should be running around here, laughing at us."

"I know," he said, his voice choked, too. "We will help him through this, Adi. We have got to help him through this," he added, more to himself than to her.

He found a clean pile of hay in the corner "Let us sit for a while."

She curled up next to him.

Without giving it much thought, he asked, "Do you miss...anyone...back in Hamiltonia?"

She hesitated. "I don't want you to be angry."

He shifted so that he could search her face. "Why would I be mad?"

She shrugged, and wriggled a little. "I miss Garin," she said quietly. "I know he is a beast, but he was my best friend, and I miss him."

She paused, but then continued, even more quietly. "But, mostly, I miss my father."

When he was silent, she continued. "I know you hate him, and I understand that. I would probably hate him, too, if I were you. But the side of him that he shared with me was much different from the one you saw. He was kind, and funny...loving, *overprotective*—" she smiled over some unspoken memory "—patient..."

She stared off for a minute, and then giggled unexpectedly. He liked the sound of it.

She continued "He would give me rides up and down the halls of Ramport on his shoulders, both of us laughing. I am not sure which one of us was having the most fun."

But then, as her memories changed, she sighed. "After my mother died, he was miserable. He came to me one night—I knew he had been drinking—and told me he planned to remarry. He told me she was not the woman my mother was, that she could never be, but he was terribly lonely and needed someone. I gave him my blessing. But when she and her children moved into the castle, she sided with them over me, and belittled me constantly. She even struck me. She made the mistake of doing that in front of my father one time, and he was so furious with her. He jumped out of his chair and had her up against the wall with his hands around her neck before any of the rest of us even knew what was happening. I thought he was going to kill her. He told her coldly if he ever found out she had spoken to me like that again, or so much as laid a finger on me, that he, himself, would throw her bodily out of the castle along with all of her 'brood.'"

Adi shook her head, still marveling over the incident. "So, Father has always been my protector, my hero. Up until the day he allowed Garin to lock me away. And still, I think he only thought he was doing it for my own good." She closed her mouth. She seemed as if she was trying to gauge Seth's reaction.

"I wish my father had been more like that," he said slowly. "He was mostly distant. Hayden was actually more of a father to me than my own father was. He was six years older than I was and had been out on his own for some time before I met him."

He sighed as he came out of his reverie to the present. "I guess I should go and help Lea. But you need to get some sleep. You have taken on more than your fair share of the work."

As she parted from him, he asked her, "Do you feel better?"

She nodded, and he lifted her chin to kiss her.

As they rose, Adi suggested, "Your arms felt so good and reassuring around me...Lea doesn't have someone like that anymore. Perhaps she could use a shoulder to cry on, too."

"I think that is a good idea," Seth replied, escorting her out. "But right at this moment, my concerns are for you. I want you to sleep in the other cabin. You will sleep better."

She nodded tiredly.

WHEN ADI AWOKE SHE immediately rose and went to the other cottage. As she was entering the back door, Seth was opening the front door.

"Where are you going?" she asked urgently.

"To get the doctor. He is worse." Without further explanation, Seth settled his hat on his head and walked out to where he already had Champion saddled and waiting.

Champion's hoofbeats had hardly faded before Adi was up the ladder to the loft. Lea was on her knees, praying fervently. Tristan's face was pale and drawn and he seemed to be having trouble breathing.

Adi crossed to Lea's side and knelt beside her, beginning to pray, too.

The minutes seemed to pass like hours, each woman listening intently for sounds of Seth's return. Lea stole the washcloth from Tristan's forehead, but when she dunked it, she said, her voice unsteady, "'Tis too hot. I am going to get some fresh water from the well."

Adi could tell that Lea wanted to get outside where she could be by alone for a minute, and probably cry, so she did not offer to take the chore on for her. She gave Lea's hand a squeeze as she rose, and tried to give her a encouraging smile. After Lea left, it seemed to Adi that Tristan's breathing worsened. The noise filled the small loft and she watched him anxiously. His body began to seize, rising several inches above the mattress with each convulsion.

"Oh, my Lord!" she cried out, trying to push him onto the mattress to keep him from crashing his head against the headboard. She heard Seth call from below.

"Seth! Seth!" she screamed in a panic.

Seth heard the terror in Adriana's voice and flew up the ladder, the doctor not far behind. When he reached the top, he saw her struggling to restrain Tristan as he thrashed about. Seth froze for a minute, and then hurried over to help her.

"Go!" the doctor ordered Adi as she set her bag on a chair. "Get a spoon."

Adi was still in shock, but she did what she was told. When she reentered the loft, the doctor had several vials lined up on the chair.

The doctor took the spoon from her. "We have to wedge this in his mouth, to prevent him from biting his tongue or swallowing it."

Seth was practically on top of Tristan now, and he was able to hold his head still while the doctor forced the spoon between his teeth.

"Good. Good."

She called out to Adi, who stood looking on helplessly, "Get me some water and a rag."

Without hesitating, Adi scrambled down the ladder again, and out the door. As she had done the night before, Lea had filled the bucket and left it on the doorstep, retreating somewhere to be alone.

"Lea!" Adi shouted, but she did not wait for a response. She whirled and headed in as fast as she could.

When she entered she noticed immediately how much quieter it had become. In the loft, Tristan had calmed and Seth was wedged between him and his headboard, lifting him up a little so the doctor could get some medicine into his mouth.

Seth glanced up as she came near, the relief evident in his eyes. She rushed forward to bathe Tristan's face in cool water as they set him against his pillows, Seth scooting over to sit on the edge of the bed frame. Tristan lay limply on the bed.

"Good girl," the doctor said, patting her hand.

Adi studied her for the first time. She was an elderly lady, draped in a black cape that she had not bothered to push the hood back from, but Adi could still see her gentle, steel-grey curls and twinkling blue eyes. The doctor turned her attention to her patient, and Seth gazed up at Adi with a hopeful smile. She was rubbing her arms, spent and sore from having to hold Tristan—who was nearly her size now—still.

Lea rushed up behind them. "Adi, you called...? Oh, Doctor, you are here already."

"Yes, dear, I am." She pulled the covers away to examine Tristan, *tut-tutting* sympathetically as she worked. "He has not awoken? Has not eaten anything?"

Seth shook his head.

The wise older lady, whose only medical training came through raising ten children of her own, felt his neck and flipped his wrist over to feel for his pulse. Her features took on a strange pallor. "Had Tristan been doing any painting before he took ill?"

Seth peered at Lea questioningly, although he knew the answer was no.

Lea hurried around to the front of the bed. "Nay. Why do you ask?"

The doctor closed her eyes briefly. "Lea...I'm afraid this isn't good."

The blood drained from Lea's face and Adi reached up from where she was kneeling beside the bed and took her hand.

"I believe he has Morris Fever."

Lea's eyes closed for a minute and Adi thought she was going to swoon. Seth must have thought so too, as he stood up to support her; but after a moment, she opened her eyes again, and asked weakly, "Are you sure?"

The doctor nodded solemnly, lifting one of Tristan's hands. She scraped underneath one of the boy's fingernails, but could not remove the orange tinge to them.

"This discoloring is a certain indicator. I am sorry, Lea."

Seth stood behind Lea, gripping her shoulders. Both their faces showed the same horrified expression. The doctor began to pack all of her little vials into her bag without further comment. Adi looked from face to face with confusion and when the doctor picked up her bag, she yelled, "What are you doing? You cannot just leave."

"I am afraid there is nothing I can—"

"Do not say that!" Adi screamed fiercely. "There must be something, *something* you can do."

"I am sorry, young lady, but there is nothing—"

Adi couldn't bear to hear it. "Nothing? Nothing at all? But what will happen? He is not getting any better."

The doctor glanced at Seth.

"Adi...the Morris Fever..."

"It is fatal," Lea finished, her voice dead.

"What?" Adi shrieked, her chin quivering. She grabbed the doctor's hands. "Please, *please,* is there not some pill, some concoction, which will make him better? You have to do something. We cannot just—" She brought a hand to her mouth to cover a sob.

"There is nothing that can be done at this point," the woman responded firmly, though not unkindly. But as she turned to leave, she muttered, "The only medicine in the world that could help him is unavailable to him. And even if it were not, it may even be too late for that."

"What medicine?" she asked hopefully.

"Oh, well..." she seemed hesitant to speak of it any further. "A long time ago, when the Morris Fever first swept through the kingdom, there was a concoction of sorts. But the royals only kept it to themselves, while commoners, like ourselves, were dropping like flies. But it hardly matters, even if such a thing still existed, which I doubt it does, the House of Morris would *never* part with it. I am sorry I even brought it up. It is not even in the realm of the possible."

As the doctor talked, Seth's eyes lit up, too, and he and Adi exchanged a meaningful look.

"I know I could get him to help us."

"What is she talking about?" Lea asked Seth.

"King Lawrence. He is a childhood friend of Adriana's," Seth explained without taking his eyes from Adi's. "Are you sure?"

"Wait a minute," the doctor warned, trying to shoot down any flights of fancy. "I am not even certain this medicine still exists, or for that matter, ever existed. The chance is so remote—"

"Still," Adi said firmly, "it is a chance. I will leave immediately." She spun to go, but Seth called her back.

"Hold it, Adi. You are not going by yourself. Do you not remember being shot in the shoulder?"

"King Lawrence's childhood friend," the doctor mused out loud, "you are not Princess Adriana?"

"One and the same," she announced, cheered by the prospect of possibly being able to help Tristan out.

"Well, then. You are even more foolish than I thought," the old woman said abruptly. "Do you not realize your father is at war with King Lawrence? Why would the king want to help you?"

Adriana's heart fell for a minute, but then she responded confidently, "I am not banking on my father's friendship with Lawry, I am betting on mine. He will help me. I am certain of it. Besides which, Lawry took quite a shine to Tristan. So if not for my sake, he will do it for Tristan's."

"Still," Lea said slowly, "you would be taking a mighty big risk. What if they decide to capture you as leverage against your father?"

A wave of sadness washed over her. "Whatever leverage my capture might once have had over my father, I am afraid vanished when I left. And even if that weren't so, I have to take my chances—" her eyes fell on Tristan's pale face "—there is no other way."

Lea gazed at her son, too, but still hesitated. "I do not know. If you got hurt again..."

"Lea, I cannot just stay here and watch Tristan get sicker." Her voice broke and she grabbed Lea's hand desperately. "Please, Lea, *please*. You have got to let me at least try," she pleaded.

Lea was clearly torn. She peered up at Seth.

"I will keep her safe. With my life, I will."

"Oh, and that should reassure me?" All eyes were fixed on her as she again studied the wan, lifeless form on the bed. "Aye," she said weakly, "there is no other way." She raised her eyes quickly to catch the expression on her little brother's face. He seemed confident. "Let us hope this little reckless mission does not end in disaster for us all."

SETH AND ADRIANA TRAVELED noiselessly through the inky blackness together. At first the horses seemed skittish, sensing the danger inherent in their late-night journey, and in the haste with which they had left the house. But after a while, it seemed the younger horse, Champion, placed his trust in the older, more-experienced Lancer. He quieted some, though still remaining close to his counterpart's side.

Adriana and Seth, too, were silent, having let go of their former show of confidence after saying goodbye to Lea. Seth had insisted that Adi go in disguise, until he could determine the amount of hostility they would face when it was discovered she was a princess from the House of Hamil. And so, the princess had hidden her long, brown hair beneath one of his hats and donned one of Tristan's loose-fitting shirts. She had originally worn it as he usually did, tucked in at the waist into a pair of his pants they had cinched. But the curves of her bust had been readily evident, so they untucked it instead. Even so, Seth had added an over-sized, bulky coat to conceal her figure more, and still thought she would fool no one if they got close enough. He wagered on the absolute dark, and his own wits, to protect her.

As they drew near to the Castle Glindimore, he halted his horse. "Adi," he tried to peer into her face through the surrounding gloom, "this may be your last chance to change your mind. The castle is down the road a piece...are you certain you want to do this?"

"I've never been more certain of anything, Seth."

"Humpf. I wish I could say the same," he retorted, afraid for her. "If I give you the signal, I want you to bolt away from here as fast as Lancer will take you. Do you understand?"

"Aye, Captain," Adi answered mockingly, giving him a smart salute, though he could barely make it out.

"Come here," he said more softly.

She leaned sideways in her saddle toward him and, as he reached for her, his hands accidentally brushed against her breasts. He took her shoulders and led her to him. His heart seemed to thunder against his lips as he kissed her, her warmth taking him by surprise in the chill air. "I love you, Adi...always."

"And I, you." Lancer pranced nervously. "Let us go."

Adriana hung in the shadows as they approached the wide, iron gates of Glindimore.

"Halt!" a loud voice shouted through the stillness. "Who is there, at this time of night?"

"It is I, Seth Hobbes, come to speak to the king on an important matter."

A short, pudgy guard in helmet and chainmail stepped forward, lifting a lantern while his tall and lanky partner stood back a distance, his sword drawn.

"Well, Seth Hobbes, what could be so all-fired important that you would have us wake the king at *this* hour?"

"It concerns a possible epidemic of the Morris Fever in the kingdom."

"Morris Fever?" The guard laughed. "Why man, no one has seen a case of that in years."

"That may be, but a case has just been confirmed by a doctor in the far northwest corner of the kingdom."

Lancer, recognizing the familiar setting of the castle, began to dance around in anticipation of returning home, snorting loudly several times.

"Who is that with you?" the guard asked, raising his lantern in Adi's direction.

Seth subtly steered Champion into the path of the light. "'Tis my little brother. He came to keep me company."

"Humpf." He studied them.

Seth decided to bluff. "Listen, man, King Lawrence will not be happy if he finds that I have been kept waiting. I am a friend."

The podgy guard straightened and the taller one tightened his grip on his sword. "Well, if it is King Lawrence you have come to see, then you are out of luck, *friend,* as our king has been captured by the Hamiltonians, as all loyal citizens of the kingdom know."

Adi unconsciously gasped in surprise. Immediately the guard raised his lantern again, and shot his hand out farther, to try to capture her face in the light, but Seth moved quickly to place himself between the guards and the princess.

"Who, then, is in charge?" he demanded. "I live out in the country a way. I had no idea King Lawrence had been captured."

The guard hesitated, but then seemed to decide it would do no harm to release information that was common knowledge, to anyone but this country bumpkin, that is.

"Sir Arthur Goodwin. And he would object to being awoken at this hour, I can assure you."

The other guard snickered his consent.

Seth weighed his options. "Aye. Thank you, then. I will call again in the morning."

He waited until the guards had turned before spinning Champion around to Adi. Once the guards were out of earshot, they discussed the new-found information.

"Lawry captured. I cannot believe it!"

"Aye. I know. 'Tis incredible. Do you know this Sir Goodwin they spoke of?"

"Aye," she said, her teeth on edge. She remembered the man making some highly inappropriate, suggestive comments to her once when she was young, when he had caught Lawrence, Garin, and her returning, dripping, from the pond. Lawry had been furious, but they decided not to broach the subject with his father, fearing they would get in trouble for going to the pond. Adriana convinced him to drop it, albeit with great reluctance on his part. The older man's leering grin had followed her for days afterwards. But it was not only that incident that upset her, it was the fact that the man had a certain general menace to him that blackened his name in her book.

"I might be able to get him to listen to me," she answered vaguely.

"Nay. 'Tis too dangerous, Adi. Especially if you have any qualms about him not being as friendly to you as King Lawrence would have been."

"Oh, his being friendly toward me is not a problem, believe me," Adi muttered under her breath, but then she spoke up, "I could probably convince him—"

"What do you not like about the man?"

Adi glanced up, surprised. Was she that transparent? She sighed. "I may be biased against him. He said something once, a long time ago..."

"What did he say to you?" Seth asked sharply.

"It was nothing, probably...I...it was a long time ago...I cannot remember exactly." But it was a lie, and he could see it. Her cheeks burned with the memory; she knew exactly the words, exactly the tone.

"It's out of the question."

"But Seth, Tristan needs—"

"Then we'll use another approach to get it. I will not sacrifice you to—"

"That is it!"

"What is it?"

She had walked a few steps closer to the castle and gazed upwards, to where a light was still on in an upper floor. "I grew up here, Seth. I know Glindimore as well as I know Ramport. Lawry was always being taken to the nursery infirmary when he even had the slightest of sniffles. His mom was extraordinarily overprotective. If there is some sort of medicine in there, that is where it would be." She whirled to face him, her eyes aglow. "I could find my path there in the pitch-black. Please, you have to let me try."

He looked up at the window, too. After several seconds, he said, "Aye. But you will not do it yourself. I am coming with you."

She nodded.

"How will we get in?"

"I know a way."

CHAPTER TWENTY-TWO

Seth followed Adi through the darkness, having tied the horses in a grove of trees not far from the front gates of the castle. After tramping around in silence for ten minutes, they came across an odd structure. A large circular enclosure, built from the same stone as Glindimore, stood yards from the castle walls. There was an arched opening with a wrought-iron gate.

"What is this place? A garden?"

Adi shivered. "Hardly. Long ago, Lawry's grandmother, Queen Veronica—some called her Queen Veronica the Good—insisted her husband, King Hubert, build this. She did not want the prisoners to be executed on the castle grounds. Did not want to see it, or even know of it."

Seth peered through the bars on the gate. "A gallows?"

"Aye."

"But I do not understand how this helps us get into the castle." He spun to find her feeling the bark of a big elm tree. "What are you doing?"

"It was here...I know it was," she mumbled.

"What was?" He came closer.

"There was a hole. We used to hide our treasures in it."

Now that he knew what he was hunting for, Seth easily found the hole. He drew out a key with a dingy pink satin ribbon on it, tied in a bow.

"That is it! Why didn't I think of that? It was lower than I remembered it. Perhaps because I grew." She was about to head for the gate, but turned. She hesitated. "Is there anything else in there?"

Seth reached in again and dragged out a long chain with a delicate, gold heart on it. In the center of the heart was a letter "A" made out of diamonds.

"Ooh," Adi cooed softly. "It's still there."

She traced the "A" reverently with a fingertip. When she realized Seth was watching her, she blushed. "Just a silly little trinket from when we were children. Lawry gave it to me." She slipped it over her head.

She then tried the key in the lock. It opened easily, swinging in on its rusty hinges, despite the years of disuse. She led the way through, closing it behind them. The area looked like it had been abandoned for some time. Grass grew between the flagstones of a courtyard and a stage of sorts at the edge of the stones sagged in the middle.

Seth followed Adriana up the few steps at the back of the stage. "Where are you going?"

She squatted and tugged on an iron ring recessed into the floor.

"In," she said with a smile, and pulled open a trap door.

Seth came around to peer into a musty hole at a staircase that led downwards. "Where does it go?"

"To the castle. There is a tunnel where the prisoners were brought from the dungeon to be executed. Thus Queen Veronica would be none the wiser. It was also a good method for Lawry, Garin, and I to escape outdoors unnoticed by our parents."

Without hesitation Adi climbed into the darkness, disappearing before Seth's eyes. He clambered behind her, losing himself in the dank blackness as well. They moved slowly in the general direction of the castle, with him resting his hands on Adi's hips so that they could stay together and not bump into each other. She sputtered in disgust.

"Ooh!"

"What is it?"

"Ugh! Cobwebs. They are so thick. I got some in my mouth. Pth-pth-pth. Bluck! Ick!"

"Here, let me lead."

"Nay, I can—"

"I am taller. I will clear a path," he insisted.

They stumbled around, bumping into the walls and each other as they changed positions. His mind leapt to other places and he purposefully pressed her against the cold stone wall. His hands cruised up her body to her neck to guide him and his head bent to touch his lips to hers. The stale abyss charged with the fire of passion as he allowed his hands to wander back over her body, finding comfort in her warmth. He recklessly explored under the thin fabric of her shirt, daring to touch the bare skin of her stomach as his lips wreaked their own havoc. His mouth forced hers open more, demanding, and seeking, as he placed his hands on either side of her on the wall, and his lips left hers to travel along her throat. She moaned, her body quivering in response to his fevered touch. Her hands found either side of his face.

"Oh, Seth! They stopped, the only sound the rasping of their breath and the rapid bass beat of their hearts. "I wish you could take me now. In the dark. I know that a lady is not supposed to think such things. But, when you kiss me like that, I cannot help myself. I want so badly to be with you." She stroked his face. "What if we never have the chance? What if we never make it out of here alive?"

"Then I will still love you forever and ever, my love," he rumbled, his voice reverberating in the stillness. "Marry me. Marry me when we get out of here. Share my life with me. This isn't exactly how I wanted to ask you—"

"Oh, Seth! I want nothing more."

He kissed her again.

"Let us get this over with and get out of here then so that I can take you home and make you my wife."

With one final kiss, he moved forward, and she placed her hands on his hips as he waved away the cobwebs.

She broke the silence after a few minutes. "Soon we will reach a staircase going up."

Shortly later, his feet bumped against the bottom stair, and he stumbled forward. "I found the stairs," he muttered sarcastically.

"We need to stay to the left. That side leads to the executioner's bedroom, which is on the floor with the other servants' bedrooms. If we stray to the right, we'll end up on a separate staircase that leads to the dungeon itself."

After a few minutes, they could see a slim stick of light coming in under the bottom of a door. They listened, then cautiously creaked the door open. Adriana led now, but after a few turns down long corridors, she seemed confused.

"This does not seem right. They have changed things." But, within moments she began to pick up the pace. "I know where we are now. It is just a little further."

He was amazed by her sense of direction, as all of the halls looked the same to him. Finally, she chose one of the doors on the right. When they had entered and lit a wall sconce, Seth could see they were in a long, narrow room with six beds lined up— three on each side of the room—and a desk at the near end. Behind the desk, hanging on the wall, was a cabinet. Adriana rushed to it and began searching through vials of various sizes and colors.

They were so engrossed, they did not, at first, hear the sound of feet approaching. But voices soon forewarned them. Seth doused the light, but it was too late. They heard shouts and someone began to bang on the door.

"Hurry!" He hustled over to a window and noted they were only about three floors up, but no handy rope stood nearby. He began to tear the sheets off the beds and knot them together.

"Here it is!" She took a bottle of amber-colored liquid from the cabinet.

Rushing over, she began to help Seth tie. It was quiet on the other side the door, but they felt certain someone would return. Seth secured one end of their makeshift rope to a hook on the wall.

"I am going first. If it will hold my weight, it will hold you." He swung one leg over the window ledge and began to descend.

A key slipped into the lock.

"Wait," she called before Seth was out of reach. "Take this. Just in case." She leaned out to press the vial into his hand and closed his fingers around it.

He froze for a minute, frightened by the implication, but then began to move even faster to get to the bottom. When he touched the ground, he felt the length of bed sheets go limp in his hand and looked up to see the rope falling toward him.

"I love you, Seth," Adi called down to him, her face pale but determined.

"Nay!" He scanned the vicinity for a path up. "I am coming back for you."

"Do not be a fool!" she cried sharply. "You get that dram to Tristan as fast as you can. I will be fine."

To contradict her words, four enormous hands seemed to appear out of nowhere and grabbed her shoulders, pulling her from the window.

Seth ducked behind a bush and hoped he could not be seen from above.

When he took a chance and gazed up, the window was empty.

CHAPTER TWENTY-THREE

The two men grabbed her arms and Adi heard an all-too-familiar voice behind her. She spun to see Sir Arthur Goodwin coming out of the room on the opposite side of the hall, pulling a robe over his bare chest and securing it at his waist. She quickly lowered her gaze, fear seizing her heart.

"What is happening here?" the short, grey-haired man demanded.

"We caught this commoner sneaking around in the royal infirmary, sir."

Sir Arthur focused his attention on Adi as she struggled with the two men. "Raise your head, man," he ordered. When she did not move, he repeated, "I said, raise your head!"

She did not see the blow coming, so was caught completely off-guard when the knight's hand hit her squarely on the side of her face. Her hat flew halfway across the room and her hair tumbled down in front of her face, hiding her from view for a minute.

"A woman?"

Sir Arthur grabbed her chin roughly, lifting her head to get the hair out of her face.

"Well! Adriana Hamil. It has been a *long* time," he added in an overly-familiar fashion that made her cringe. "And what were you doing here? Come to sneak into King Lawrence's bed behind sweet Sariah's back?"

He took a step to one side, and she could see into the other room through the door he had left open behind him. In the enormous bed, Lawrence's wife Sariah, obviously naked, sat clutching a sheet to her chest. She seemed ashamed and sorrowful.

Adriana gasped.

Sir Arthur circled her slowly, sizing her up like some prize piece of beef. He touched the coarse fabric of her coat and noted, with pleasure, she flinched. He removed it to better scrutinize her, brushing her purposefully as he did so. "My, how the mighty have fallen." His voice was velvety soft and sinister, "Eh, *princess?*" He peered at her with falcon eyes, not bothering to conceal the lust that lay within them.

"Princess?" interrupted one of the big men at her elbow. "Princess Adriana, of the House of Hamil? Maybe we can trade her for King Lawrence."

A ghost of alarm flitted through Sir Arthur's eyes, but he quickly recovered.

"A brilliant idea, my dear Shep...if King Henry or that stupid sidekick of his, Sir Garin, had any interest in her return. But from what I heard," he said, centering his attention on her again, "it was good riddance to bad rubbish."

She craved one chance to wipe the smirk from his angular face.

"Keep her locked in here. When I'm...*finished,*" he said, with feigned delicacy, "in there," he gestured to Sariah and she averted her face, "I'll come back here."

He trailed a finger slowly along Adriana's cheek. She twisted, but he grabbed her chin in his viselike grip, and stepped up so close she could feel his warm breath on her skin.

"You are *mine*, this time, Adriana. No Garin, no Lawrence to defend you." With his free hand, he slowly pulled the string that gathered her shirt at the neck, then slid the one gripping her chin painfully along her neck and dipped it just inside the fabric.

She fought against her captors fiercely, trying to break free from their hold.

Sir Arthur laughed. "I will be back, my dear Adriana. I will be back." He untied his robe and let it fall open as he swung around to retrace his steps to the bedroom. As he closed the door slowly Adi could see Sariah look up at him.

The two guards pushed Adriana into the room, and left, locking the door behind them.

She laid her shaking hands over her chest as she stumbled back a few steps, rocking in an effort to find comfort. Wiping at the few hot tears that had escaped onto her cheeks, she crossed to an oval carpet between the rows of beds. Her heart beating wildly, she yanked it away, to reveal the trapdoor she had hoped was still there. She threw it open and descended the rope ladder attached to the floor below it. Long before she first explored the castle, some smart servant had installed the door so they had quick access to the room if one of the royal children should cry.

She tried, as best she could, to slip the rug back into place as she closed the door above her.

Carefully she traversed the hall. Lucky for her, Lawrence and Sariah had not had any children yet, so no servant had taken up residency under the nursery. She scurried through the halls and found the entrance to the staircase she had climbed earlier, diving again into the blackness.

In the dark, she missed the hall to the outer door, and continued downwards until she stumbled onto flat ground in the dungeon.

She bit back a cry as she fell, hard, onto the stone floor.

"Is it already time for more torture?" a wry voice asked.

She sought for something she could use to help get to her feet and found the cold, iron bars of a prison cell. The voice was as familiar as her own.

"Lawry? Is that truly you?"

"In the flesh, or what is left of it," he joked. "Adi. What in the world are you doing here?"

"What am *I* doing here? What are *you* doing here? I thought you had been captured by my father."

"Oh, so that is what he's telling people. Nay. Just tricked by my head minister, Sir Arthur Goodwin."

"He imprisoned you?" she asked, incredulous.

"Aye. And I am certain he would have killed me by now, too, if I had told him where I have my royal treasury secured."

"Well, we have to get you out of here."

"There are keys on a ring at the bottom of the stairs to your left." While she worked her way in that direction, feeling the cell bars, he asked, "So...you did not answer my question. Why are you wandering through my castle?"

She bumped into the stairs and her fingers traversed the stone wall, trying to find the ring.

"I came because Tristan is ill, and you have the medicine to make him better, which I...kind of...stole from you," she added apologetically.

"Nonsense. Had I known, I would have given it to you freely. I could deny you nothing. And that Tristan, he is a great boy. He is not very ill, I hope?"

"Actually, he is quite ill. I hope Seth makes it in time," she murmured. After several minutes of fruitless searching, she asked, "Are you sure they left the keys here?"

"They had torches and I saw them hanging on a spike. Feel higher, maybe."

She stretched as high as she could, and then when that did not work, she jumped. With her first hop she touched the ring and, it sounded—from the rhythmic scraping noise it made against the stone—as if she had set it swinging against the wall. She jumped again and knocked the keys from their peg.

"That a girl, Adi! Come let me out."

She smiled at the renewed energy in his voice.

Hunting about on her hands and knees she recovered the keys and reversed her course in order to free the king. As soon as the key turned in the lock he opened the door, stepped out and grabbed her up in a fierce hug. He gave her a resounding kiss on the mouth and she could feel his whiskered chin and wondered how many weeks had passed while he had been held below in the dark.

"So you found your Seth, eh?"

"I did!" she exclaimed, her joy ringing in the emptiness.

"That is my Adi," he said, patting her cheek. He grabbed her hand and felt, like she had, along the bars to the stair. "Just like old times, eh?" He laughed, clearly ecstatic to be free.

She squeezed his hand and they followed the walls up and stumbled out into a hallway which was dimly lit by torches, but seemed as bright as day after their time in the dungeon. "New look for you?" Lawrence joked, gesturing to her pants and shirt.

"New look for you?" she retorted, rubbing his whiskered face.

He felt his own face ruefully. "Aye. I wonder if my Sariah cares for a man with a beard?"

In her mind's eye, Adi saw the last image she had of Sariah in Lawrence's bed with a half-dressed Sir Goodwin closing the door. She was grateful her friend was too distracted to notice the pained expression on her face.

Just then, a guard came around the corner.

"King Lawrence!" he shouted. "How did you get free and return?" He rushed forward with a huge smile.

"Get back here?" Lawrence responded jovially. "I have been here all along, man. Sir Goodwin's had me locked in the dungeon."

"Here, Sire? Oh, my gracious! I'm so sorry, your highness."

"Not your fault, Jenks." He chuckled, clapping the big man on the shoulder. "Not your fault at all."

"Your Majesty!"

"Sire!"

Two more men rounded the corner and greeted their lost king joyously. After exchanging a few words, Lawrence interjected, "Now, Gentlemen, if someone would please hand me a sword, I have a castle to win back. Oh, and Jenks, could you see Princess Adriana safely out of the castle?"

"Aye, Sire. Your word is my command."

"Oh, ho, ho!" Lawry laughed heartily. "I've missed the ring of that."

As his men made exuberant plans about what they would do to Sir Goodwin when they found him, Lawry swung back to Adi, sheathing the sword he had been given and taking both of her hands.

"You and Seth will come back to see Sariah and I soon?"

She nodded, wincing again at the mention of his wife's name.

"And Adi, do not worry, I will send out the royal physician at first light. Where do they live?"

"The far northwest corner of your kingdom, near Morriston."

"Very good. I will send him. And I am certain Tristan will be fine."

She nodded tearfully and he raised her hands to kiss them, then, handed her over to the care of his servant, Edwin Jenks. "Good luck, my dear."

"And to you," she replied sincerely.

CHAPTER TWENTY-FOUR

Jenks saw Adi to the castle gates, and then, anxious to return inside, wished her well and left her. She hustled through the woods to the spot where the horses had been tied, but just as she came into the clearing, she was grabbed from behind.

Seth swallowed her up in his embrace. "Oh, Adi! Do not ever do that to me again." He kissed her face repeatedly.

"I promise. Never again." She released him. "You still have the medicine?"

He opened his palm where the vial was yet pressed. The sound of a single cannon firing exploded through the night.

"What was that?"

She laughed lightheartedly. "Just Lawry letting me know he has retaken the castle. I will explain later," she replied to his quizzical look. "Let us go."

Lancer and Champion thundered away through the night, seeming to understand the need for speed. Their riders crouched over their necks, urging them on.

When they arrived at the cabins, Seth and Adi did not bother to tie the horses, just jumped off and rushed into the house. When they reached the loft, they understood the deathly quiet that had descended over the house. Tristan remained in his bed, and Lea was in the other, her hair wet with sweat, her face ghostly white. Seth lifted her hands and showed them to Adi. Her fingernails had the familiar orange tint.

Seth administered the dram to both of their patients. They sat and waited impatiently for a change in their demeanors.

"I hope I did not give them too much."

"I am certain you did fine," she reassured him, taking his hand. "Besides, Lawry said that he would send his physician as soon as he could."

They settled in to wait, Adi curling up on the floor by Seth's feet. After some time, the warmth of the cabin combined with the fatigue from their brisk ride and the lengthy amount of time they had been up, began to seduce them into sleep. Seth's head was on his chest, and one of his hands rested on Adi's shoulder. Adi had her legs curled to one side, her head lying on her folded arms in his lap.

"Hail, my Lady Adi."

She blinked her eyes open.

"Trist!" She flew from Seth's side to his in an instant.

Her cry woke both Seth and Lea, Seth springing from his seat in alarm. Adi was hugging Tristan fiercely and sobbing.

"Why is she crying?" Tristan mouthed over her shoulder, and Seth clapped him on the back heartily.

"Welcome back, Trist." His smile broad, he sat weakly on the side of Lea's bed. His sister squeezed him around the waist and laid her head on his back.

"Thank you, Seth. Thank you!"

"It wasn't me, it was Adi."

Lea lifted her head and smiled in Adi's direction. "I will thank her when she quits blubbering."

Seth laughed and held his sister.

IT WAS THE BIG DAY.

Adriana woke to the sound of Lea bustling below, scouring everything for the umpteenth time in preparation for the king's visit. She sat and gazed lovingly on her dress hanging in the corner. She had spent hours laboring over it, though it was really a simple enough dress.

This was the day she was to wed Seth and her life was going to begin in earnest. She swung her legs out of bed, but had to grab the bedpost to keep from falling. Whoo! She would need to remember to get out of bed more slowly to avoid these head rushes. She placed a hand on her forehead but a sudden burst of pain in her shoulder made her wince. *I must have hurt it when I fell into the dungeon when I found Lawry,* she thought ruefully. Nothing to fret about.

She would not let anything ruin this day.

In the next cabin, Seth sat at the kitchen table, fidgeting with the high-necked collar of his shirt, and feeling like a man with a noose around his neck. Not because he felt marrying Adi was a death sentence, but simply because he hated formal wear, and being the center of attention. On top of that, Tristan was getting a certain sick pleasure out of his discomfort and Seth felt the need to cuff him around the ears but restrained himself.

Tristan was dressed in similar garb, and was probably nearly as uncomfortable, but was not about to let on. He was taking his role as best man—a role that would have gone to his father—seriously.

"Now, Uncle Seth, is there any advice you need about—" he cleared his throat, smiling, "—your wedding night...."

Seth swatted him with a snort.

"Just because you have been seeing that Smithson girl for a whole...what, three weeks is it? That does not mean you know more about women than I do, half-pint."

Tristan chortled and rubbed the spot where Seth had hit him. Seth became serious again, twirling the cuff links at his wrists. They had been Hayden's. Lea had given them to him that morning.

Tristan sat next to him, suddenly sober, too. "Do you miss Father?"

Seth looked up, surprised by how intuitive Tristan had become. Trist had been surprising him a lot lately. "Aye. It is days like this that I miss him most."

"He would have loved Adi," Tristan said after a few minutes.

Seth smiled. "Aye, he would have."

Everyone loved Adi. One could not help but love her. And soon, he would be allowed to love her for the rest of his life. It seemed incredibly right.

Outside the friendly and familiar clomping of horse hooves could be heard coming down the dirt lane leading to their house. Both men leapt up and went to the window.

"King Lawrence is here."

Tristan and the king had become close after his bout with the Morris Fever. Lawrence had visited several times to check on everyone and had even played a game or two of chess with Tristan.

He and Seth went out to greet the coach. When it pulled up, the door was opened by the king himself. "Seth, Tristan, hello," he called out merrily as he assisted a dark-haired woman as she left the coach. "You remember my wife, Sariah."

Seth gave a short bow. "Your Majesty. Welcome."

"We are so excited to be here," the queen responded, giving her husband's arm a squeeze.

"So...you ready for the big day, Seth?" Lawrence teased.

"Aye, Sire, I am."

"Ahh...good, good. Uhh...do you think I could steal your bride-to-be for a few minutes? I would like to talk to her in private, if I could."

"Of course, of course. She's right this way, Your Majesty."

"Uh-uh-uh," he chided. "The groom is not supposed to see the bride on their wedding day. Even I know that, Hobbes. I will find her. You will entertain my wife?"

"Of course. May I escort you inside, Your Highness?"

Their voices faded behind him as Lawry crossed the yard and knocked on the front door of the smaller cottage. He shook his head. Adi must really love this man if she were choosing to live here with him, he thought. Lea opened the door and curtsied.

"Lea!" he roared. "How good to see you." He took her hand and kissed it.

"And you, too, Your Majesty."

"Oh, forget all that rot, now. You are to call me Lawrence, remember?"

"Yes, Sire." She visibly relaxed.

They both turned as Adi descended from the loft. She had on a long, simple, flowing white gown. Her hair was pulled up, and intertwined with little white flowers and white satin ribbon which trailed behind her. She was breathtaking.

"Lawry."

The king felt as if he had been struck by lightning. "Adi...you are...utterly sensational."

"Oh, Lawry," she said, swatting him and blushing profusely. "Stop it." She squeezed him.

"I was wondering if we might take a short walk. There is time, is there not?" he asked Lea, sensing that it was she who was really in charge.

"Take all the time you need, Your Majesty." He frowned and she corrected, "Lawrence. We do not have a set schedule."

Lawry appreciated the lie. "I will only take a few minutes, I swear."

But once they were out in the sunshine, the king could not help but amble, enjoying their rare, quiet time together. He sighed.

"I cannot help thinking that this is an end to an era."

"Oh, nay, Lawry. This is just the beginning of the best part of our lives."

He chuckled and patted her hand where it rested on his arm.

"Adi," he said after a brief silence, sounding like he was reciting a rehearsed speech, "I take my job of walking you down the aisle very seriously, and, as a stand-in for your father, I want to ask you if you have any questions, any qualms about being married today?"

She stopped, looking up at him with a radiant smile. "None whatsoever."

"Hmm... Well then, mind if I offer some free advice?"

She shook her head, listening attentively as he began.

"Marriage...is not always easy," he said, staring off in the distance. "Sariah and I have had a tough time of late. Sir Goodwin..." He winced, and paused for a moment. "He took more from me than my castle."

Adi paled.

"Sariah...went to his bed...willingly. She confessed it to me, and told me it never would have happened if he had not coaxed her, but...she *was* willing."

He ducked to avoid a branch and then continued.

"You see, she believed that I was not coming back. Had she known I was but *twenty-some-odd feet under her bed...*" he said, his teeth gritted. He left his thought unfinished, sighing. "But...after seven years, like Sariah and I have enjoyed together...sometimes, I guess, one begins to wonder what it would be like..." His voice faded. "And I have to take some of the blame—"

"Oh, nay, Lawry."

"Oh, yes, Adi," he insisted. "I was not as attentive to her as I should have been. I had begun to take her for granted...not making her believe on a daily basis, as I should have, she was the most beautiful woman in the kingdom, and the most important thing in the world, to me. Rather than traipsing off on hunting trips too frequently, I should have been trying to keep the spark alive. But—" he sighed "—we are starting again, because, I love her, Adi, I really do."

Adi smiled at Lawrence, despite the throbbing that seemed to be getting worse in her shoulder. She knew it would take her a little longer to forgive Sariah. When she thought of Lawry in that cell and Sariah upstairs with the man who had put him there... But she knew her friend loved his wife, and she was just going to have to get over it.

"I am glad things are working out for you two," she said truthfully.

"All relationships have their problems. Like you and Seth, he told me about some of the things you two have been through, and, frankly Adi, I never knew you were such a handful."

"What? I have not..." she began, but then she noted the twinkle in his eyes. "Oh, Lawry." She laughed, nudging him.

He chuckled, too. "Seriously, Adi, after the things you have gone through, I think it is all downhill from here. And anyone who sees the way Seth and you look at each other would know this is the real thing. And, I like him. He is an honorable man...much better than that Garin. I never thought he was good enough for you. And, if I cannot have you, then I guess Seth will have to do." His smile was broad. "You are wearing my necklace." He lifted the diamond "A" into his hand.

"Aye." Adi suddenly felt faint. "Oh, my. It is warm out here." She fanned herself with her hand.

"Do you think so? You are kind of flushed, too. Must be all the excitement. Well, if I do not get you back soon, I think Lea will skin me alive."

She slipped her hand through his arm. "Lawry...thank you."

"For what? You are the one who showed up like an angel and freed me from my prison cell."

"For coming here, and...just for being you." She stretched up on her toes and kissed him on the cheek.

He cleared his throat.

"Come. Let us get you married."

CHAPTER TWENTY-FIVE

Adi's aisle wove through apple trees that threw white confetti blossoms all along her path. Standing twenty yards away was the man who would become her husband. His eyes were riveted on her without regard for anyone else present. Tristan stood beside him, as bursting with excitement as his uncle was serious.

Adriana pushed aside the wave of pain that threatened to bring her to her knees.

By now it was clear to her that something was wrong. It was equally clear to her she could not go another day without becoming Seth's bride.

Her heart leapt with the first glimpse of him through the trees, and she knew she could endure any kind of pain, if only to get through the ceremony.

Seth noted Lawry was talking with her as they walked through the trees together, her hand on the sleeve of his elaborate velvet coat. She seemed relaxed, and happy, and he had never seen her look more beautiful than she did this very moment. Her flowing white dress reminded him of the nightgown she had worn on the night they first met, and from that image, a series of others paraded through his mind...Adi, her face determined as Lea held the knife over her lustrous hair the night they had escaped together from Ramport...her face, creased with pain when he broke the arrow from her shoulder in his cottage...her face, full of sacrificial love as she stood above him in the window of Glindimore, having just thrown down the sheet rope, her only means of escape.

He then remembered moments when he simply watched her in everyday actions—playing with Tristan, or helping Lea around the house, and then she had glanced up, catching him watching her, and given him that special, secret smile that she kept just for him. He remembered every detail of her face when he had first kissed her, sitting together in her bed, while she was still tender from her arrow wound, and moments, like in the nearby meadow, when he had seen the passion cloud her eyes when they had touched, and he had kissed her.

He became aware the face he so loved was now drawing near to him. He studied her again, never failing to be taken by her. Her cheeks were pink; her lips soft and moist. She had a sort of breathless glow about her, as if she had been holding her breath all of her life for this one moment. He felt a warmth explode in him, splitting his lips into a smile as brilliant as the rays of the sun that filtered through the trees, splashing the ground with radiant light all about them.

A short, nondescript minister dressed in black and holding a Bible stood before them, but as he took Adriana's hands, he was almost surprised by the man's voice, coming, as it seemed, from his elbow, interrupting his personal trance.

As the minister began the familiar words of the wedding ceremony, Seth gazed on her face, soaking in each detail. So absorbed was he in her that he became aware, after a while, something was wrong. Though her eyes glowed with love for him during much of the ceremony, there were moments when they seemed to drift off to some unpleasant memory. Although her smile was, at first, bright and genuine, at moments he recognized a tightness at the edges.

When the minister turned to get the rings from Tristan, Seth leaned in and whispered. "Are you well?"

"Aye, I am wonderful, Seth," she said with such earnestness, he believed her. *Maybe it is nerves*, he told himself, but even as he did, he knew it to not be true. Adi was not one to get nervous. Even so, he patted her hand on his arm in a sign of comfort, and found it to be hot. But before he could think much about it, he realized that the preacher was handing him the ring.

"With this ring, I thee wed, Adriana," Seth peered into her eyes as he slipped the silver band onto her finger. He had designed it for her with an arrow through a heart.

He saw the tears of happiness well up in her eyes as she hesitated a moment, before taking his ring, and placing it on his finger with trembling hands.

"With this ring, I *thee* wed, Seth Hobbes."

Even the minister, who had at first, appeared as if he would rather be doing something else, seemed to get caught up in the warmth and strength of their love.

"You may kiss your bride, Mr. Hobbes."

Seth drew Adi in and kissed her as cheers went up from the small party gathered there, Tristan and Lea, Lawry and Sariah, the Smithsons, the Parishes, and Utey Deadlow and his wife, Virginia.

As the newlyweds walked back along the path to the house, their guests covered them in apple blossoms. Seth kissed his wife again.

Then they were encircled by happy well-wishers, everyone commenting on how beautiful the ceremony was. When Lawry got to Adriana, he wrapped her up in one of his infamous bear hugs, only to have her go limp.

"Seth! Seth!" he cried out, his voice panicked.

The crowd parted in front of Seth as he rushed over, swooping her up in one smooth motion. His worried eyes met Lawry's.

"Let us get her inside."

He took her in and laid her on the bed that had been his wedding present to her. He had carved it painstakingly from a combination of oak and apple tree wood from the orchard, from a tree felled in a storm.

Tristan was right behind him. "What is it? The Morris Fever?"

"I do not know, Trist." Seth checked her fingernails but found they were without the orange tint. Still, he couldn't know for sure. "Get the medicine." He immediately began to bathe her wrists in cool water, and dab it on her face and neck.

Tristan scurried off and Lawry took his place. "What can I do? What is wrong with her?"

"I am not sure. She is burning up. Has she been ill all morning?"

"She did not mention anything. But, now I consider it, she did seem rather flushed and...weak, for Adi, that is."

"Hmm..." Seth responded, frowning. "She must have been trying to hide it so that she could make it through the ceremony."

Lawrence's footman appeared in the doorway. "Your Highness?"

"Get back to Glindimore at once, and bring Dr. Redding back here as fast as you can."

"Aye."

The man sped from the room just as Tristan rushed in yelling, "Here it is, Uncle Seth." He handed him the vial that was half gone.

"I need to wake her first," Seth mumbled to himself. He was uncomfortably aware of the king's presence as he undid a few of the buttons on her dress, parting the fabric near her throat and chest, but she was wet with sweat now and he had to do it. He dabbled cool water on her upper chest and put his wet hands to the back of her neck.

Adi moaned and shook her head back and forth, eventually opening her eyes weakly. "Oh, Seth! I am so sorry." She seemed near tears.

"Nonsense," he said, relief painting his voice. He helped her to lift her head, and poured some of the medicine down her throat.

"I have ruined our wedding."

"Nay. Nay, you did not, silly," he chided. "You made it through the important part," he added with a smile.

"I did, did I not?" she said dreamily, closing her eyes as if the effort of keeping them open was too much. She lapsed into either unconsciousness, or sleep, Seth couldn't tell which. All he knew was that she was taking in even, shallow breaths.

"Now what do we do?" Lawry asked, wringing his hands.

"We wait," Seth answered with a sigh. He drew a chair up to the side of the bed, putting his elbows on his knees. Folding his hands, he watched her face with resignation, ready for a difficult night.

"We wait," Lawry repeated unhappily. He was not used to having to wait for anything and it didn't suit him. He pulled a chair beside Seth and mirrored his posture.

Hours later, they switched to pacing separate paths beside the bed as they listened hopefully for the sound of the doctor approaching.

Adi was not sleeping comfortably. She thrashed around and moaned pitifully, making her newlywed husband and old friend desperate and frustrated in their helplessness.

"I do not understand," Seth mumbled, miserable. "The medicine worked quickly the last time."

They turned at the sound of footsteps on the stairs. It was Lea, followed by the queen. Lea brought a bowl of water and a rag. Seth was grateful that she had agreed to entertain the queen and allow him to take care of Adi, though he could tell it tested her.

"How is she?"

"Worse," was all Seth said. He immediately took the water and wet the rag to wipe her face. It seemed to help her relax a little, although her brow was still creased with the effort of absorbing the pain and she did not open her eyes at all.

"Lawry?" the queen asked quietly. "Do you not think we should be going? It is late."

"I am not going anywhere until I see that Adi is better," he said firmly, without looking up at his wife.

"But I am tired, Lawrence."

"Your Majesty, we have a cottage next door you are welcome to use—"

"You can hardly expect me to sleep there," the queen responded, appalled.

"Sariah. Hold your tongue," Lawry snapped, startling everyone. "If you cannot be polite to these people, then I suggest that you—"

"I did not mean anything by it," she responded tearfully. "I only...I am just so tired."

There was an awkward moment of silence, then, Lawry sighed, closing his eyes for a long moment. "I am sorry, Sariah. I am just worried."

"I know you are," she said, coming over to rest her hand on his shoulder. He reached up to squeeze it, and just then, they all heard the sound of a carriage approaching. Seth's and Lawry's gazes locked.

"I will see the doctor in," Lea offered, and disappeared.

"I will just go lie down next door," Sariah said. "I'd just be in the way."

"Perhaps that would be best," Lawry responded still focused on Adi.

Sariah waited at the top of the ladder for the doctor to come up and then left. Dr. Redding was a short staid man with thinning grey hair and a bushy mustache. He bustled into the room and directly to Adi's side without any preliminary comments.

"Hmm...." he murmured, his mustache twitching as he examined her.

"She was exposed to the Morris Fever. We gave her the medicine, but that was a while ago."

The doctor did not comment.

"It should have worked by now," Seth repeated like some mantra.

"It did not work because this woman does not have Morris Fever," the doctor said matter-of-factly. He continued to examine her, folding back the covers to inspect her feet.

"You the husband?"

"Aye."

"I may have to remove some of her clothing." He glanced up at the king.

Lawry peered at Seth inquiringly from across the bed. Seth, whose jaw was set, took measure of the king at length. "He can stay, *for now*."

His internal debate was unnecessary though, as the doctor had to unbutton only a few more buttons before asking, "What is this?" He pointed to a red, oval, saucer-sized area. In the middle was a dark red section the size of a large coin.

Seth paled. "She was shot by an arrow."

Lawry's brows went up, but he did not ask any questions.

"How long has this swelling been here?"

"I do not know," Seth answered, his face becoming red. He had not seen Adi's bare shoulder since the night he found her in the orchard. "We were only married today. This was to be our wedding night," he explained.

"Hmm..." the doctor said again, annoying both Seth and Lawry, if the king's snarl was any indication. The doctor pressed on the swollen section and Adi screamed out, shocking everyone.

"When was she shot?"

"Several months ago."

"The arrow, how was it extracted?"

Seth eyed Lawry nervously, and spoke to him instead of the doctor.

"She was bleeding everywhere. I did not know what to do. I broke the shaft off, and left it in her. I had to bind the wound to stop the bleeding."

"Just right," the doctor said, nodding his head. He twisted to consider Seth. "I would have done the same thing, son. Did you clean the wound?"

"I did the best I could, but it just kept bleeding."

"Well...normally the bleeding itself will clear out any contamination, but in this case, my guess is, something is causing an infection. It could be something as small as a cinder from the blacksmith's fire that created the tip of the arrow. We will never know."

Lawry caught Seth's distraught look. "You did your best, Seth."

"Nay, you do not understand. *I* made the arrow."

"You shot her?" the doctor asked, aghast.

"Nay. Nay. Of course not. But I am a blacksmith. I make arrow tips, and I recognized my own work. I sold it, and it ended up in the hands of the man who shot Adi."

"Not your fault, my man," the doctor said dismissively, patting Seth's arm.

Seth remained unconvinced and remorseful. After a minute, he asked, "What do we do?"

"Well..." The older man sighed. "I can give her something for the pain," he said, shaking his head sadly, "but all we can do is hope that her body fights off the infection."

She moaned, and the doctor again turned his attention to his patient. He took a vial from a drawstring purse inside a bigger bag he carried.

"Help me," he said to Lawry, forgetting, as he often seemed to do in his work, that he was speaking to the king.

From the other side of the bed, Lawry helped him to raise Adi so he could get her to drink a little.

"There," he said finally, after she had been laid back down. He pulled the covers up to her chin.

Seth's gaze had never left her. "Now what?"

"Now we wait."

Seth and Lawry exchanged a glance. "Isn't there anything else that can be done, Martin?" the king queried.

The doctor put a hand up and smoothed his mustache. "There is one way..." he said vaguely, looking off into the distance.

"What are you talking about, man?"

The doctor looked evenly at Lawry for a second, unaccustomed to being snapped at. "There is a man who is supposed to be an expert at these kinds of things. He would cut open the wound, and clear away any debris...in this case, the arrow, and any infected tissue surrounding it, then, bind it and let it heal."

"Is that not dangerous?" Seth asked.

"It can be," the doctor admitted. "But this man has saved many people's lives in this fashion."

He took in Adi's pale face. She seemed to be sleeping more comfortably. "Where is this man?"

"The last I heard, and this was just a few months ago, he was in the king's court in Hamiltonia." He checked Adi again. "I am afraid there is nothing I can do for her, except give you this." He pressed the bottle with the drought for pain into his hand. "If she gets much worse, the man I speak of, Dr. Godfrey Lancing, would be your only hope."

The doctor left and the men stood looking at each other from opposite sides of Adi's bed. They were silent until they heard the front door close.

"I do not want to wait," Seth said in his bass voice.

The king nodded vigorously. "What do you need from me?"

Seth thought. "A wagon."

"'Tis yours."

CHAPTER TWENTY-SIX

Thus it was, well before dawn, Seth loaded Adi into the back of a wagon that he had padded with hay and placed a mattress into.

"We will take good care of Tristan at Glindimore," Lawry said to Lea, who was already in the back of the wagon watching over Adi. Clasping Seth's shoulder, he added, "Good luck, my man."

"Thank you. Thank you for everything."

"Do not think twice about it. I only wish I could do more. Now get on out of here and you will be halfway there before noon."

Seth shook his hand and then stopped by the side of the wagon before climbing up to the driver's seat, peering into the bed. He wished he could touch his wife's hand where it lay limply in the hay.

"Take care of her," he said to Lea, his voice tight.

Lea swallowed. "I will, Seth," she reassured him.

He took a deep breath and climbed up to his seat, taking the reins and shouting a "hah!" to the horses.

Lea looked back toward their cottages as they rolled away at a quick clip. Tristan stood beside the king, Lawry's hand on the boy's shoulder. Tristan waved tentatively. She waved back. Despite the fact he was almost as tall as Lawry, her son looked so young to her, his face drawn with worry.

When she could no longer make out Tristan's features, she turned her attention to trying to keep Adi still, so that the jarring motion of the wagon would not hurt her. She gripped the bottle of pain medication tightly. It had to last them a while, so she knew she would have to ration it carefully and make some tough decisions on her friend's behalf as she watched her writhe in pain.

For Adi's part, she had become familiar with her pain. She felt the waves of agony rise, becoming more fearful with each second. As they built, higher and higher, hot and searing, she knew she would not be able to stand much more. When it would, at times, mercifully recede, she would brace for the next wave, knowing it would come, waiting, anxiously, for the mind-numbing pain only she could recognize. She wanted to cry out, to scream, to curse the man who had done this to her. But she knew her cries were like blows to Seth, so she endured her torture with silence, or sometimes, when she couldn't stand it, with low whimpers. At times, she would slip into a blessed blackness, a temporary escape from her reality. But when she would awaken, the pain was always there, her constant companion and tormentor.

She knew Seth was concentrating on steering the horses to the smoothest parts of the road, but the ride was still bumpy. After a particularly hard bounce, a cry escaped from her tightly pressed lips. She knew it pierced through him as surely as the arrow had pierced her. He drew the horses in and spun around.

"I missed seeing that rut in the dark," he said apologetically. "How is she?"

"In anguish," Lea answered, her brow furrowed. "Come help me administer this drug," she added urgently.

Seth hopped down and climbed up into the bed of the wagon.

His presence broke through the wall of Adi's suffering. She moaned, "Oh, Seth! I am sorry."

"What? Honey, you have nothing to be sorry for." He hastened to her side.

"I know how worried you are. I have been trying...not to call out...but that one just sort of...caught me by surprise..." Her words were broken by her labored breathing as she fought to steady her voice and not slip from him into the comforting darkness.

He stroked her hair.

"You do not need to worry about me, Adi. I am tough." He smiled at her. She smiled weakly in return, although her eyes were shut.

"Lea," Seth said with a note of pleading, "could you take the horses for a drink? I hear a stream in the brush to the right. I just want—"

"I understand, Seth."

Lea knew that her brother wanted a moment alone with his new wife.

The strain of their separation was showing on his face. He needed Adi as much as she needed him.

Lea understood that only too well. She wondered, briefly, about the old saying, "It is better to have loved and lost than never to have loved at all." Seeing him now with his face tight, his eyes swimming with worry, she wondered if it would have been better if he had never met Adriana at all. But she knew, in her heart, she would not have denied him what Adi brought into his life, the side of him she awakened, that only she could have awakened. Lea believed assuredly that just as she would have never parted with one second of her time with Hayden, Seth would say the same of his short time with Adriana.

Lea looked back as she scrambled from the wagon at the loving look the couple gave one another, remembering the moving vows they exchanged some hours before. Her heart squeezed inside her chest. As she unhooked the horses to lead them through the woods to the water, she listened to the sound of their soft, tender voices, though she could not make out their words, until it faded off behind her. When she got to the bank of the little creek, she sat and cried, getting it out of her system before she had to go back to them.

Seth gazed into Adriana's face as it was lit by the moonlight. Although her hair was tousled and her skin an unnatural shade of white, he could not help but think of the night he first saw her asleep in the castle. She still looked as beautiful now, or even more so, because his heart was fully won over by her, for he now knew her strength of spirit and fortitude, her simple generosity, the sound of her laughter, the taste of her lips.

"Adi?" he whispered, his voice choked.

"Mmm..."

He stroked her hair. "I love you, sweetheart."

"I love you, too," she breathed, the corners of her lips lifting despite the tension on her face.

"I am sorry, honey." He hated to see her go through this. Hated, more, that it was his arrow that had caused her harm.

"Nay," she retorted, her voice stronger. "I am sorry, Seth." For the first time, she started to cry. "This was to be our wedding night."

"Oh, nay, Adi. Please do not do that," he begged, almost at breaking point himself, too. "Shh. Shh." He shifted so that he could lie by her side. "See. See. I am here beside you, honey. There is no need to fret. I am here."

"Nay, you fool," she replied, chuckling and crying at the same time. "We were to be making love to one another right now."

"Oh, now." He laughed, low in his throat. "There will be plenty of time for that. We have a lifetime, Adi."

She laughed again, burying the sharp pains it caused. "You always say that."

"That's because it's true."

She began to cry harder. "What if it is not true? What if there is no time left for us?"

"Adi, do not say that." He was crying now, too. "Please, do not say that."

"Oh!" she cried out. "I am sorry. Shh. Shh. It is fine, now."

He marveled that through her pain, she was still able to worry about him. "Hold me, Seth."

"But what about your shoulder?"

"I do not care. Hold me."

He gingerly slid his arm under her. He could feel her fevered body against his and wanted to cry again for love of her.

"There," she said, with a note of relief. "There. That is what I needed. That is all I needed."

She turned her head into his chest and gave in to the peaceful blackness.

When Lea returned, she was stunned to find them lying together. In the moonlight she could see the glint of tears on Seth's face.

"Is she well?" she asked, swallowing a half-sob.

"Aye," he said, getting up carefully and laying her back. He kissed her forehead, resting his head there a moment. "I have to get going," he said to her still form, or to himself, Lea could not be sure which. His reluctance was palpable. He climbed down next to his sister.

She stretched to put a hand on his cheek, searching her mind for comforting words, but finding none.

His expression was worn and haggard. He smiled at her wanly, unable to say anything. He patted her clumsily on the shoulder and then helped her up into the back of the wagon. He latched the gate in place, and stood for a moment with his hands resting on the top of it, watching Lea get settled in next to his wife.

He walked to the front of the wagon as if he was wearing lead boots.

"Well, then." The words struggled out of his mouth. "Let us get going."

CHAPTER TWENTY-SEVEN

"This is where you get out," Seth told Lea.

"What are you talking about?"

He had pulled in front of the gates of Glindimore and held his hand out to help her out of the wagon.

"You will not be going any further with me."

"And just who says that I won't?" Lea retorted.

"I do." He slanted his head toward the road. "It is only an hour's ride from here. And I will not take you into a war zone."

"Well, who says I am giving you any choice?" She crossed her arms, refusing his outstretched hand.

Seth sighed. "Lea, you can get out of the wagon, or I can haul you out," he said simply.

Lea tried to stare him down but after looking into his eyes and no doubt seeing the determination there she must have decided she was fighting a losing battle. She moved over to kneel in the hay by Adi.

"Be strong, my girl," she whispered.

She had not awoken in hours. They had used the last of the pain medication and it was clear she was fading away from them. Lea, perhaps wondering if this would be the last time she would see her friend, lost control, hanging her head and sobbing.

Seth climbed in and put his hands on her shoulders. He waited patiently for her to calm. Helping her to her feet, they walked, with Lea's hand in his, to the back of the wagon. He hopped out, reaching back to swing Lea to the ground. Wordlessly he closed and latched the gate. Lea's trembling hand grasped the top edge of the gate, as she rose on her toes to take one last look at the sleeping princess in the hay. Seth looked too.

For a minute, it was easy to imagine that the beautiful princess was just sleeping an enchanted sleep. That, if only Seth would steal up to her and kiss her cheek, she would wake and her laughter would fill the air again. But, in the blink of an eye, the dream disappeared, and he knew by the deathly pallor of her skin, Adi may only have hours to live.

Lea closed her eyes and seemed to gather herself. Then, she turned to embrace him and held on to him. Seconds passed. Seth laid his head on her shoulder, just as he had when he was a little boy, and then he released her.

"I have to go, Lea."

She nodded, peering at their joined hands for a second, and then lifting her head to look him in the eye earnestly. "Godspeed," she croaked hoarsely, squeezing his hands.

Not trusting his voice, he only nodded and left her, dragging himself onto his perch atop the wagon, and snapping the reins. He looked back once; Lea still stood in the road, covering her face with her hands. Seth drove on.

A HALF-HOUR FURTHER into their journey, Seth ran into a roadblock in the form of two sentries and a humongous felled tree that spanned the width of the road.

"State your business, Morristonian."

"I am a Hamiltonian, and I wish to see the king."

Seth heard the faint sound of an arrow being drawn to a bow. Searching the woods to his left, he counted four archers, partially hidden by the trees. There were at least three more on the right.

The sentry laughed heartily, elbowing his partner in the ribs. "He wishes to see the king."

Seth glared and his jaw became like stone. Here was the test. Did the king still have love in his heart for his daughter? If so, he could get Adi the help she needed; if not, he might be putting her in further danger.

Seth made his decision.

His tongue was sweating, and he could not form the words at first. "I have Princess Adriana in the back. She is deathly ill. We need to see the king's physician."

The sentry's face sobered. He approached the wagon, keeping his eyes on Seth, who kept his hands in his lap, loosely holding the reins. When the man came to the side of the wagon, he chanced a quick glance in the back.

"Well, why did you not say so? Let him through," he called to those behind him, waving them off as he did so.

Seth urged the horses forward, watching the arrows still strung and pointed toward him from the trees.

"Stand down!" came the shouted order. "The princess is on board and needs medical help. Stand down, I say!"

Gradually the archers lowered their bows, while keeping their arrows strung and watching him with suspicious eyes.

Seth heard a horseman take flight through the woods on his right, a messenger, no doubt.

He ran into no more trouble until he hit the bridge he helped to build. The guard there raised a hand to stop him.

"Are you the one that carries the princess?"

"Aye."

The man nodded. "You will have to leave your wagon here, by the king's order. He is out, but Sir Lucian will see you through." He jerked his head to indicate the young runner who had brought the news of his arrival as far as the bridge. The young man's horse skittered on the bridge.

"But the princess is unable to walk, I tell you. She is gravely injured."

"'Tis the king's order," the guard shrugged indifferently.

Seth swung from his seat, staring furiously at the man. Why could these sentries not learn to think for themselves a little? Surely the king would have let a wagon through with his injured daughter aboard. He worried further jostling would send Adriana over the edge, but he had no real choice. He made a move to unhitch Champion.

"No horse either."

He stood, dumbfounded, but then climbed into the back of the wagon, murmuring to Adi, though he knew she could not hear him.

"Here we are, sweetheart. You hang on. Not much longer now."

He bent to scoop her up. When he reached the back of the wagon, two guards scurried over to help him out, but he stubbornly stared them down and they backed away. He jumped, trying to absorb the impact himself, but still, he knew it pained her, even though she did not wince or cry out or show any change whatsoever. This worried him. Was he too late? Forgetting for a second where he was, he feathered a kiss over her forehead. Then, remembering himself, he straightened and walked with her toward the bridge, his back held straight.

Watching him, it seemed the sentry finally felt a twinge of guilt. "I could have one of my men take her on his horse...?"

Seth glowered defiantly at him and strode past without commenting. But after a bit, he began to pay a price for his stubbornness. Although Adi was light, and he was strong, the castle was still quite a distance and his muscles strained with his burden. He was afraid to adjust her much, too, which would have helped his tired muscles; but he did not want the shifting to add to her discomfort.

Two horsemen flanked him on either side, hanging back and watching the display of strength and love.

By the time he crossed the long lawn toward the castle, his arms were beginning to shake and his legs felt as tight as a bow string.

Across the lawn, Garin was having breakfast with several of his advisors on a wide terrace. Their loud laughter carried on the wind to where Seth struggled forward with Adi.

When the man Garin was speaking with gawked, staring fixedly over his shoulder at some unknown sight, Garin spun to see the strange parade headed in his direction. A man was carrying a woman, who appeared to be dead, while two of his men followed at a little bit of a distance. The man held his head high, and walked resolutely across the grounds. When he got closer, Garin recognized the blacksmith Adi left him for. The man's veins stood out on his arms and his muscles shook and, though he still despised him, Garin had to admire the commoner. After all, it was insane for the man to have entered his court when he had spirited Adi off, a death wish, in fact.

"Well I'll be damned," Garin said under his breath.

He stepped down the two broad steps of the terrace and onto the grass as the conversation ceased behind him, all eyes now on the stranger carrying the woman across the lawn. Again the Commander had to respect a man whose strength of love would carry him to such extremes. And that was when it dawned on him. The woman that he loved, that he brought forward, must be... He stumbled forward a few steps, his face no doubt advertising his shock. He closed the gap between them.

"What have you done?" he cried out. His eyes were wide with horror, as he gazed at the princess's face.

"It is not what I have done!" Seth's voice thundered, veins bulging in his neck. "It's what *you* have done, you and your men."

He looked accusingly at Derrick who stood a few feet to his right, looking green. Then his hard stare swung back to Garin's face.

"Did you order them to shoot her?"

"What? Of course not! And anyone who did something like that will suffer for it." Garin twisted a little to glare at Derrick, his look meant to feel like the cold edge of a blade. Two men stepped behind Derrick as if to bar his retreat.

Garin turned back to Seth.

"'Tis as much your fault as mine. If you had not taken her away—"

"'Tis true. It was an arrow made with my own hands that pierced her," Seth admitted. The pain that admission caused him was clear in his eyes.

Garin almost felt sorry for him. He reached out involuntarily to stroke Adi's hair and felt the heat radiating out from her. His gaze flew to Seth.

"What? She is still alive?"

He dropped his eyes to her face, with a bewildered look, as if just realizing she was there. "Barely," he answered, his voice choked with grief.

Garin snapped his fingers and a man ran to his side.

"You there. You." He pointed at two other men behind him. "Get that tablecloth and use it like a sling to carry her inside. "Get Dr. Lancing immediately," he ordered the first man who had answered his call.

The men did as they were told, stretching the cloth on the ground in front of Seth and then began to take Adi from him, but they hesitated when they saw the fierce look on his face.

When he seemed certain they would come no farther, he looked at Garin.

"I want your promise, your *word,* you will not hurt her."

"Look," Garin replied with irritation, "I know you fancy you love Adi, but surely you understand you are not the only man who does. You have

known her for...what? A year or two? I have known and loved her all my life."
By the time he finished, his voice trembled with fury and pain.

Seth studied his face for a long minute, and then nodded. He bent and gently laid Adi on the tablecloth and kissed her face.

Garin swallowed, amazed at the man's gall to kiss his Adi right in front of him. But, at the same time, he was moved by the love he saw reflected in Seth's tear-filled eyes.

Seth stood back, and let the men carry Adi away. He made an attempt to follow them, but Garin stepped into his path.

"I'm sorry, *friend*, but commoners, such as yourself, are not allowed inside the palace. I am certain you understand," he added sarcastically.

Seth had known there would be a price Garin would exact for having taken Adi from him. So this was to be it, then; he would not be allowed to be with her while they administered to her.

He swallowed. He looked again at Garin. He wanted to wipe the sneer from his face with his fist, but he knew he would have to curb both his temper and his pride in order to get Adi the help she needed.

"You will help her? Your doctor will make her better?"

Garin assessed him, his eyes now hard as the marble stairs beneath his feet. He twisted away from Seth, raising his goblet and taking a sip from it. He stared at the dark doorway his men had taken Adi through.

"Why should I?" he asked without turning. "After all, she left me to go to your bed."

Seth lunged forward but was immediately caught by three of the men.

"You will *not* speak of my wife like that!" he spat, as he struggled to free himself and attack Garin, despite his former resolution not to.

Garin whirled around. "Your *wife*?" he screamed, incredulous. "She..." He seemed unable to bring himself to say it. "She married *you*?" His distaste for the man he considered vastly inferior was evident. "Oh, ho, ho!" he chuckled mirthlessly. "This changes the situation. This changes it."

Seth cursed himself for telling him.

Garin paced back and forth in front of him, rubbing his chin thoughtfully.

"When did this...*marriage*," he said, as if the point was in question, "take place?"

"Yesterday," Seth answered grimly.

Garin stopped midway through the circuit he had been walking in the grass and stared at him. "What, when she was out of her mind with fever?"

"She was better then," he growled in response.

"Of course she was," Garin threw out. He continued to pace for a minute.

Seth shifted his weight, trying to see through the doorway where they had taken Adi, but could not make out anything.

Garin stopped, as if he had arrived at a decision. He came to stand in front of Seth.

"I will take care of Adi. I will nurse her back to health, get her any medicine she should need, and provide the finest doctors. But, there is one condition."

Seth looked at Garin blandly, although inside his heart was pounding. So there was even a higher price to pay.

"You must leave here. Leave her with me, and never return."

"What?" he balked. "Did you not hear me say that she is my *wife*?"

Garin recoiled at the word.

"I heard, blacksmith, but she was to be *my* wife. Do you not remember?" he fumed, stepping up to within inches of his face. "Or maybe you try not to think of the vow she made to me, maybe it is easier on your conscience that way."

"*She made no vow to you!*" he roared, his eyes sparking. "It was a vow her father made to your father. She did not choose you at all. She chose me." Seth regretted the words the instant he had uttered them, but his grief and exhaustion had muddled his head. "And we did not break that vow in any case. We waited until she was twenty-one."

"Well, that is cold comfort to me, now, is it not?" Garin replied deadly soft, his gaze shifting between Seth's eyes. He pivoted. He waited a minute or two while Seth silently considered his ultimatum, but then, suddenly, he spun on his heel to face him again.

"Enough! It is time for you to make your decision. You may take your...*wife*...with you, to bury her, or you can leave her here with me, so she can live. What will it be?"

Seth stared at him in disbelief. Could Garin really be that cruel? Could he really sentence the woman he once loved to death for loving another? Because that was what it came down to, he knew. He thought about the scars on Adi's hands. A man that would do that in jealousy might dismiss her now for spite, if she was to leave with *him*.

He turned his back to Garin, his hands on his hips, head lowered.

Can I do that? Just let her go?

She was dying, he knew...if he took her away from the help she needed, it was really him sentencing her to death then, was it not?

He slowly swung back, broken. "Aye."

"Aye? Aye what?"

"Aye. I will leave, and never return, as long as you help her."

"I have your word?"

Seth looked off to the side, fighting the tears back, then again looked at Garin.

"I have said it, man! Must you hear it again? Aye, then. You have my word."

He whipped around and left so quickly the men behind him, who had dismounted from their horses, had to jump out of his way. He never looked back, just strode across the lawn as he had come in, a lone figure on the field of green.

ADI'S EYES OPENED SLOWLY. The first thing that she noticed was an astonishing absence of pain. The next was she was in her own bedroom in Ramport. She twisted her head and saw Garin leaning against the door to the balcony, staring off across the fields.

"Garin?"

His head snapped around and his posture relaxed, but he remained remote.

"Aye."

She looked around the room again as if to verify what she had already surmised. "I am at Ramport?"

"Aye."

"Where is...?" She hesitated.

"The blacksmith? That is fine, you can say his name. You have been calling it out in your sleep for hours now," he snapped.

She blushed, searching for words to say that would not anger him, but before she could, he spoke again.

"You *married* him, Adi?" The betrayal he felt was written on his face.

"I am sorry," she answered softly. "I love—"

He slammed his hand against the door jam. "You love him! I know! That has never been more evident than when I sat here, losing sleep, worrying over you, while you called out for *him*."

She understood now why his face was haggard, his eyes bloodshot. "I am sorry."

"I know. You have said that," he fumed. "Did you...consummate...your marriage?"

"Garin!"

"Answer me, Adi!" he screamed, furious. "Answer me!"

He advanced on her threateningly, and she cried out, "Nay. Nay. Is that what you wanted to hear?" Tears spilled from her eyes as she lost her composure. "I could barely make it through the wedding itself."

"I suppose you passed out in his arms?" he spat sarcastically.

"Nay—" she tried to rein in her emotions "—into Lawry's, actually."

"Lawry was there?"

Garin could not help the look of pleasure that crossed his face when he spoke his old friend's name, but it was coupled with hurt. Lawry had been his best friend in his youth, and he had been the one who was constantly there for Adi. Garin wished, in a way, that he could have been there for her, too. He cursed the fact that, where once, everything in his life had seemed so clear to him, now, since the blacksmith had entered the picture, he felt perpetually confused.

He took another step forward. "Adi, I love you," he blurted out.

"And I love you, Garin. That has not changed." She reached out for his hand, and he could hardly doubt her sincerity. "It is just..."

"You are *in* love with him," he murmured sadly.

She nodded.

"Why, Adi? Why him and not me? What do I lack?" He kissed her hand, and laid his cheek on it.

Adi seemed moved, she stroked his hair briefly.

"You lack nothing, Garin. It is just...it is hard to explain. It is like...remember when you tried to teach me how to play backgammon?" She smiled.

He snorted. "Do I ever? You were completely hopeless."

She laughed. "You say that because you based your plays totally on logic, while I made mine by caprice. And you tried to explain to me why you enjoyed it so much, and could not."

"Aye," he said with a sigh. "I remember." He paused. "You are not truly comparing your husband to a backgammon game, are you?" He couldn't help but smile. This was what she did to him.

She laughed. "You know what I mean. Sometimes it is hard to explain why something is so special to you, it just is."

Garin lightly kissed her fingers.

"I am not the man you left behind, Adi."

She started to protest.

"Hear me out. In the war I...saw things that no man should have to see. I considered myself a soldier before, but a man is not a soldier until he has had to fight." He looked off in the distance, his heart squeezing. "There was this boy...he was probably fourteen, but he had told me he was sixteen in order to join my troops. I had to—" his voice became choked, "—tell his mother... I tried to protect him, but, there were too many of them. He died in my arms, Adi. That kind of thing changes you. I began to examine my life, and I did not like what I saw. Especially when it came to you. I took you for granted, and worse," he turned her palm over and traced the scars tenderly, "I hurt you. I do not want to be that man anymore. And I want to make it up to you."

SETH STROLLED MOROSELY through the orchard at dusk. This had become his habit again. It was the place where he felt Adi most, where he had been reunited with her, where he had wed her. For the hundredth time, he revisited his decision to leave her in Garin's hands. But, in all reality, it had not been a decision, he told himself again. She was dying, he simply had no choice. He wondered how she was now, where she was, what she was doing. Now the sun was nearly down, the air grew cooler. Autumn was approaching fast; the thought depressed him even more. How many lonely autumns would he spend thinking about Adi?

As he shuffled through the orchard, dragging his feet in the dirt, he heard the distant sound of a horse approaching. Curious as to who would be travelling in the gloom, he lifted his head. He could hear the hoofbeats more clearly now. The traveler was flying over the ground, a dangerous mistake in the low-hanging branches. They must be desperate to reach their destination, he concluded.

Minutes later, the horse came into view, a woman aboard wearing a thick travelling cape with the hood raised. She reined the horse in about ten yards from him and slid from the saddle, seemingly in one motion. She stood frozen for a minute, and that is when Seth recognized the horse. It was Lancer. He had left him in the hands of the bridge guard, telling the man the steed belonged to Princess Adriana. Had they sent word of her recovery?

The woman pulled back the hood, her chestnut hair flowing out recklessly. His heart was in his throat. Adi ran forward and embraced him tightly, too emotional to speak. He buried his big hands in her tumble of hair, clasping her to himself desperately for fear of her disappearing again. After minutes of struggling with their emotions, he tilted her head back, rubbing his thumbs across her skin, and gazed into her face.

"How?" he uttered brokenly.

"He set me free!" She sobbed. "Garin set me free."

He drew her in again, his face in her hair, almost afraid to believe it. "Why?" he whispered in her ear.

"I do not know. It does not matter." She leaned away. "He told me you left me there in exchange for him getting me the medical attention I needed."

He pushed the hair back from her face urgently, hoping that he could make her understand. "It was the hardest thing I have ever done, Adi, I—"

"I know. I know," she breathed, closing her eyes for a minute.

He fingered the arrowhead she wore on a chain around her neck. "Is this...?" She nodded. "I would have thought you would want to be through with it forever."

"Oh, nay," she exclaimed, clasping it. "'Twas this arrow that brought me to you. If not for it, I would have never wound up on your doorstep."

He looked at her with a slight frown. "You have an odd fashion of looking at things, you know."

"I know," she replied with an impish grin. They stood gazing at each other for several seconds.

"I missed you," Seth finally whispered, kissing her forehead, and her cheeks, and then beginning to cover her whole face with fast, desperate kisses, that she matched with kisses of her own, until their lips collided. "Oh, Adi! I have waited so long for you." Her eyes were misty, as drugged with desire as he. He bent and swept her off of her feet, kissing her again. "I want to take you home." His voice was hoarse.

She laughed freely. "You cannot carry me all the way back to the cottage, silly."

He laughed in return. "You want to wager on that? I carried you from the bridge over the River Astri to Ramport."

"What?"

"You probably do not remember much. You were in bad shape." His heart squeezed at the thought. "But you are well now? Totally well?"

"Aye." She played with a lock of his hair. "Still a tad sore, but, all-in-all, a much faster and easier recovery than the first time around."

"I cannot believe you are back. That you are actually here, in my arms."

"I know." She sighed, laying her head on his chest.

"Here we are," he announced at his door. "Now I get to carry you over the threshold, as I should have on our wedding day. Well, I guess I did, actually. But it was only because you had passed out."

"I wish I could remember. I do not want to have missed even one moment with you."

He set her down, moving one hand to the back of her neck, one to her face. He could not stop touching her. "There are some moments you would not want to remember. You were in a lot of pain."

"I am sorry," she murmured, looking at her hands as they glided along the edges of his jacket. "I know that was difficult for you."

"None of that matters." He caressed her cheeks. "All that matters is you are here with me, now and for—"

"For a lifetime," she finished.

He held her close once more. "Oh, my Adi," he murmured, squeezing his eyes shut. "Welcome home." He kissed her again, tenderly at first, but growing more passionate.

She lifted her chin as he kissed her neck. "Take me to your bed."

He needed no further urging, and he did not have far to go in his little one-room cottage. He took her cloak from her shoulders, placing it on a kitchen chair, then led her, silently, holding her hand, to the bed he carved for her.

"I did not have time to make the bed," he muttered apologetically.

"'Tis fine." She smoothed the sheets, as if trying to imagine the warmth his body would have given them. "I like the idea of your having slept here." She lifted her gaze, her lips parted, desire swimming in her eyes. The intensity between them was almost painful.

He could not wait a second more. He slid his hands beneath her soft, thick hair and kissed her, hard, on the mouth, wanting to make her truly his, as he had from the start. His hands went to the buttons on her dress and he patiently undid them, until he could push it from her shoulders. "You are so beautiful," he whispered in awe. She wore only a thin, linen shift, white, with thick straps. He ran his hands along her bare shoulders, trailing his fingertips across her skin. She trembled. "Are ye cold? I should stoke the fire." He turned to leave and she yanked him back by the lapels of his coat.

"You have already," she said hoarsely, hauling him in for a kiss.

Adi tugged at his jacket, and Seth stepped back to shrug it off. He ripped his loose-fitting shirt off over his head.

"Mmm..." she murmured with approval. Her hands slid up the center of his chest slowly, and out to his shoulders as she watched them skim along his bronzed skin, taking in every chiseled inch of the physique that had set her atremble since the beginning. Now that she could touch him, she was appreciative of each swing of his hammer that made his body so solid and toned. Her hands continued to his shoulders and down. Her next moan was caught in his mouth as he pressed his to hers again, pushing her back against the bed frame.

She grabbed the post behind her head, arching her back as he lowered his head to her chest, feverishly working at the buttons on her shift to free the rest of her to him. As soon as the garment was open below her breasts he cupped them possessively. Her nipples were hard even before he brought his thumbs to circle them, but she pressed into his hands even so. He squeezed and her urgency was almost unbearable until his hands slid around beneath her clothing to her buttocks, letting her relax for a second and take a breath. Then, with a jolt that forced the breath from her, he pulled her closer so that her pelvis was against his groin, heat to heat.

She felt the bed behind her, folding the covers back so she could lie in it. He climbed next to her on his side, continuing to unbutton. When, at last, she was completely naked on the bed, his hands journeyed over every inch of her skin, testing each curve. She felt his lips and tongue on the flat of her stomach, and threaded her fingers through his hair, her body humming beneath him as he traveled even lower. He came back to kiss her, long and deep, and his hand between her legs. With strong fingers, he rhythmically drew circles until she cried out and her world was full of a soft, golden light that spread from her hair to the tips of her toes.

Seth watched her breathe in deeply, a new and fascinating creature.

"Mmm, more."

She tugged at his pants and he complied with her request. Soon that piece of clothing, too, lay abandoned somewhere. On the floor? On the bed? His lips cruised over her again, tasting the inner curve of her thigh, then higher, crossing her stomach. He reveled in the feel of the ultra-soft skin below each breast before sucking a nipple into his mouth, loving the sensations it gave him, and relishing how much it affected her.

With only the moon lighting her face, he could see her eyes squeezed shut in sweet pain, watch the corners of her lips rise when he hit a particularly pleasant spot. Though her body was ready, he still entered her carefully. He felt an initial wave of satisfaction, but soon desire, the beast clawing inside of him, took the reins again, urging him on. He rose above her, thrusting forcefully and then sliding back. In. Out. She rose to meet him. The need he ignited in her had her clutching the pillows above her head and calling out his name in the dark. The sound of her voice, laced with passion and whimpering with need, drove him insane. As he drew her again toward the finish, she placed her hands to his buttocks, pulling him in desperately with each vital drive. She made a soft sound in her throat and he felt her relax beneath him. He slowed his movements to let her enjoy the sensation, but quickly found he could wait no more. He relinquished himself to the same golden light, an explosion so profound pinpoints of light flashed behind his eyelids.

He lay heavily on top of her as his heartbeat returned to normal, and she glided her fingers along his back, upwards and outwards, and down again. He enjoyed the way they were molded together as if from the same piece of clay, or like the metal, melted in his forge. They stayed like that for some time without speaking, content, until he could tell his weight had become too much and he rolled to one side. She shifted onto her side next to him, throwing a leg over his lower legs and pressing as close as possible so they were connected all along the length of their bodies. She fell asleep in his arms, just as he had dreamed of for a long time.

He delighted in the oneness they shared.

Nothing separated them now. Nothing ever could.

CHAPTER TWENTY-EIGHT

Adriana woke to shouting and confusion. Someone was dragging her out of the bed. When he switched holds to grab her under her arms, she clutched desperately at the sheets even as she opened her eyes to identify her attacker. It was a man she never met before, but she recognized the colors of his uniform. He was one of her father's men and he was not alone.

"Nay! Stop!" she cried, but she was already almost on the floor. She managed to take the sheets and a quilt with her, but before she could wrap it around body, she felt one of the men touch the bare skin of her bottom. She shrieked. As one of the soldiers finally secured her around her waist, half lifting her to her feet, she saw three other men at Seth's side of the bed. One held a sword tip at his throat.

"Seth!" she screamed, afraid of what the men might do to him.

She saw one tall, fierce-looking soldier throw Seth's pants on top of him. Then the two men struggling with her were finally able to bustle her out the door.

She was thrust forward and fell awkwardly to her knees. Fighting her way to her feet, she accidentally stepped on the sheets. When she righted herself, she tugged again at them to make certain she was not exposed. Her hair was a wild jumble of curls as she shook it out of her face, unable to use her hands to push it back.

She stood in the middle of the yard, facing a large, dark-haired, bearded man on an enormous horse.

"Ana! You have shamed me!" her father roared, swinging out of his saddle to stand before her.

She was shaking with rage.

"Nay, Father! It is you who has shamed me. How dare you come here and drag me out of my bed—"

Behind her, Seth was shoved out the door, his hands bound behind him. His lip was bleeding. Hair in his eyes, he glowered at the soldiers and still fought to free himself.

"A bed you shared with this commoner!" the king spat angrily, glaring at him.

"This commoner, as you called him, is my husband!"

While the word still hung on her lips, the king struck her brutally, knocking her off her feet.

Seth cursed him and strained against his captors, breaking free for a moment, but his momentum caused him to stumble forward. The metallic sound of a sword being released from its sheath accompanied his fall, and before he could get to his feet he found the edge of a blade again at his throat.

Slowly, painstakingly, Adi rose from the ground. She gathered her covers, but not before giving the men behind her a quick view of her despite her best efforts.

To add to her utter embarrassment, she saw Lea and Tristan had been dragged from their house to watch the proceedings.

Her voice quivered. "Why did you come here to humiliate me like this?"

"I have come to take you home. No daughter of mine is going to roll around between the sheets with some commoner."

Something snapped inside her.

"There is nothing common about this man!" she shrieked, "He is uncommonly good. And uncommonly loving. He has supported his sister, and her son—" she looked in their direction, becoming a little choked up when she caught Lea's eyes "—ever since she lost her husband. He is kind to everyone he meets, and decent, with a strong sense of right and wrong and the will to follow his conscience, even when it hurts him to do so."

She looked back at Seth, and her gaze softened, a look he returned.

"If that were true, he would have left you alone instead of seducing you and making you into his little whore."

There was a shout from Seth and two more soldiers rushed forward as he battled. One grabbed the back of his hair and jerked his head back to expose his neck more, which was cut a little. Blood dripped down his chest.

"Seth!" She moved toward him, but was barred by a soldier's arm.

"Papa!" she called out in her distress, looking at him with tears in her eyes.

"Stop!" he ordered. And then more quietly, "Not here."

His meaning was clear.

"Papa!" she begged, hearing the sound of Lea's gasp behind her. "You cannot do this. You cannot!" She sobbed.

The soldiers made an effort to drag Seth away.

"DON'T!" she shouted, falling again to her knees. "Please, Father, please."

The king hesitated for a second.

Inside, she tightened with resolve. She stared unflinchingly into her father's eyes.

"If you kill him, I will kill myself. No matter how hard your men try to guard me, I will find a way, and you know I will." Her voice came out flat and low but definite.

"Adriana, you do not mean this. You are being irrational. You think you have feelings for this man, but what you are feeling is simply lust."

"Nay, Father. I love him with my whole heart. This is no flight of fancy. He is the man I have pledged myself to." She peered at Seth now, for a moment, forgetting all the others and spoke directly to him.

"The man who I am to share a lifetime with."

"ENOUGH!" the king bellowed. "I will not listen to this rubbish."

She knew better than to press further.

The king ran his hand through his thick hair as he considered his options.

"So be it, Ana. You win," he spat. "But you will not receive one farthing from me." He whirled around to mount his horse, then looked her directly in the eyes. "As far as I am concerned—" he continued, his voice as cold as the steel at Seth's neck "—you are no longer my daughter."

A strange whimpering noise came out of her mouth. She tried to collect herself, though the tears rolled unchecked.

"Father. The money means nothing to me, but...surely you do not mean I cannot come to visit you from time to time."

His voice was harsh and distant, but his eyes revealed his deep sorrow. "From this day forward I will not speak another word to you."

He turned his horse around and started forward.

"Papa. Papa! *Please!*" Adi tried to get to her feet to follow him. She stretched out one trembling hand but the king spurred his horse into a run.

The soldier who had his sword to Seth's throat lifted it, and brought the hilt crashing down onto his head before leaving with the others.

Lea rushed to Adi, while Tristan went to Seth, who moaned and shook his head, trying to clear it.

Adi was folded in two, sobbing as if her heart had been split open. None of Lea's efforts to console reached her.

Seth stared at his wife, huddled in front of him, as Tristan quickly worked the cords binding him with a pocketknife. He sawed back and forth until they lay, useless, on the ground. Seth staggered forward, falling to his knees at her side. It was not until he spoke that she reacted, his words penetrating the grief that engulfed her. She twisted to clutch on to him, further distraught when she saw the condition he was in.

"I am so s-sorry," she choked out between sobs. She continued to utter apology after apology, unable to stop the words from spilling out of her mouth.

"Sh-sh-sh. Adi, honey...I am fine. Shh." He sat back on his heels, gathering her closer as she wept unrestrainedly. He kissed the top of her head. "Let us get you inside, now."

Lea and Tristan helped them inside, where they collapsed onto the bed together, wrapped in each other's arms. They were alone, finally able to seek and find comfort in one another.

SETH WHISTLED AS HE ducked under the branches threatening to snag his hair in the orchard. He had seen Adi disappear into the trees from his blacksmith's shop, and followed her. Ahead, he caught sight of her leaning against a tree trunk. The last rays of the dying sun made her outline shimmer. He was struck by her beauty, as he so often was, and stopped dead in his tracks to just watch her.

Over the past few weeks, he had come to know that gorgeous body well. Their bed had become their haven—a port in a storm—where they were learning to weather anything that came their way.

Seth knew she was still grieving the loss of her father. Although she tried to act as if nothing was wrong throughout the day, he had noticed how quiet she had become. And at night, her passion burned out of control. She took from him all the love he would give her, hoping to somehow fill the gaping hole in her heart. He knew, in a sense, she was using him to fill that void. But if being used felt like this, he thought, he was all for it.

He let his gaze slide along each familiar subtle curve of her figure and allowed his imagination to run away with him for a few minutes.

As he watched, she stooped to pluck a leaf from the patchwork gathered on the ground. She twirled it by the stem and he noted it had chosen to go out in a blaze of red. But then, he saw her shoulders begin to shake and his heart became heavy. Her hands moved to cover her face, as if to hide from the world, even here, in the stillness of the orchard.

He started forward, but at the sound of a stick breaking beneath his boot, Adi jumped, twisting her back to him a little and furiously rubbing at her face.

"Oh, Seth." She tried to sound lighthearted. "I did not hear you coming."

She faced him, more composed. He strode to her, taking the leaf from her hand and spinning it.

"Aye, I know." He held up the leaf. "'Tis pretty—" he brushed her face softly with the back of his hand "—like you."

She blushed but said nothing. He leaned in, resting his forearm on the tree behind her, much as he had that day outside of Ramport's walls when he came to understand he was falling in love with her. He bent his head, noting the quickening of her breath as he took her lips with his, pulling at them gently with his own, as though he were reaching into her core and tugging on her heartstrings. He could feel the rapid beating of her heart against his chest and was pleased he could still excite her like he had in the beginning of their time together.

He separated from her, and she opened her eyes slowly, unable to hide the pain in their blue-grey depths. He ached for her. He played with her hair, then looked steadily at her, shifting his gaze from one eye to the other.

"You have been crying," he noted. A statement, not a question.

She looked down and the mask she had been wearing slid a little, the forced smile fading, her face crumpling with the crushing sorrow she could not avoid. She nodded slightly. He put a fist underneath her chin and lifted it, seeing the tears pooling in her eyes.

"Adi," he breathed, completely captivated by her. He swallowed and looked down himself, trying to come to grips with his own feelings for her. "You do not need to hide this from me. We are to share all now, as man and wife."

"I know," she said. "I am sorry."

"Stop saying that," he insisted.

"I just...I did not need to upset anyone else."

"But that is what I am here for. I am supposed to support you."

Their conversation was interrupted by the sound of a horse approaching at a rapid pace. Both Seth and Adi turned toward the sound, and in a minute a lone horseman appeared. As he came to a stop and dismounted, Seth stepped in front of Adi protectively. After all, the last time her father had visited he had struck her. But she ducked around him, staring at her father wide-eyed.

"Father? Something is wrong. Is it Garin? It is not Garin, is it?"

The king noticed how Adriana instinctively reached for Seth's hand and how he, in return, very naturally rubbed his thumb across the top of her hand to comfort her, even as he stood rigid, in protective mode.

"Nay, it is not Garin."

"Lawry, then...it is Lawry, is it not?"

"Nay, it is not Lawrence, either. As far as I know, he is well."

She relaxed a little, but studied his face intently. She retreated a step and took Seth's other hand.

"What then?"

The king gazed at her, then looked at Seth pointedly. "I came to talk to *you*."

"If you think I am going to leave you alone with—"

Adi cut in. "Anything you need to say to me can be said in front of my husband."

King Henry looked at Seth again.

"Aye," he replied.

Surprise registered on their faces as he took a tentative step forward, his eyes only on Adi now.

"I was wrong, Ana, horribly wrong, about you and what is best for you. Garin, actually," he said, chagrined, "brought me up short when he found out about what happened the last time I was here." He felt the heat rush to his face at the thought. "And he made me see sense."

They stood as if dumbstruck.

He turned and walked in a circle. "I see, now, that this blacksmith—"

"His name is Seth," Adi muttered.

"Seth," he repeated slowly. "I see what you have here with Seth is something quite uncommon." He sighed. "Garin asked me if it would have mattered if my dear Victoria had been a villager, and I knew that the answer was, not at all. I loved her, as you love Seth." He paused, looking behind her now. "I owe you an apology, too, son. I never gave you a fair chance. I would like to...beg your forgiveness."

Seth stood frozen, reading his face. He saw sorrow and regret, but not treachery. He released Adi's hand and held his out to the king.

"You have it, Sir."

The king visibly relaxed, shaking his hand warmly and covering it with his other hand.

"What about you, Ana?" he asked tentatively. "Can you forgive your old Papa?"

Instead of speaking, she stepped forward, encircling his waist with her arms and laying her head on his chest, weeping.

"Oh, now," he said, appearing surprised. "There, there, Ana. Everything is fine now."

The king glanced at Seth, looking uncomfortable. He smiled and took two big steps backward before whirling and walking off, leaving them alone.

As Seth walked, ducking his head under branches every so often, he began to examine what he had with Adi too. It was rare, to be sure, a love like theirs. He chuckled. Who would have ever thought that he would fall in love with, and marry, a princess? The thought was absolutely ridiculous.

He smiled and headed home.

NOTE FROM THE AUTHOR

Thank you for reading AN UNCOMMON LOVE, part of my RO-
MANTIC REALMS COLLECTION. I hope you enjoyed it. Now that
you've read the book, won't you please consider writing a review? Reviews
are one of the best ways readers discover great new books. They don't need to
be fancy or long, just a sentence or two honestly describing your opinion of/
experience with the book. I would sincerely appreciate it.

Want more from M.J. Schiller?
Page forward for an excerpt from
TO HELL IN A COACH BAG
DEVILISH DIVAS SERIES, Book One

TO HELL IN A COACH BAG

Tucker

The heads popped up in unison, and Maxine stared at Sam who was pale as a ghost. "I am *so* sorry."

"That's okay," Sam answered quickly.

"Okay?" Alex screamed. "That's a four-hundred-dollar Coach purse."

That got my attention. I stuck out my head. "Excuse me, ladies, but I couldn't help but overhear. Did you say four-hundred-dollar purse?"

"Oh, Tucker," Maxine wailed, taking ahold of my shirt with both fists. "You *have* to get that purse."

"O-o-okay." Was she the next to crack? I started to leave, but Max called me back.

"Oh, and Tucker, be careful."

"I will," I replied, bewildered. It wasn't like I was going to have to scale the edge of the building to get it. There were stairs.

It was not until I got below that I understood her statement. The billion-dollar purse was stuck on a tree branch hanging over a muddy ravine separating the tennis courts from the outer courtyard. Here and there, quaint little bridges crossed the ravine. There had been some recent mountain storms, and it was plenty full at that point. I looked to the balcony where the three women watched me.

"How much did you say this purse cost?" I yelled.

"Four-hundred dollars," they yelled in unison.

As I leaned against the tree trunk and took off my loafers, I glared at them, wondering about the twisty path that brought me to this. I jumped and caught a low branch, then muscled my way to sit on it.

"Oh, my!" Maxine exclaimed.

I analyzed the branch the purse was hooked on and noted no branches were near enough to it. One above it appeared questionable, with patches of stripped bark. I climbed higher, hoping to angle in its direction, and finally made it to a position where I was directly above it. I laid flat on the branch, holding on with one hand. The other I tried to extend to the purse. I was within inches. Pushing a little farther, I leaned to my right and gave my reach the added inch, and I snagged it.

"Got it!" I called triumphantly. But as I did, my weight carried me around the branch, and I found myself hanging upside down, with my arms and legs wrapped around the branch. Squeals of delight came from the Musketeers, but I ignored them and concentrated on my predicament.

I needed to free my hands to walk myself back in, so I stuck the strap of the purse in my mouth, careful not to leave bite marks on the expensive leather. But when I grabbed the branch again, an unpleasant noise sounded over the rush of the water below. I prayed the snapping came from another branch, and held very still, just in case. To my relief, nothing happened.

Until I began to inch back toward the trunk, at which point a very loud *crack* rent the air. Oh shit. My stomach lurched as I fell through the air, hitting several smaller branches on my way to the ground. I landed with a thud on the soggy bank.

From above came a threefold gasp, followed by a hushed silence.

I assessed my condition, moving to determine if anything was broken. Sore yes, broken no. So, I rose, covered in mud like a horror movie swamp monster. It was smeared on my face, in my hair, and all over my white shirt. I held out my arms as they dripped and looked at my trio of spectators.

"Oh, good. You still have it," Sam yelled happily.

TO HELL IN A COACH BAG can be purchased at: https://books2read.com/ToHellInACoachBag

ALSO FROM M.J. SCHILLER

ROMANTIC REALMS COLLECTION:

TAKEN BY STORM
AN UNCOMMON LOVE
LEAP INTO THE KNIGHT
LADY OF THE KNIGHT
A KNIGHT TO REMEMBER

ROCKING ROMANCE COLLECTION:

TRAPPED UNDER ICE
ABANDON ALL HOPE
BETWEEN ROCK AND A HARD PLACE
ROCK ME, GENTLY
MIDNIGHT MELODY

REAL ROMANCE COLLECTION:

UPON A MIDNIGHT CLEAR
THE HEART TEACHES BEST
DAMAGE DONE
HOMETOWN HEARTACHE
TAKE A CHANCE ON ME
BLACKOUT

DEVILISH DESIRES SERIES:

TO HELL IN A COACH BAG
DAMNED IF I DO
THE DEVIL YOU KNOW
SATAN, LINE ONE
PITCHFORK IN THE ROAD

SIN WORTH THE PENANCE
HELL HATH NO FURY
SATAN'S SPAWN
TEN MINUTES IN THE SIN BIN
DEVIL'S IN THE DETAILS (*Coming soon!*)
DEVIL'S ADVOCATE (*Coming soon!*)
HADES NIGHT (*Coming soon!*)

LOVE AND CHAOS SERIES:

ROCKED BY GRACE
ROCKED BY LOVE
ROCK IT TO THE MOON
ROCK OF SALVATION

LAST CHANCE BEACH ROMANCE/INSATIABLE FIRE SERIES:

BEATING IN TIME
LEAD ME ON
ROCK TO THE RHYTHM
BASSIST'S INSTINCTS (*Coming soon!*)

ABOUT THE AUTHOR

BESTSELLING AUTHOR M.J. Schiller is a retired lunch lady/romance-romantic suspense writer. She enjoys writing novels whose characters include rock stars, desert princes, teachers, futuristic Knights, construction workers, cops, and a wide variety of others. In her mind everybody has a romance. She is the mother of a twenty-seven-year-old and three twenty-five-year-olds. That's right, triplets! So having recently taught four children to drive, she likes to escape from life on occasion by pretending to be a rock star at karaoke. However...you won't be seeing her name on any record labels soon.

www.ingramcontent.com/pod-product-compliance
Lightning Source LLC
Chambersburg PA
CBHW061156170626
46809CB00003B/1126